A Soul Reclaimed

sands press
Brockville, Ontario

A Soul Reclaimed

Shayna Grissom

sands press

sands press

A Division of 10361976 Canada Inc.
300 Central Avenue West
Brockville, Ontario
K6V 5V2

Toll Free 1-800-563-0911 or 613-345-2687
http://www.sandspress.com

ISBN 978-1-988281-69-8

Cover Design by
Edited by Laurie Carter
Formatting by Renee Hare
Publisher Sands Press

Publisher's Note

This book is a work of fiction. References to real people, events, establishments, organizations, or locales, are intended only to provide as a sense of authenticity, and are used fictitiously. All other characters, and all incidents and dialogue, are drawn from the authors' imaginations and are not to be construed as real.

For information on bulk purchases of this book or any book published by Sands Press, please call 1-800-563-0911.

1st Printing April 2019

To book an author for your live event, please call: 1-800-563-0911

Sands Press is a literary publisher interested in new and established authors wishing to develop and market their product. For more information please visit our website at www.sandspress.com.

Chapter One

"Don't think I've forgotten," Peter said.

I knew he hadn't. My birthday wasn't a widely celebrated event, but Peter had a small cake waiting for me on my desk every year. My mother would never celebrate the day I ruined her life, but at least my tutor loved me.

"You know how I feel about my birthday," I told him.

"I do, which is why I insist on making a day of it. Besides, you know how much Sarah loves the castle market."

The second part of my birthday tradition was visiting the open market. He was right. Sarah loved all things luxurious and extravagant. It was something that reminded her of the fourth region, the place she once called home. Every year, Peter and Sarah would take me to the castle market, and we would see the most exotic wares.

It wasn't that I disliked the market. I enjoyed it. Peter could be a wild card at times, my mother and stepfather didn't approve of him. Within the confines of our classroom, no one could find the rumor to whisper in the steward's ear. Out here, in the public eye, Peter's presence could draw unwanted attention.

"Just don't stir up any trouble." I said.

Peter cocked his head and gave a mischievous grin. "Trouble? Me?"

He knew what I meant.

"Nora, Myrtle was dismissed ten years ago. I don't think your parents want to hurt you. They didn't realize how much it would upset you."

He was lying. Whenever he started a sentence with my name, whatever followed was a lie. Myrtle was the first maid I had at the castle, before Peter and Sarah. A chubby midlife woman who didn't lecture me for wetting the sheets or crying without reason. Myrtle was dismissed to punish me, and Peter knew it.

Peter sat on the edge of his desk to look at me. "I can't promise everything will be fine, that everything will stay the same. But I *can* promise that you will always find your way."

I wanted to believe him, but I am nothing but my mother's old baggage, a remnant of a mistake Bella made as a teenager. The "something" she left at her parent's house when she met the steward. The item she packed up and took with her from the fifth region of Hell when she moved into the castle. I should have considered myself lucky with my rags-to-riches story, but I'm an ungrateful child.

My mother found her happily-ever-after. Away from my grandparents with their rules and judgments, far from the fifth region, where zealots burned the heretics. The ruler of Hell had whisked Mother away from all her troubles—all but one.

Sarah rushed into the classroom. Her dark hair was wrapped ornately around her head, and she was wearing a blue velvet dress today. It looked nice on her; it matched her icy blue eyes and the coolness of her skin.

"It's time for supper," she said.

The three of us ate together at the small wooden table in my bedroom while Peter read poetry and funny short stories from the castle library. The rain tapped against the glass of my window that overlooked the garden. It only added to Peter's poetry reading.

Sarah never showed any interest in this ritual. I didn't typically laugh, but if I liked something, I would make a comment. Sarah's cold demeanor was mostly ignored. It wasn't that she was uncaring, Sarah simply did not express herself outwardly. Peter never asked me to change, so I didn't expect it of Sarah.

"Are we planning on going to the market tomorrow?" Sarah asked.

"Seems so," Peter said. "Are you going to get permission from the steward?"

Sarah nodded. "There have been reports of some strange activity at the border."

I knew what they were talking about. The borders of the seven regions that divided Hell were coming undone. No one knew why. The steward had doubled patrols, but it wasn't helping. More than ever, the souls of the seventh region were escaping and attacking the rest of the population.

Peter shook his head. "Outlanders roaming around the first region unchecked."

"Choose your words carefully," Sarah said.

Peter pushed his plate away and wiped his face with his napkin. His long, wrinkled fingers clawed around the napkin, balling it up before throwing it onto his plate.

"Until tomorrow, then," Peter said. "Goodnight, Nora." He winked.

When I stepped outside the room the next morning, I only saw a tracker. His soft leather uniform was covered with a chainmail vest. The vest not only served to protect the hunter, but it also allowed his hawk to perch on his shoulder without damaging his leather. The patch on his chest indicated he was a hawk hunter, but his bird was likely roosting in the barracks.

His gray eyes shifted nervously in my presence. "Where is Peter?" I asked.

"He's gone."

"Where did he go?"

"He's just gone."

I didn't like the way the man answered me, but it wasn't his fault. He was likely instructed to answer this way. "Should I go ask my stepfather?" I asked.

I received no reply.

That night, I insisted on having dinner with Mother and Vinicio. My wish was greeted with opposition from my mother, whose eyes watered right away, knowing why I was intruding on her romantic dinner. If Vinicio understood why I attended, he didn't show it.

He motioned to a chair at the long dining table. "Please, join us, Nora."

The food was extravagantly displayed in heaps. The massive fireplace gave the entire stone room a soft glow. The table had a red and black embroidered runner, and fruits were stacked in glossy wooden bowls. A giant roasted boar was in the center of the long wooden table. Mother was wearing a red ball gown, her full skirt overflowing in her seat. She was wearing a little red hat with a veil pinned to her curly blonde hair. She had cut her hair since I'd last seen her; it was now bouncing freely just below her chin.

"You've grown into quite the young lady," Vinicio said. He picked up several vegetables with his fork before placing them in his mouth.

"Funny how that happens."

"Nora, please don't," Bella pleaded.

"I wouldn't be here, upsetting your dinner, if you hadn't dismissed my tutor," I told her.

"I'm sorry we didn't talk to you about it first," Vinicio said. "But you're a young lady now, and you need a more mature teacher. You've outgrown him, my dear."

"And Sarah?" I asked.

"She left on her own." He said.

"Peter says that only dictators fear opposition."

"He would teach you such nonsense, wouldn't he? I should have dealt with him years ago. Who knows what other stupidity he's filled your head with . . ."

The steward's hand rested within range, and I imagined stabbing him with a salad fork and watching him scream and flounder around in pain. The thin skin would perforate, giving way to the blood and bone underneath. The images were so vivid that I blinked hard to make them go away, but they wouldn't quit. My head was indeed filled, filled with visions of the only man who gave a shit about me—Peter.

Vinicio jerked his hand away and let out a stifled cry of pain. He held pressure on it, and my mother looked over with concern.

"What's wrong, my love?" she asked.

"I got another cramp in my hand," Vinicio told her, but his green eyes remained on me.

Liar, my other voice mocked.

"It's all those late nights writing." Bella pouted.

I shouldn't have thought something so morbid, but I couldn't stop myself from thinking it. For a moment, it seemed like Vinicio was reacting to what I'd imagined, but that couldn't be. The truth was all too blatant. I am powerless and subjected to the whims of my mother and stepfather. They had given me Peter, Sarah, and Myrtle, and they had taken them away without a second thought.

"We'll get you a new tutor soon," Mother promised.

The steward excused himself. "Ladies, it's been a privilege, but I'm afraid I have some soul placement to do. Please stay and enjoy dessert." He kissed my mother and left.

Chocolate cake with cherries was served, and I glared at her.

"Please don't look at me like that."

"Was it because I was happy?" I asked.

"Sweetheart, I want you to be happy. Why can't you understand? I'm doing the best I can for you."

"This is your best?"

All I wanted was Peter; why was that so hard? I could forgive the dismissal of Myrtle all those years ago, but not Peter. They couldn't take Peter away from me.

A servant walked in with two small drinks. "Special compliments of the steward—honeyed wine."

I couldn't stand being in the same room as my mother and her pathetic counter-guilt trip. I drank the sweet, fermented drink as fast as I could before I got up from the table. Mother was crying as she always did. I hated seeing her cry, but I couldn't back down this time. I didn't want to punish her; I just wanted Peter back.

I didn't remember returning to my bedroom. The wine went to my head, and I felt nauseous. I rippled beneath the surface of consciousness. I heard the crunching of steps and faint whispers. No matter how hard I tried, I couldn't fight sleep. Even the chill of night air and the feeling of soft, damp grass could not rouse me.

Chapter Two

I opened my eyes to a full moon and a pitch-black sky. I played with the grass between my fingers, still drowsy from the wine.

No, poison, a familiar voice echoed within my mind, and I knew it to be the truth. Vinicio had drugged me and left me here, but where was "here"?

When I sat up, I saw the edge of the Starry Wood. Great ancient trees towered over me, casting shadows in the moonlight. I understood Vinicio's intentions. He was going to leave me to the beasts of the Starry Wood.

Peter's lecture on this place stirred in my mind.

"Do you know why they call it the Starry Wood?" he'd asked all those years ago.

I'd shaken my head.

"The woodsmen are invisible during the day. At night, they glow with starlight. Some say they swallowed our stars, but I don't think it's true. Anyway, with the woodsmen glowing, the woods look like they have stars."

"Stars?" I'd asked.

"Invisible, except they are covered in bright little specks," he'd clarified. "In the other life, stars are in the sky, but we don't have them here."

Woodsmen made no noise, with bodies that were completely invisible but for the stardust that covered them. They were enormous men who ate any soul, no matter who they were.

It was true what people said—the woodsmen made no noise. It seemed nothing more than the wind rustling the dense forest at first. It was sort of majestic when they emerged from the tree line, the way they sparkled and were illuminated against the trees and the solid black sky.

Three of them were running straight towards me, and all I could do was stand there like an idiot, frozen in terror. Even if I did run, they would outpace me. How long would it take for Mother to realize I was gone? I shut my eyes and hoped I would be swallowed whole. It would be preferable to being ripped apart.

I felt the impact of something hitting my left side at full force, sweeping me upward. The gravity-defying moment was jarring, but together, we landed solidly on thick branch several hundred feet from the ground. My savior was a shadowy figure for the most part, but a gruff male voice said, "Don't move," before he bolted towards the woodsmen.

Could he be one of the vampires Peter had told me about? My eyes struggled to follow him under the light of the moon. He was a blur bolting in and out of sight as he headed towards my attackers. He jumped onto a nearby tree and scaled several hundred feet before diving at an angle towards the first woodsman. The woodsman didn't see him coming.

The vampire pierced through the creature's belly and leaped at the next starry giant before the body of the first fell to the ground. The woodsmen seemed completely unaware of one another. While the vampire scaled the second one, the third continued in my direction. It was oblivious to the first one's death and the second one's plight.

Panic filled my chest as the thing drew near, and my rescuer was still embroiled with the second woodsman. I had to move; I had to get away from the creature before it could find me. I headed towards the trunk of the tree. I wanted to climb higher, but I couldn't reach the next branch. I grabbed ahold of the bark and tried to shimmy my way up, but the bark was too jagged and stabbed into my hands.

Sliding back down the trunk, I looked over to see the woodsman feeling through the trees. Its eyes were closed. It couldn't see me; it was trying to find me by scent. My scent must have been difficult to make out with all the resin on the massive trees. The smell of pine was overwhelming, but, under the circumstances, I was grateful.

That's it! The resin!

Instead of jumping and risking injury, I ran to the trunk of the tree, found a large glob of resin, and stepped into it. It felt gross, and I wasn't sure if I would be able to get back out of it. Completely submerged in the sap with only my head and hair exposed, I watched the woodsman search in vain. Its desperate fingers searched for me in the branches. Combing the canopy, it looked right at me, but it couldn't detect me.

I could no longer see the vampire; he may have been killed. It was best that I waited till dawn before trying to climb down and make my way back to the castle—if I could even get down. It was dark, but I could feel the distance the way one could feel an oncoming storm. I didn't like heights.

That voice in my head wouldn't quit. *He's not going to stop, you know. Vinicio will try to kill you again. Mother won't protect you just because you wish she would.*

The woodsman's search was cut short as the dark figure jumped onto the back of his neck and bore into the creature until it too fell silently.

"Girl, girl, where are you?" the vampire called.

"I'm here," I called back.

He didn't climb the tree; it was more like he was suddenly walking on the branch towards me. It was visibly jarring, and it was then I understood why the vampires were said to be excellent guards. With so few of them, they were strongly encouraged to enlist—though this was the first time I had ever seen one.

He looked no different than a soul. His hair was a dark brown wavy mass that barely touched his shoulders. His nose was slightly crooked, and his eyes were blue and full of kindness. He was slender and of average height. He wore hide pants, a plain white tunic, and a worn brown coat that trailed around his leather boots. He looked more like a pirate than a blood-drinking, sharp-toothed undead guy. He was nothing like the books or rumors described.

He was clearly amused with my predicament. "That was some smart thinking, but how did you plan on getting out of there?"

"I only planned on not getting eaten," I said, defending my strategy.

"Hmm." He tilted his head to one side, trying to determine the best course of action. "I was saving this for a special occasion, but I guess you need it more."

In the light of the moon, I noticed a large scar on the inside of his hand. He reached in and pulled me out by my left arm. With the other hand, he reached into the side pocket of his coat and produced a water skin. "It's not enough to clean you up entirely, but it should help."

I opened the water skin, expecting water, only to find it was a strong alcohol. My face twisted involuntarily at the smell, and he laughed apologetically.

"You're not a fan of moonshine, I take it? That's okay; neither am I. It will wash the sap off, though."

I looked at him before looking down at myself. "Not sure where to start."

"I know a place that will have some clothing for a girl your age. I'll take you there before I get you back home. Your mother must be worried sick. How did you get out here in the first place?"

Two strong hands held me at arm's length as he dropped us to the ground. He unstuck his hands from under my arms, and together we walked into the sunrise.

Vinicio

"I don't wish to cause any alarm, but Nora is nowhere to be found," Bella whispered to Vinicio over their breakfast. Bella's blonde curls bounced freely and smelled of roses. Her hair hid some of the creases on her face, a face that perfected desperate and pleading expressions.

The steward was sucking the marrow from a large bone. When Bella mentioned Nora, he stopped and wiped his face fastidiously. "Do you think she ran away?" he asked.

"She was so upset about Peter being dismissed. I wanted to talk to her about it this morning, but she was gone."

Vinicio looked down, contemplating how to say the next few words. "You know, if she had walked out the front entrance, we would have been alerted. That means if she did indeed run away, she would have had to go by the Starry Wood."

Bella's eyes watered. "She's too smart for that. I'm sure of it."

"I will see to it that she is found," Vinicio promised. Bella embraced him, and he warmly accepted. "I know it's been a difficult transition. Everything will be right in time."

"I'm so sorry she has been such a bother." Bella fidgeted nervously, twirling a ringlet around her index finger.

"She's nothing of the sort." Vinicio kissed Bella's forehead as he stood. "I'm going to alert the trackers to look for her. I'll spare no expense. As he strode out of the dining room, he called, "I'll have the top trackers looking for her." He could feel Bella watching him as he went.

In the court hall stood Rebus—an old man, but efficient and wise. His beard was long, and his red silk robes flowed along the floors.

"My lord?" Rebus asked.

"Rebus, my stepdaughter has run away. Hacia and Alfie are the tracking generals, yes?"

"You're only sending the two, my lord?"

"I don't want rumors spreading. If the girl is still alive, the last thing we need is a ransom or retaliation murder."

"Of course; is there a portrait I can show Alfie and Hacia?"

"Yes, there is one in Bella's room. I'll see that it gets to you. Now, if you'll excuse me, I promised my wife an excursion on the river."

The advisor's heavy eyelids lifted in curiosity, but he said nothing.

"I need to take her mind off her daughter." Vinicio moved closer to the advisor to speak. "It is possible that she ran away with her former tutor, or maybe he kidnapped her. I think it more likely that she ran away alone. I fear she wandered too close to the woods."

"Oh, sir, I am so sorry." Rebus knew that if the girl had left in that direction, she was as good as dead.

"She never truly adjusted to life here. I shouldn't have dismissed her tutor the way I did."

"You cannot blame yourself for a child's folly, sir."

Vinicio looked up from the floor. "Thank you, my friend. I worry more for her mother. She is a fragile woman. I hope this upcoming trip on the river will be productive. If her daughter is gone, the only thing that could console her is another child."

Bella had struggled with infertility since they married. She was young and healthy enough for children, but over the years, she'd suffered several miscarriages. It had been a while since they last tried to conceive, so Vinicio hoped they would be successful this time. He'd hate to dispose of his wife for the sake of his legacy.

The advisor's head bobbled in a nod. With the entire situation explained, he knew that the search was more for Bella's sake than it was for the child. Nevertheless, they would search every corner of the world to find the remains of a little girl lost.

The hawk hunters and the trackers were the two branches of the military in Hell. Vinicio would send the two generals out to find and dispose of Nora. Both were loyal to him—Hacia proved as much when the hawk hunters attempted a rebellion during his father's reign. Instead of siding with the hunters, she instructed her trackers to move against them. She had been distant and mostly elusive since then, but she was also much older and likely trying to hide it.

Alfie had gotten his promotion recently. When the last hawk hunter general died suddenly, it only made sense that Alfie was promoted to the general ranking. While some thought the death of his predecessor suspicious, Vinicio applauded Alfie for his ambition. He had a general of his choosing, and that prevented future rebellions.

It seemed Vinicio had killed Nora's maid all too late. It had been Sarah's job to report anything suspicious to him, but it seemed she'd forgotten. The first maid, Myrtle, had sympathized with the child right away, but Vinicio had been sure Sarah would do better. All the while, Bella's arms pulled him into a false sense of security. For ten years, Nora had posed no threat to anyone.

Last night changed all of that.

Vinicio went to the bathroom and removed his dark leather gloves. Bella thought it was a fashion of sorts, but the gloves hid a stab wound on his left hand. Four small punctures side by side were purple and angry. Vinicio redressed his wounds and put the gloves on once more. He did not wish to explain the injury and risk Bella's suspicion.

Chapter Three

Nora

Dawn's light was edging the horizon by the time we reached our destination. It was a cottage yard littered with children's toys and an overburdened clothesline. A stump with a hatchet and a small stack of wood sat several paces away from the door. Before the vampire could knock, a young boy with white blond hair opened the door.

"Mum! Mum, Aegis is here!"

Moments later, several children emerged, all chanting the vampire's name. "Don't touch that one," Aegis said, pointing at me. "She is covered in sap."

One of the boys nodded. "You were playing in the forest too. I had a drop of sap fall on me once; I still have pieces in my hair! Mum!"

I counted seven children before a tired woman emerged from the stairway. She had a full figure and frizzy red hair that poked out from under the scarf wrapped around her head. "What's this?"

"I'm sorry to wake you, Gerta," Aegis said. "I found her in the woods while hunting. She hid in the sap to escape three woodsmen."

The woman gasped. "Did you finish all three of them?"

"I did."

"You're lucky Aegis found you," the woman told me. "Poor girl, you must be scared out of your wits. Jess! Alexa!"

Gerta's two daughters were near my age. One was taller and broader than her little sister, who had braids. Both had pale blonde hair like their brothers. The girls took one look at me and seemed to understand what their mother wanted.

I couldn't wait to get the sap off. Getting up the stairs proved to be a daunting task as the sap was heavy and clung to my clothes and skin as I moved. Each time I extended my leg, a sticky noise would squeak from my pants. The resin stiffened my clothes whenever I wasn't moving, but moving was painful, as the sap stuck to every fiber on my skin.

"Did you really see the woodsmen?" the shorter girl asked. The taller one was pouring a jug of alcohol into the stained bathtub. I wanted to be cautious with my steps, but there were clothes everywhere that were impossible to avoid.

"No, go ahead and step on the clothes," the bigger girl instructed me. "They will be easier to clean than the floor."

I did as she said. Fully dressed and with various garments stuck to my shoes, I got into the tub. The bathroom was small for the number of people who used it, but it had a big window, making the room feel bright and cheery. It felt like home, though perhaps not my home.

"Did you really see the woodsmen?" the girl with the braids asked loudly.

"Yes, I guess I did," I answered.

"I heard they were see-through but freckled with light."

"Yes, those spots of light are called stars," I explained. The alcohol felt cool on my skin, and it was indeed loosening the sap.

The younger girl tilted her head. "What are stars?"

"Well . . ." I wasn't sure how to explain them. "There are other places, like this place, except they can see the distant light of other worlds. They look like little light spots, and they call them stars. That is why the forest is called the Starry Wood."

"We've only known it as the forest. How do you know such things?" the older girl asked. Her curiosity had been piqued.

"I'm from the castle." The words choked me for some reason.

"I'm Jess; this is Alexa," the older sister interjected.

"It's nice to meet you both."

"We will let you bathe," said Jess. "Here are some scissors if you just need to cut some of it off. Under the towel are some of my clothes; they should fit you. If you need anything, just give a shout." The girls left, shutting the door behind them.

I tried to pull my pants off, but between the sap and the wetness, it was impossible. At first, I didn't want Jess and Alexa to leave, but decided it was for the best. It would have been embarrassing to have the girls in the room with me. I didn't have much experience with girls my own age.

With a little effort, slicing my pants off in strips with large kitchen shears worked the best. I did the same to my shirt, but the sap stuck to my long hair. Pulling on the strands got annoying. I cut my hair along with the shirt. I saved as much length as I could, but it felt liberating to be able to move my neck without the pull on my hair.

After what seemed like hours in a very cold tub, I finally freed myself from the sap and was able to dry off. What was left of my pants and white shirt remained in the tub. I looked in the mirror to see the damage I had done to my hair. Inspecting it carefully, I saw that I would need to cut it to my shoulders to even it out. Using the large pair of shears, I clipped the best I could. My hair fell jaggedly around my shoulders, but it was better than wearing clumps of resin. After putting on Jess's clothes, I felt like someone far removed from the castle. The sack dress was big, with a faded floral print, but I was happy to be wearing it. As I moved down the stairs, I could hear Gerta talking to Aegis.

"Why would you want to take a small girl with you?" Gerta's cheeks flushed pink. "Just leave her here with me."

"I'm not leaving her." There was a desperate tone to his voice. Why would he want me to go with him?

Gerta's arms were crossed, and she shook her head in solid opposition.

I did my best to pretend I didn't hear, but I spoke up before they could continue fighting over me. "Um, I didn't know how you would want to clean up the mess . . ."

"Oh, don't worry about that, my dear. Between the sap and the alcohol, your clothes will make excellent fire starters." Gerta smiled and motioned for me to come. "I'll pack you some supplies. You'll be traveling with Aeg for a while."

I looked at the vampire sitting on the sofa, and he nodded. Gerta led me into the kitchen, where she grabbed a brown traveler's knapsack and began loading it with bread, cheese, and beef jerky. She had so many children that I wondered if she regretted it.

The house was a mess, and she was just as disheveled, but she kissed the heads of her children every time one walked by, and she didn't seem frustrated with all the noise and the mess they made. I would have been happy here. I knew they were probably struggling to get by with so many mouths to feed, but I didn't want to leave with the vampire. I knew I could be happy here.

"I can work hard. I don't know how to cook, but I can wash clothes and look after the little ones," I offered.

Gerta smiled at me. "I'd love to have you. Aegis will bring you to visit, I'm sure."

I was frightened by the idea of traveling alone with a strange man. What did he want from me? I could feel his eyes on me as he sat on the couch. He was watching through the doorway, and it made me uneasy. I wondered how far I was from my grandparent's home.

It occurred to me that we were on the outskirts of the fifth region. When I was left in the wood, I could still see the tallest tower of the castle. We skirted along the forest during the day, which meant we couldn't have been far from the town I was born in.

"This is still the fifth region?" I asked.

She nodded. "I can't stand all those burnings. I won't let my children near them. I only go to town when I must."

Gerta was nothing like my grandparents or the town folks. My mother was like that too. She hated seeing the burnings and the hangings. Gerta didn't follow any sort of religion, and Mother didn't either. The only thing the two women seemed obsessed with was love. Of all the things to be drawn to, love didn't seem like such a bad thing.

It was better to feel all-consuming love than it was to burn people alive. Then again, my mother's devotion to love was what almost got me killed. Love wasn't any better an obsession if you hurt people in the process. It was easier to justify, but not necessarily healthier.

"Where is he going to take me?" I whispered.

"Aegis is a good man. He would never do anything to hurt you; he is just a little rough around the edges. He's lived a long time and seen a lot of things, and sometimes that makes a person hard on the outside. You understand?"

"Vampires don't eat souls?" I asked, trying to mask my concern.

"Goodness, no!" Gerta laughed. "I don't think they eat at all, actually."

With the knapsack filled, I was led from the kitchen to a man who looked just as reluctant as I felt.

"All set?" he asked as softly as he could manage.

I gave him a nod, and we left Gerta's home. All nine of her children were peeking from windows and waving. I didn't want to leave. Those girls could have been my friends, but I could never have a normal life like them. I didn't belong here.

We walked for what felt like forever. The sun was well-established in the sky, and the ground's coolness had long diminished, yet we were still walking.

"Where are we going?" I asked.

"To see a friend of mine in Metropolis; he might be able to help us."

"Help us do what?"

Ignoring my question, Aegis stopped and pointed off the dirt road toward the horizon. "There's a creek that way." We changed our course towards the water. "We should rest there, have some lunch, and top off our water skins."

The creek was small, but patches of grass and weeds were growing in an otherwise inhospitable place. "Is everything here so—"

"Dry?" Aegis finished. "Yes. It's not as hot in this area as some places, but hardly anything grows."

I didn't understand why. "But the woods and the plain of grass . . ."

Aegis nodded while stoking a small fire with a stick. "It's said that the Wood has an underground cavern that is filled with water—the purest water known. The plains I found you on and the Wood draw from that water source, as do the inhabitants of the castle."

I understood what he was prodding at. It was obvious I came from the castle. I had no knowledge of the world around me. I only knew the royal names for things, names no one else seemed to use. The castle was the closest inhabitance to where the vampire had found me. I didn't know how to answer.

"Do the people here dislike those who live in the castle?" I asked.

"I don't think anyone cares anymore," Aegis said noncommittedly as his fire grew weak. "Without the king, the castle means nothing to the people in this land." He continued to poke and blow on the small flame until it was once again roaring.

"I'm from the castle," I admitted.

Aegis's eyes glimmered strangely in the firelight. They reflected the light the way a cat's eyes would. He wore a carved stone pendant around his neck. The carving was of a dagger and nothing else. It reminded me of something, but I couldn't quite recall what it was.

I remembered most of my lessons about the king of Hell, though history wasn't one of my strong points. Peter had been insistent that I know the history. When the king of Hell died, a new king always emerged, except for the day he hadn't. From that day forward, a steward had been appointed, and his descendants ruled in succession.

"How did they know if a soul was the new king?" I asked.

Peter looked confused. "Did your mother not tell you of the soul bank?"

I shook my head, and Peter's puzzled expression made me feel stupid. He looked towards the door for a long moment. "I'm a little surprised she didn't teach you about the soul bank."

"Mother doesn't tell me anything; she's too busy."

Peter's eyes grew sad, and he nodded. "Very well. I'll tell you."

Returning to his chalkboard, Peter drew a box with bars arranged in a star on the front. "This is what the soul bank looks like. It was the duty of the king, and now the Steward, to ensure that it is not tampered with in any way. You remember those worlds elsewhere? The ones with the stars?"

I nodded eagerly.

"Good. When the people in those worlds die, they come to this world and remain in their incorporeal form until the king places them."

I was all too familiar with the caste system of our world. Our status was determined before we were born into the world, and it meant that bad people would continue to reproduce bad people. I was something in between. I didn't belong anywhere.

It was then that Vinicio stepped into the classroom.

"Will you excuse us a moment?" He dismissed Peter.

Vinicio always scared me. He wasn't a large or imposing man by any means, but he still scared me. He was slender and shorter than Peter. His hair was dark, and his skin was a golden tone. Vinicio was by all accounts a handsome and soft-spoken man, but Mother feared him. She always fussed and worried whenever he seemed unhappy with something. I seldom saw the steward of Hell; Mother never wanted me around when they were together.

"Do you like your tutor, Nora?" Vinicio asked. He leaned against the desk and folded his delicate hands in front.

"Yes, sir."

"That's good. I want you to be happy here. If your tutor makes you happy, then he shall remain. I do have one request, however."

I swallowed hard and nodded.

"Your mother and I agreed to retire the history of the soul bank. At one point, such information was relevant, but now—"

Vinicio walked over to the globe on the desk and it a spin. "Now things are different. Kings are long gone, and they have left me and my legacy the burden of ruling. There is no use in spreading such mythology anymore. Do you understand?"

"Yes, sir."

"Good. You may resume your lessons."

He'd left the room, and it felt as though all the warmth had gone with him. I'd shivered, and Peter had returned to the room. He couldn't meet my eyes, but he'd resumed instruction.

"We will pick up where we left off yesterday with math."

Three months after that conversation, Peter was gone, and I was alone. Not entirely alone—the vampire stood only a few steps ahead.

"What do I call you?" Aegis asked.

"What? It's Nora." I was still halfway in the past when I answered. If Aegis knew, he didn't let on.

"We should get moving soon."

I didn't understand the need to rush; maybe he had changed his mind and decided he didn't want me around after all. Maybe he wanted to sell me. Perhaps he wasn't as good as Gerta thought.

"Where are you taking me?" I asked.

"Away from the castle, for one," Aegis replied as he stomped out the fire. "The second biggest city is in the next region over. I know people there, people who have inside knowledge of the castle. Maybe we can find out who wanted you dead," he said.

"I already know who." I said as I absently kicked around the knapsack that hung from my wrist.

Aegis stopped for a moment to look at me with his pale blue eyes. "Who wants to kill you, Nora? Why would anyone want to kill a little girl?"

He looked so sad and forlorn at the thought of someone wanting me dead. Ripples of anger surfaced across his stubbled face before he returned to his stoic self. I wanted to keep my guard up and be wary of him, but I suddenly found myself feeling guilty of ill thoughts towards him.

"Vinicio is my stepfather," I told him. "He never wanted me around, just like my mother. He's trying to get rid of me."

"There's more to it than that."

"Like what?" I feigned stupidity. If he knew I came from the outlands, he would understand why.

"I don't know, but we will find out," Aegis said.

Liar, liar, my other voice called from within.

Aegis was lying about how much he knew, but he wanted to be sure before admitting such to me. To have outlanders in the castle would likely anger people. Was Mother looking for me? Did she miss me? Was I so bad that she would abandon me? What had I done wrong? I put the knapsack on and followed Aegis to the dirt road and onward to a city with answers, away from my mother and a place she told me was home.

"Come on, girl!" Aegis called, and I ran to his side.

"Gerta said you didn't eat," I started.

"No." He laughed. "I don't eat, and I don't drink blood. I don't melt in the sun, and I'm not allergic to garlic or crosses."

I laughed at the absurdity of the idea. He seemed to think it was funny, too, because his face crinkled around his eyes when he smiled.

"How long do you live if you're not killed?"

"Forever, I suppose," Aegis said, lifting his arms to the sky.

"Are there girl vampires?"

At this, Aegis laughed fully. "Sure there are, but I haven't seen any in a long time."

I realized the trajectory of my questions was getting awkward, but how many souls encountered a vampire and woodsmen in one day? Even Peter didn't know as much as Aegis must. Despite the bombardment of questions, Aegis was good-natured, and he seemed to enjoy the conversation. It made me wonder when he had last had a conversation with another person.

"Do vampires have children?"

"No." Aegis kept his eyes on the road ahead as he spoke. "We're not souls. We don't have a reserve of living essence waiting in a safe somewhere. When we die, that's it."

"How did you get here?" I asked.

"We were here all along. We were buried deep in the ground. I woke to the sounds of people screaming and crawled to the surface. That's when I saw a woodsman devouring a soul for the first time." His eyes narrowed as he wandered in his own past.

"How awful."

"After I killed him, I saw other holes in the ground—the vampires that came before me. I was a slow riser."

"Do you remember anything from before you woke up?"

"No, it's been far too long." Aegis looked at me and smiled sadly. "Minerva said that when our memories become too much of a burden, we sleep in the dirt. It's impossible to live with nothing but death, so it's easier to forget."

"You're nothing like you're described," I offered cheerily, but Aegis didn't respond.

I had more questions, but Aegis was pulling away. He was in his own thoughts, and I could sense he didn't want to talk anymore.

We followed the dusty trail toward the sun until it began to set. Aegis set up another bare fire and spent the better half of the night coddling the weak flame. If only Peter had taught me how to start a fire or forage for food. I'd never imagined I would need to know such things, but Peter should have known.

After my first terrifying lesson with Peter, I had sat in my room and looked out the window just as I had at my grandparent's home. Who had selected this room for me? They had chosen a room with a beautiful view and scenery I could watch forever. However, something within me had changed. I was no longer content to look out the window. I knew better than to wander—if my grandparents had been there, they would have sent me to the closet for punishment.

But my grandparents were not there. I looked outside my door and saw one of the trackers several feet away. She saw me and gave a polite nod, but otherwise remained unmoved. No one had said I had to stay in my room, so I left. I felt the flush on my face, but I ignored it and pressed on. I passed the tracker slowly. I tried to appear confident, but my mouth felt dry, and it made me swallow a lot.

The castle was a maze of stories etched in glass, some I remembered and some I'd never known. Grandmother used to tell me the stories about the kings of old, but they were described as fairy tales and not actual history. If they were just stories, why would people go to all the trouble of etching them in the glass?

I found myself standing before the image of the king and the monster again. The monster was sitting across from the king with cards in his hand. Its skin was yellow with red cracks throughout its body and a huge set of horns that branched out towards the sky. The king's black crown glimmered in the sunlight despite being the darkest color on the glass, and a small dagger with a bejeweled hilt was at his side.

"Have you ever heard this story?" a voice said from behind me.

I whirled around to see Peter. His hands were in his pockets as he observed the glass.

I shook my head.

"In the time before kings, Titans ruled Hell. They loved to torment souls—beat them and enslave them, among other unspeakably cruel things. When the king of souls manifested his powers, he set out to defeat the Titans. With the help of the vampires,"—Peter pointed at the men in the picture—"the king ended the rule of the Titans."

"Vampires?"

"They are like souls, except they are immortal," Peter explained.

I had heard stories. "They drink blood and only come out at night."

Peter laughed. "I think those are rumors. The vampires are said to be incredibly strong, however."

"Are there any still around?" I asked.

"It's possible. After the last of the Titans was subdued by the first king in a game of cards, the vampires found themselves in another war. The vampires and woodsmen have been killing each other over their territory. It's been years since we've had reported sightings of either creature."

"What kind of king would use a game to end a war?" I asked.

"The kind that learns an enemy's weaknesses. You see, each Titan was said to have a fatal flaw, and this Titan could only be controlled by those who knew his name."

I smiled at the ploy. "So that king made a bet and won the Titan's name."

Peter chuckled. "Pretty clever."

"What was its name?" I asked.

"No idea. Only the king and the vampires present knew."

Peter was still looking up at the stained glass. He seemed sad in a way. As I explored, Peter roamed the castle with me, telling me the story behind each of the stained-glass pictures. His eyes were still wild, and they flickered as we spoke, but it was then that I decided I liked him.

If Peter knew so much, he should have given me tools to survive on my own. I always wanted to be self-reliant, but I was never big enough and never smart enough. Still, he had no more way of knowing the future than I did. I was feeling sorry for myself, and I wanted someone to blame. I had spent my life relying on people who didn't want me.

I couldn't remember how old I was when I learned to dress. I had to have been young, but I had managed to put on my undergarments, stockings, dress, and shoes all by myself. When my mother came home, she had been thrilled. Initially, I thought she was excited about my efforts, but instead, she told me she had met someone.

"He is the steward! Can you believe it? This could change everything. No more living with your grandparents! He wants to see me again tomorrow." Mother had paused and looked me over. "Nora, what happened to you? Your clothes are on backwards and inside out. Your shoes are on the wrong feet…"

"Come back to me, Nora," Aegis said.

I wiped the moisture from my eyes and refocused on the present.

"Sorry, I—"

"Don't be sorry. I don't know what you've been through, but I know the road can be tough."

Aegis was whittling a stick and started to quietly sing a song. It was a lovely melody, but I didn't understand the words—vampires must have their own language. I wished there were more of his kind. I curled up near the fire and rested my head on the knapsack. Aegis continued to sing, and I let his song lull me to sleep.

It wasn't until I woke the next morning that I realized I was covered by an old, worn trench coat, and the fire was burning hot. There was an animal on a spit over the fire.

Aegis was turning the carcass.

"We need to find every opportunity for fresh food," he said. "Reserve the food from Gerta's for the days we can't find anything else."

"How do you know how to cook and hunt when you don't eat anything?"

"Sometimes people pay me to escort them from region to region," Aegis replied. "Not many are willing to tangle with a vampire."

I sat up, and he handed me the stick. I wanted to ask why anyone would need an escort. It had been over a day and not once had we seen another soul aside from Gerta's family, but I didn't have the courage to ask. After I had breakfast, we put out the fire and continued.

"We should reach the border by the afternoon if we keep a good pace, and the city gates by nightfall," Aegis explained.

"The border?" I asked. I'd heard of them, but never seen one.

"Each region has a gate of sorts," Aegis explained. "Some are harder to get through than others."

"What about this one?" I asked.

"This is one of the easier ones to slip past. It's easy to get in; you just need a lot of silver to get out. The people that live in the sixth region of Hell tend to dislike the folks of the fifth layer."

"I don't blame them," I said.

Aegis looked at me curiously. "You've seen the fifth region?"

"It's the only place I've known outside the castle. I lived there until I was six."

"You don't strike me as a fifth-region soul," Aegis observed.

"I didn't belong there," I said, more to myself than to Aegis.

He said nothing in response.

The border between the fifth and sixth regions of Hell wasn't exactly a border. It was more like a small fence made with rounded stones and mud mortar. Hawk hunters and trackers patrolled lightly, but for the most part, they seemed at ease. The rock fence went on as far as I could see along a flat and desolate plain.

Along the wall, there was crumbled debris and rocks laying around. The trackers just stepped around it. As we approached, I saw some small rocks fall from the wall onto the ground. The closer we got, the more apparent it was that the wall was crumbling. The mortar was dry and cracked and could no longer hold the stones in place.

"It's falling down."

"Yeah. Most of the borders are. There's nothing the steward can do to prevent it, so he just adds more patrols. But patrolmen can be bribed, so it doesn't help anyone, really," Aegis explained.

"Are the trackers going to stop us?" I asked as we drew closer.

"People visit the sixth region all the time. They are more concerned with people trying to get into the fifth region from here."

I tried to hide my fear, but the idea of being caught and sent back to the castle made it hard to breathe.

"Hey, it's okay," Aegis said as he held my hand.

A new sort of fear took the place of the former. Why was Aegis helping me? I'd never known anyone to do anything so high stake without a reason. What did he want from me? Was I a fool to blindly trust this vampire I knew nothing about? I needed to be careful; Aegis was leading me to a place known for thuggery and prostitution.

Gerta said he was a good man. He probably didn't have the same interest in girls that soul men did. Peter had tried to protect me from the awful things that happened in other regions, but I knew of them from the fifth region. Many of the religious groups had laws that justified forced marriage. Rape was generally not considered a crime just so long as there was an indication of ownership.

I knew it to be wrong because my grandparents disapproved of it. I didn't understand the cruelty and the devastation it wrought until I was away from the region long enough to see how much better people were when they were not enslaved by their beliefs.

We walked through a gap between the rock wall without any incident. The trackers on patrol were a fair distance from us and did not seem moved by our passing. I let out a sigh of relief and pulled my hand from Aegis's. He gave a silent laugh at the motion, but he let the awkward moment go.

Chapter Four

Aegis was almost correct. We reached the city just after dusk. We would have made it sooner, but we had to stop several times because of something I had eaten or drunk. He kept his distance as I squatted in the bushes or behind a tree, but the embarrassment left my ears red.

"It could have been the water," Aegis suggested.

While I appreciated his kindness, I didn't care to respond. He picked up my water bag and gave it a smell. With the water seemingly approved, he picked up the knapsack and inspected the jerky. "Did you eat any of this?" Aegis asked as he lifted a chunk of dehydrated meat.

"Yeah."

Aegis threw it as far as he could. "That meat was spoiled. Too thick a piece of meat to properly smoke. Good thing it wasn't the water. I don't trust the water in this city. It smells strange, and the people always seem sickly. Are you about finished out there?" he nagged.

"Yeah," I responded while pulling up my undergarments. He seemed much more talkative as we approached the Metropolis. Perhaps it was more fun to talk to me when I was squatting in the bushes.

The land around the walls was sandy and even more barren than the road we had been on. Sandstone walls ascended well into the night sky.

"Were those walls built for the woodsmen?" I asked, but I got no response. The vampire was staring at the gate intently. "Aegis?"

"Shh." His fingertips stopped just short of my lips. "We need to camp here for the night and get into the city tomorrow."

"Why?"

"The guards won't let people in at night without asking some questions. During the day, it would be more common for a man and his daughter to want into a city."

I looked at the stationed guards and saw several dozen on post at various points. "Are there normally that many guards?"

"I can't say for certain," Aegis admitted, "but it seems like more than I've seen in the past."

"They won't be afraid of you, will they?" I asked.

"No. People don't know what I am unless they know what to look for."

We retreated away from the city and out of sight. It wasn't cold out, but I was getting hungry, and Aegis wanted to have a fire before the temperature dropped during the night. I waited by the determined campsite while he set traps in the brush and collected wood. Aegis was so fast and so strong that he often restrained his movements in my presence. I tried not to be startled, but it was outright scary to see a person dodging around quicker than my eyes could follow. It made collecting and hunting much easier. His sense of smell was so acute he could detect nearby animals.

I was tired of doing absolutely nothing. I dug into the ground with my bare hands to create a pit for the fire. There weren't many rocks around me, but I was able to make a small stone circle around the little pit. I heard some footsteps—no doubt Aegis was trying to make deliberate noise so as to not startle me. It wasn't until I felt a hand on my shoulder that I felt the chill of an uninvited guest.

I looked over my shoulder to see two men, both thin and dirty. They smiled. The shorter one's teeth were stumped by decay.

"What is a little girl like you doing out here?" the shorter man asked.

"She looks so clean and pretty," the taller man said, his hand still on my shoulder.

"You guys better run before my father comes back. You won't like him." I tried to keep my voice as even as possible. Neither man seemed concerned with my father's return.

"You think we could get enough to cross regions with her?" the shorter one asked.

"Depends on what circle we take her to. If we get her to the outlands unscathed, we could afford three or four border jumps."

"You're outlanders?" I prodded.

Neither man answered me. Instead, they looted my knapsack, looking for goods. "Right, well let's get out of here before her dear old pappy returns." The taller man said as he pushed me forward. "Start walking, girl. You don't want to give us any trouble."

"No, you don't—we'd be forced to sample the goods," the shorter one sneered.

Aegis's mention of being an escort for souls suddenly made sense. He hadn't wanted to tell me what happened to girls who wandered alone outside the cities and more than Peter had. I'd learned about the slave trades and region-hopping by overhearing things people said in the castle.

One afternoon, I'd been playing in the garden when I overheard an old man talking to someone I didn't know. The stranger had a bald head, and he towered over the old man who I saw was Rebus, the steward's advisor.

"The regions are increasingly unstable," the tall man said. "Only a true king can determine a soul's place."

The advisor's head stopped bobbing. "Well, we have no king, so what would you suggest?"

"All due respect to the steward, but when was the last time someone actually looked?"

"He assigns souls to regions several times a day; he would surely notice if one was glowing as they say a king's soul glows."

The bald man rolled his eyes, but did not refute the old man. "Father, the borders are weakening. The outlanders are bringing souls from other regions and selling them as slaves. In the past, the outlanders could escape, but it was never possible for a first or second region soul to end up in the seventh."

"We will increase patrols and consider ways to make this more difficult," Rebus promised.

"A bandage on what will be an ongoing issue."

"What would you have me do? The steward simply does not have the power to control the barriers as the kings once did."

I watched the two men walk away as their argument continued. When I returned to the classroom, Peter seemed to know I had been up to no good.

"Where have you been?" Peter asked.

"I was exploring again."

Peter's face wore an expression of disapproval, but I knew he didn't truly think it was bad. He thought lots of things were bad, but curiosity and exploration were not. I told him about what I'd heard from the two men in the garden. His face grew sullen, and he closed the classroom door.

"I know about the barriers weakening," Peter confirmed.

"What does it mean?"

Peter took the globe off the table and set it on my desk. "You know how we have seven regions? The outlands are where the worst of the souls go, and the first region is where the purest souls are placed." Peter's long slightly wrinkled finger traced the regions.

"Yes."

"The king was said to have powers beyond an ordinary soul. Not only did he have the ability to truly identify where a soul belonged, but he also strengthened the barriers between regions. While the steward is reasonably able to assign souls to regions, he cannot control the borders. Instead, he relies on the military."

"But . . ." I didn't know how to ask the question, and my eyes welled up as Peter continued to explain. I was part outlander, so if the barriers kept people in their regions, how did I come to exist?

"You see, souls can ascend their region. It is difficult, but it can sometimes happen. Say an outlander decides never to hurt another being ever again and crosses the border. The patrols and trackers won't make any move on him until he breaks the law. In time, with perseverance, an outlander soul can redeem itself and even move up a few regions."

"So, when good souls are bad, they are demoted?" I asked.

"Clever girl," Peter replied. "Of course, the souls won't accept an outlander to their region. They're not welcomed until the dirt is scrubbed off and the soul fills out and can find clothing that doesn't give it away." Peter was no longer looking at me, but he continued. "If a soul in a lesser region works hard, and makes sacrifices, redemption is possible. Only true repentance can deliver a soul to a better region just as a truly evil deed can push a soul into a lesser region."

"It sounds hard," I interrupted.

"Yes, I suppose it would be." Peter had responded . "The barriers are not to keep souls in; they are to keep souls out so that the pure souls cannot be forced into lower regions. If we had a king, slavery wouldn't be an issue."

Another shove on my back forced me to walk into the present. The two men were pushing me away from the city and toward the arid deserts. I had no idea where Aegis had gone. I looked around without moving my head. If I saw a way to escape, I didn't want them to catch on. There was nothing but dry dirt and the occasional half-dead shrub. I couldn't outrun both men, and I couldn't rely on Aegis to come save me. Fear coiled so tightly within my center that I thought my insides would break.

It wasn't just fear; it was anger. How many times had these men taken good souls back to the outlands? Where were those people now? I wanted revenge, but I wasn't sure why. I started seeing images of toxic black venom surging though their veins, burning them slowly, painfully. It would slither towards the heart before striking fast and hard, pumping that venom into every fiber of their beings.

I just needed something. Something, something, something…

And then there it was—a snake perfectly camouflaged in the dust. I didn't know if it was poisonous or not, but it could be enough of a distraction. I watched its coils move along the dirt, but both men seemed oblivious. The shorter man talked on and on, only to be interrupted by the occasional grunt of the taller man.

"You know," said the shorter man, "I bet we could find ourselves a nice little spot out here one day…" Suddenly his chatter was replaced by a scream.

That was my cue to run.

When the taller man also screamed, I didn't look back to see if it was me he was yelling at. I didn't look back at all until I got within range of the city walls. Neither man attempted to follow me. Their bones would be picked clean before morning. Satisfaction swelled in my chest. I had taken care of the situation myself.

I made it to my little camp and found Aegis sitting beside the fire. I could have been raped or killed—or both—and my fierce protector sat picking his teeth. I felt the blood rise to my head and I stomped towards him. When he turned to look at me, I kicked at the ground, sending dirt and dust hurtling at his face.

"What was that for?" Aegis asked, wiping dirt from his face.

"Where were you?" My fists were balled up so hard I could no longer relax them.

Aegis turned towards the fire and put a snake on the spit. "I was around."

Tan scales and a large, flat head lay beside him. Its vicious fangs were exposed, and its black eyes stared at me.

"You were there the entire time."

"It didn't look to me like you needed much rescuing, but you do need dinner." He motioned towards the spit.

"You killed the snake that saved me."

"Well, looks like he'll be saving you again."

We broke camp the next morning just before dawn. I ate the remainder of my snake friend for breakfast. As we backtracked away from the city, I wondered absently if it were young or old. After a few hours, the sun had dried any residual moisture the night had given, and we met with the gravel dirt road heading toward Metropolis.

A caravan drawn by a pair of mules overtook us. The mules plodded by slowly and Aegis appeared to get an idea.

"Say, friend," he called to the driver. "Do you have room for some passengers?

"Maybe," the driver replied stiffly.

"My daughter and I have been walking for days; could we catch a ride with you?" Aegis implored.

The man said nothing for a moment. "You got any weapons?"

"No, sir."

"I do." The man pulled back his jacket to show a large hunting knife.

"We won't cause you any trouble," Aegis promised.

The man looked at Aegis hard for a moment before he hauled on the reins and letting us onto the caravan. Aegis thanked him several times, but the man said nothing as he resumed driving the mules towards the city.

The bench was hard, and the ride was bumpy, but I was more than happy not to be walking. My feet stung and when I pulled one shoe off, I could see that blisters had formed. Some had already popped and were oozing. The fabric that covered the cargo hold was scratchy against my back, even through my clothes, and I couldn't help but be curious about the contents.

I peeked inside the caravan through the opening flap. The man noticed me looking but said nothing. Inside, were a bunch of crates filled with rocks and a little old lady asleep sitting up. Her hair was covered with a black scarf that matched her black frock.

It didn't take long to reach the city. Aegis was right—the daytime guards seemed much more relaxed and waved people by without barely a glance. Although they seemed especially familiar with the man we traveled with—the two guards smiled and nodded, and he returned the nod.

The city of Metropolis had more dust inside its walls than the desert we had just left behind. Children bathed in the streets with buckets while the elderly sat outside their hovels and stared off into the distance. I was overwhelmed by all the noise and smell of bodily fluids. It was like the stink of all the bodily functions a person could exude were condensed in the air of this city. The heat only exacerbated the condition. It wasn't overpoweringly hot, but it was much warmer than the castle.

"This is our stop," the man said as he pulled on the reins, bringing the cart to a halt.

"Much obliged, stranger." Aegis shook the man's hand before looking back at the cargo. "Say, you wouldn't by chance need some help unloading all those rocks, would you?"

"Nah, that's how the boys around here earn a little money."

"I see; then we will be off. Thanks again."

I looked back at the old lady. She was still fast asleep in the covered wagon. When we walked away, a question came bubbling up. "You could have unloaded that wagon in minutes; why didn't you?"

"Didn't you hear? That's how the neighborhood boys make money. For some of those boys, that's the difference between eating or not this week."

I had never gone hungry before. "What do they do with the rocks?" I asked as we navigated among the clay hovels towards the inner city.

Aegis walked a few steps ahead of me, his coat now covered in a sheen of bronze from the dust. "This city's major export is gravel," he said as he paused before an enormous wheel. Several dozen people worked around the great wheel, which was propelling water to power a ladder shaft. They were making what looked like giant bricks.

"The city of Metropolis came to fame for having the strongest and largest wall," he continued. "Before the vampires came, souls flocked to this city for protection. They would give up their lives in the outskirts for the safety of its walls."

"But you said the woodsmen are gone." I didn't understand.

"I said they might be—no one can say for sure," Aegis corrected me.

"There hasn't been an attack in centuries; why continue to build their walls?" When I looked around, all I saw was disarray and poverty. Why would the people of Metropolis spend so much effort on a wall instead of working to make their homes and living conditions better?

Aegis took a sideways glance at me, knowing there were more questions. "Without proper leadership, people build walls and nothing else."

The city became more populated and dense as we moved forward. Beggars and street entertainers clogged the arteries that led to the center. The shops bled into one another as merchants fought for space. I noticed their wares were much more expensive and scarce than what was available at region one or even region five.

Yet, despite the sparse offerings, the Metropolis market reminded me of the one outside the castle. Sarah loved the markets outside the castle. She wasn't all bad. She was cold and reserved, but she did seem to care for me on some level. I refused to let my mother interact with my maid or Peter if I could help it. The best way to protect them was to stay out of trouble and out of sight. Mother had the power to rip away people I loved. I wouldn't risk losing Peter.

On my ninth birthday, I found a small cake waiting for me at my desk. He was wearing a party hat and spun a pink noise-maker around in his hand. It rattled loudly, but he thought it was funny, so I smiled.

"Thank you, Peter."

"Seeing's how it's your birthday, I thought we could play hooky—"

"No," I said firmly.

"Still refuse to let your guard down?"

"Not after what happened with Myrtle."

Peter nodded. While Sarah was an adequate maid, she was a reminder that, if I loved someone, they would be taken away. I'd only seen my mother a few times since she'd dismissed Myrtle. I'd fought to keep her as my maid, but Mother refused to budge on the issue. Vinicio fully supported my mother's decision. I stopped speaking to her for years after that, but it didn't seem to affect her. She'd rather have my silence than my shadow lingering behind her.

"All right, then," Peter interrupted my thoughts, "—student's choice. What do you want to learn about today?"

"Mythology."

"Mythology," he repeated. "About the other life?"

I nodded.

"It is said that when we die, our souls are reborn somewhere else. Occasionally, souls claim to remember parts of their other life, and they publish their memories. Some accounts are rather strange and less reputable, but some seem to match up with others."

"Couldn't they just make up a story like the other stories?"

"A copy? They could if they had access to the private library. Only castle officials and scholars have such access."

"So, several people recall the same things from the other life. It must be real then."

"The stewards have such information under lock and key, but I believe it to be real."

"What is the other life like?"

"It is more of the same from what I understand. People are born; people die. Rulers squabble over territory…" Peter's face lit up at the mention of rulers. "They don't just have kings. They have presidents, prime ministers, god-kings, and queens."

"Aren't they just the same thing?"

"For the most part. Presidents and prime ministers are elected leaders. The people cast votes to give them power. God-kings are just kings, but they are revered as gods. Queens are female kings."

"That can happen?"

"Oh, yes, it most certainly can. There is no reason why it couldn't happen here as well. We've just had no such luck yet."

Sarah knocked at the door before rolling lunch into the classroom.

"Just what are you teaching her?" Sarah teased. Her wry smile did nothing to diminish the serious tone of her voice. Her pale skin and long dark hair made her blue eyes so unnerving. She had a slight cleft on her chin and a scar on her lip.

"Oh, it's her birthday, so I'm telling her fairy tales."

"You'd rather stay cooped up in here with this old geezer when you could be playing outside?" she said with a smile that looked forced.

"I didn't know I could take the day off."

"Would you like me to ask?"

I nodded. Sarah left, and Peter shook off the tension from her visit.

"Take care with what you say around that one," he whispered.

"I always do."

"Good girl. Do you want to go outside the private chambers today? Maybe wander around outside the castle?"

"Could I do that?" I asked.

"Sure, if your stepfather gives us permission. You're old enough now not to run off or get lost. It's settled, then."

"What is settled?" Sarah asked, startling Peter and making me jump.

"If Nora can take the day off, we'd like to go on a little outing."

"Oh, how fun. I'll get my things," Sarah replied. Peter and I looked at one another with surprise.

An open-air market was set up outside the castle. Each vendor had a colorful tent that rested on thick green grass. The sky was clear and blue, unlike in the fifth region, where it was always overcast and gray. The first thing I did was take my shoes off and step on the grass. We had grass in the fifth region, but it was dry and long like hay.

Peter understood my fascination. Sarah attempted to chastise me, but he stopped her. No one seemed to care that I wasn't wearing shoes, and I liked the feel of it. We looked at the vendors; Sarah had more interest in the wares than we did.

She seemed interested in fabrics more than anything. Her eyes were glued to a lush, red taffeta. Peter and I moved on to look at other things, but she stayed behind to talk to the merchant about the fabric.

I noticed the people of region one appeared much healthier than the ones from region five. Their skin and hair looked shiny, and their complexions were soft and sort of glowing. Peter and Sarah didn't quite have the same shine to them, but then again, neither did I.

A man peddling sweets had some cookies dipped in chocolate, so Peter and I each got one. Mother was right about one thing: chocolate was divine. It seemed cruel to deny the rest of the world.

"How is it all these good things are here, but not everywhere else?" I asked Peter.

"Most of the food is produced in the third region. They refuse to send it to the seventh region of Hell for obvious reasons."

"The outlanders would attack them."

Peter nodded. "So, they send to their neighboring regions—the second and fourth—as well as to us, though we do some farming. The fifth and sixth regions are on the other side of the Starry Wood, and the only way they can get food is if the first region sends it."

"And do we?"

"Certainly, yes. But it's not always the freshest. For the most part, we send scraps, leftovers, and defective foods. We send it to the fifth region and hope it trickles over to the sixth region."

Sarah returned to us, her face stern and sullen. "If you've had enough sweets, it's time to return to the castle. Collect your shoes. I need to speak with Peter."

I ran ahead as she asked, but I wanted to know what she and Peter were talking about. Occasionally, I looked back to see their tense expressions. My shoes were in the same place I had left them. I put them back on and waited for Sarah and Peter to catch up. Sarah looked longingly at the red fabric, but didn't slow her gait.

"That fabric was pretty," I commented.

"Yes, and too rich for me," Sarah said. "Come along." She stormed past us towards the castle.

"What were you guys talking about?" I asked Peter.

"Oh, just a mouthpiece ensuring I know my place."

I wasn't sure what that meant, but it probably meant that Sarah was chastising him about something. She was always disapproving of something. Maybe she would be nicer to Peter if we did something nice for her.

"Peter, I want that red fabric Sarah was looking at."

"How much?"

"The whole bolt."

"Done. You want it sent to her room?"

I had nodded, and Peter had broken away when I reached the entrance of the castle.

In the most populated part of region six, even a yard of fabric was unseen, let alone a red taffeta. I wondered where Sarah was and if she was safe. I knew she wasn't really my friend, but I still worried about her. My worry for Sarah was like an extension of my worry for Peter, but that small voice in the back of my head told me that Sarah was beyond worrying about anymore.

Chapter Five

Aegis brushed people aside carefully so as to not give away his lineage. A flick of his arm could have sent several people sprawling. The crowd left me dazed, and I felt as if this mass of dirty, stinking people would swallow me whole. It was as if a collective, staring entity was attempting to suck the air from around me. My heart pounded, and I felt weak within the grasp of so many hands.

It was Aegis's hand that found mine once more. It wasn't a romantic action, but the touch was something I was unaccustomed to. I didn't want to pull away, but I didn't know if it was okay to rely on him too much. What he got out of this, I didn't know.

I wondered if Peter came from the sixth region—I could see him making a gamble or two. I couldn't imagine Peter being a zealot from region five. He wasn't from region one. I didn't know much about the second and third regions of Hell, so he might have been from there. I doubted he was an outlander, but then again, I knew nothing about outlanders, not even my own father. Peter painted them as survivalists, not necessarily bad people. I hoped that was true.

The only thing I knew about my father was something my grandmother had said about him when I was little. She had just made some bread and told me not to touch it. I was so hungry that I ripped a piece off the loaf and ate it the moment she walked away. Looking back now, it was obvious and a little funny, but when she came back into the room, she asked me if I had taken a piece.

I shook my head as hard as I could, but it was apparent that I was the culprit. She didn't lecture or punish me, but she bent down to meet my eyes and said one sentence.

"You're a liar just like your father."

That was the only thing I had ever learned about my father. I never stole another piece of bread from my grandparents, no matter how good it smelled. They never starved me, but I was a visitor in their home. I could never ask for food; I had to wait until they offered. They couldn't wait for me to leave. Their bread and generosity had been reserved for welcomed guests.

"Here we are," Aegis said.

We stood outside a clay residence that had a canopy entrance. There was a wooden door, old and worn by sand and heat. The fabric canopy was torn and propped with a few pieces of wood. This place looked important. For what, I didn't know, but it was the only home with a door in this city. The rest just had curtains for privacy.

"Can I trust you to stay here and not run off?" Aegis asked.

I nodded. "I don't have anywhere to run off to."

"Phineas is …" Aegis hesitated. "Interesting."

"Peter always said that interesting was a word that meant nothing."

"Just stay out here and try not to get into trouble."

And there I waited. Content to just sit in a patch of shade, I had no intention of moving. With my knees drawn under my chin, I observed the people of Metropolis. They were so busy. It seemed that most men had carts, and if they didn't have carts, they were begging from the men with carts. Their long tunics were sometimes belted, sometimes not.

Everyone wore sandals. I wished that I had sandals. The heat wasn't intolerable, but my blistered feet were further aggravated by the shoes that insulated that warmth. I took off my shoes and let my feet breathe, and the occasional wind provided some relief.

"Hey, kid, what are you doing there?" A man with a cart stood before me, looking at me curiously.

"I'm waiting for my dad; he's in there." I pointed at the door.

The man nodded. "Your papa didn't want you in there. Good, that's no place for a little girl."

I noticed his cart was full of random junk. "Do you have a pair of sandals in your cart?"

The man looked at his cart and shrugged. "I don't think so, but I'm headed to the swap market. They are bound to have some there."

"Where is it?"

"Just over there, next to the gambler's pit." The man motioned to a several-story building a few doors down. "Good luck, miss," he said before taking his wares to the market.

The idea of putting my shoes back on made me want to cry, but I knew walking on hot sand wouldn't be any better. I needed sandals, but I didn't have any money. My only option was to go to the swap market and make a trade. Ignoring the stinging rub against my heel and toes, I put my shoes back on and set off to the market.

Aegis had told me to stay where I was, but it was hot, and my feet hurt. I would be back before he knew I was missing. I was scared, but curiosity was edging me forward.

Have a look. Aegis will find you when he's done. He'll always find you, my other voice promised. Before I could stop myself, I was walking towards the building.

My other voice had a way of taking over when I was reluctant to do something. I wondered if it had any connection with the snake or with Vinicio's hand. Nothing like that had ever happened until recently. The other voice was mine—they were not my thoughts—it was like the thoughts were someone else's. When the snake and Vinicio incidents happened, it felt like how my other voice felt—like an undertow manipulating my ocean.

Inside the building were tables where various games were being played. There were games with cards and tokens, others with wheels that spun. Winners were raking small silver figures of various things I did not recognize. I overheard that the lower level held a boxing match, and several patrons were making their way to see it. It was the roof that hosted the swap market.

On the roof, the small market had little to offer. There were a dozen tents with carpeted floors and sellers guarding their wares. None looked friendly nor receptive enough to trade some dirty shoes for new sandals. What was I thinking? I needed to get back to where Aegis had told me to be. Sometimes that little voice got the best of me.

Accepting defeat, I went back downstairs. The casino was mostly vacant now except for a few stragglers finishing up their hands. An older man with large white muttonchops and a visor peered at me with his small, frameless glasses. "What is a young lady doing here in the gambling pit by herself?"

"I'm sorry, sir. I didn't know it wasn't allowed."

"Foreigner, I see. Any age is allowed, though most parents forbid their children to gamble here. This is the sixth region, after all. Many violent people reside here—the kind who would refuse to lose to a little girl."

I shrugged. "I don't have any money; I just wanted to see if I could trade my shoes for sandals at the market."

He leaned over his card table to have a look at my shoes. "Ah, I see. Come, play a round. It's on me."

I sat down. "But I don't know how to gamble."

The old man placed a silver token in front of me. "Everyone knows how to gamble; not everyone knows how to win. This token is yours. With this, you could easily afford a pair of sandals and maybe a small lunch. Or you could take a gamble—put it here." The old man pointed at a circle on the table. "And maybe, with a little luck, you can double your money."

I wanted to just walk away, but the prospect of winning suddenly felt more important than a new pair of sandals. *Sit down and play.* Something within me told me I would win, even if I didn't know how to play. "What do I do?"

The old man laughed until a coughing fit took over. "I know a gambler when I see one!" he declared. "All right. The game is Spades Fourteen. Spades are wild. Your goal is to get to fourteen with as many spades as you can within the three draws." The old man took the token I placed in the circle and exchanged it for several lesser tokens. "You place a bet and continue your bet between draws."

"What happens if no one gets fourteen?"

"The closest to fourteen wins. Good luck."

"Okay." I placed the largest of my tokens in the circle, and the dealer shuffled and dealt a card to me and then himself. My card was a seven of spades. The dealer's card remained hidden to me, but he put an additional token on the table.

I mirrored his movement by placing another token down. He eyed me cautiously, attempting to read my expression. *You have him now.* The next card placed before me turned out to be a six of spades. All spades were wild, and I needed fourteen. The voice in the back of my mind was silent but smug.

The dealer seemed to know what I was thinking because he put the smallest token into the pile. "Dealer is not allowed to fold their hand, even if the player is clearly winning."

I put another token into the amassed pile, and the dealer dealt the final card.

Aegis

Daylight filtered in through the window shades, more than enough for Aegis to see the home was filled with junk. Books were stacked from floor to ceiling. Various swathes of fabric were strewn about as a sort of makeshift carpet. Tables and chairs stood all over the room, though most were broken and had their remains scattered around.

It seems it's getting worse, Aegis noted.

Aegis stood in the middle of a messy room with a thumb resting on his belt. He said nothing and made no attempt to find Phineas. He could smell the man and knew he was nearby. It was only a few minutes before Phineas sat up from the rubble. His hair was shorn—all except for a fuzzy white tuft at the very top of his head. Paler than any man Aegis had ever seen, he had eyes that were red and bloodshot. Phineas had many problems, and his strange appearance was the least of them.

"Aegis! Chhu-Chhu!" Phineas yelled uncontrollably.

"Hello, Phineas, the years have not been kind to you."

Phineas exploded with another incoherent noise before regaining his composure. "No, everything has been getting worse, I'm afraid."

Aegis shook his head and helped the man to his feet.

"You look the same, strangely enough," said Phineas. "It's been what, fifteen years? You haven't changed at all."

"I need your help. You tried to tell me something years ago; what was it?" Aegis asked, ignoring Phineas's observation.

A series of retching noises came from Phineas. His whole body convulsed as he fought against the expulsion. After several minutes, he was finally able to remain still, but his condition left him weak. "You shouldn't have come to me; I'm getting worse. I'm dangerous to more than just myself."

"I had no choice. You're the only one who could possibly give me answers."

"You want answers about what is happening in the castle?" Phineas was straight to the point.

"You once tried to tell me something—something important. I refused to listen," Aegis said.

"Fifteen years ago," Phineas confirmed before suddenly falling into a seizure. The convulsions were much more violent than Aegis remembered. His sickly acquaintance didn't have much time left. It was useless to restrain him—Aegis would likely do more damage attempting to do so.

Several minutes passed, and he began to wonder if he had come too late. Phineas was psychic, but such an ability had awful consequences. Aegis had first encountered the man in his youth. At the time, he had a twitch and a slight case of Tourette's, but the empathic abilities charged his brain with currents not intended for any mortal, and his mind became a series of blown circuits.

It was true that the last time Aegis had seen him was fifteen years ago. He had come to Phineas to seek out more of his own kind but instead got promises of world-changing prophecy. Aegis didn't wish for such a thing; he merely sought one of his own kind. Specifically, he was looking for a sign of Minerva's whereabouts. Aegis had run out before Phineas could tell him about the kings of old.

Finally, Phineas was released from the spell. "The stewards haven't been honest." Wiping the froth from his mouth, the psychic continued. "They have indeed been looking for the king of souls, but they do not intend to crown them."

Aegis nodded, knowing as much. He had the same suspicion, but without proof or reason to move against the steward, such things went unchecked. He was also angry at the idea—not angry at the stewards for what they were doing, but rather angry that Minerva had left him to look for proof. He never saw her again.

"Without a real king, the borders are weak and allow chaos," Phineas went on. "Allowing the outlanders to kidnap souls and drag them into slavery." Aegis was aware of this as well.

"It's a rare occurrence …" Aegis began but was interrupted.

"Lies!" Phineas hissed. "The castle only wants people to think that. With each passing day, outlanders are leaving the region and entering the promised lands unchecked. Even the trackers are unable to monitor them all."

"And the steward won't look for the king, even now?"

Phineas smiled. "Oh, he's looking."

"Tell me your prophecy," Aegis demanded.

"The king's soul is awakening …" Phineas fell to the floor. His mouth foamed, and the capillaries in his eyes began to burst.

Aegis waited for him to come out of the seizure, but the longer he waited, the more he pitied the man. He knew Phineas wasn't going to recover. Instead of letting the man suffer needlessly, Aegis snapped his neck as fast as he could.

Aegis wished he could have heard the entirety of Phineas's vision. The man had held onto it for fifteen years just for him. He suffered at great lengths to spread the knowledge he had. Aegis didn't have time to grieve over Phineas, however. He had a little girl to worry about, a girl he felt inexplicably drawn to. He'd never held much concern for souls before, but this one was different. She was lost in the past just as he was.

With Phineas gone, there was nothing to keep them in Metropolis. Aegis didn't like the idea of raising a girl around thieves and gamblers. Aegis didn't know much about teenage girls, but he did know safer places than this. He'd take her to region three, perhaps. Somewhere nice and quiet where she could grow up and be happy.

Nora

"Seven of spades, six of spades, and an ace of spades." The old man nodded. "Very good, young miss. You have now doubled your token. Would you like to play again?"

"Yes," I said eagerly. Dropping another token on the circle, the old man dealt another card. It was a queen of spades, followed by an eight of spades and a six of spades. The dealer had a better hand, but my fourteen of spades with an additional spade still beat his hand.

I collected my winnings and placed yet another token on the circle. The old man wasn't smiling at me anymore.

I should have been frightened. Several men, including the game warden, were surrounding the table, attempting to discover my secret. It seemed impossible to lose. I didn't understand why. I wanted to win, and I did.

The pile of tokens in front of me only grew larger. My bets became bolder. I was unable to lose. All I could do was smile and shove another pile of tokens into the circle, compelled by my greed and the satisfaction of seeing the old man lose.

They couldn't figure out how I was winning, and the disgruntlement was growing louder with each passing deal. The thrill of the gamble surpassed any fear I once had. I'd quit after a few more rounds. I just wanted to win a big one first.

"Perhaps the lady would like to try a new game?" the game warden asked, extending a welcome to a long table with a spinner with numbers.

"Sure," I agreed. The old man exchanged my tokens with larger, more manageable tokens. He seemed happy to be rid of me, but before I moved to the next table, I gave him a token. "Thanks."

The game warden himself explained the game to me, but I didn't listen. The old man was wrong. I didn't need to know how to play the game; I merely needed the desire to win. My winning streak had attracted a crowd, and other players were now betting on my winning.

The game warden spun a reel, and the ball rolled around before landing precisely where I wished. There were cheers and hoots of excitement from the other gamblers and exasperated faces from the pit bosses. By the third round of roulette, Aegis found me. His expression was one of awe and fear. It's as if he was looking at me for the first time.

Not wasting time, Aegis grabbed me and quietly said, "We're leaving." He scooped up the winnings into a purse and nodded at the warden, who nodded back.

"Hey, I wanted to buy some sandals!" I said.

"Later." Aegis was practically dragging me out of the building.

"I can't walk in these shoes anymore; my feet are blistered so badly."

Instead of debating with me, he walked up to a caravan exiting the city. "Sir, a silver token in exchange for a ride."

The driver's face lit up under his straw hat, and his mouth dropped at the amount offered. "Lemme see."

Aegis withdrew a silver token from the purse, and the man nodded quickly. "Hop in back; there is water and some bread. Help yourselves." The man was very pleased with the token. He clearly felt he was getting an excellent deal.

I took off the worn shoes and let my feet breathe once more. Once we had settled in the back of the caravan, Aegis resumed glaring at me.

"Why are you looking at me so weird?" I asked.

"I told you to stay put."

"I was just trying to get some sandals."

"I thought you were more cautious than that. Did you forget your stepfather is looking for you?"

"I know—I just had to," I said.

Aegis looked at the driver to make sure he wasn't listening in. "You have no idea, do you?"

I didn't know what to say. I had disappointed him, and for some reason, it felt worse than when I misbehaved with my mother and grandparents. "I'm sorry; I didn't mean to cause any trouble." Tears filled my eyes. I felt so stupid crying because I got in trouble.

"Nora." Aegis moved closer, mindful of the driver's proximity. "We need to be more careful. We don't know why the steward wants you dead."

"Isn't it obvious?" I asked him, tears blurring my vision.

"It isn't—not yet, at least," Aegis said.

What was he talking about?

"I'm half outlander," I whispered. It felt good to get it off my chest. How did he not know?

Aegis's blank stare masked his confusion poorly. "You think that's why he wants to kill you?" he asked incredulously.

"Everyone in region five hated me for it."

Aegis looked away for a moment, but his responses softened. "I've never met someone who was half outlander, but I'm sure it happens more often than you think. Perhaps he doesn't want others to know about you. It would prove his reign is weakening if an outlander can get so far from the seventh region unnoticed."

"You won't tell anyone?"

"Never," Aegis promised. "But how did you win all that money?"

"I don't know," I admitted. "I've never done anything like that before."

"That's a small fortune you won. It's enough to build your own castle somewhere. What did you start with?"

"A small piece. I went all in each round and won every game," I explained.

"That's not beginner's luck; it's a miracle."

I wanted to tell him it wasn't beginner's luck, and that I had known I would win. It was that voice in my head that guided me or put words in my mouth that I normally wouldn't use. It was my voice, but at the same time, it wasn't. Telling people about voices in your head didn't end well, so I kept it to myself.

"You'll need to teach me how you win," Aegis teased.

Chapter Six

Vinicio

Vinicio watched Bella sitting at her vanity while she brushed her hair. Her daughter was still missing, and the inner conflict was beginning to show on her gentle face. Whenever she thought he wasn't looking, Bella was either crying or staring off into the distance. As Bella's husband, it was Vinicio's duty to listen to her and help her grieve. It would help her if she could talk about her daughter.

"Tell me about her," Vinicio commanded.

"Nora?" Bella asked.

He nodded slowly. "To be honest, I don't know much about her. Tell me about her father. Just what happened?"

Bella fidgeted and looked frightened by the idea, but he needed to know.

"Sweetie, there is nothing you could do that would make me feel differently about you. Go on, tell me your story."

Bella told him that Nora looked like her father, and that she resented her daughter for that. At the same time, she felt guilty for putting her own needs before the child's.

"When I looked for a husband, I told myself it was for Nora's sake," she said. "To get my daughter away from her bitter grandparents. It wasn't until I met you that I admitted to myself that I was not meant to be a parent."

There was nothing more Bella could do besides wait for Nora to grow up. When Vinicio met Bella, she seemed resigned to such a fate, but he had need of a wife, and he needed a way to watch Nora more closely. Bella could never know his true motivations, but even if she did, would she have made any other choice? Vinicio thought not.

"I've never said it out loud before," Bella said, wiping her tears away with a napkin. "You must think I'm an awful person."

"You were very young when you had Nora, yes?" he asked.

"Yes, I was fourteen. I'd never met anyone like her father before. He felt so safe and reassuring. He wasn't even afraid of my parents."

Vinicio tipped her chin up so that her eyes met his. "I'm not afraid of your parents." That made Bella laugh. She knew the slightest annoyance in his voice sent people scattering. She'd seen him in action.

"You're from the fifth region—the region of zealots, fundamentalists, and those prone to obsession," Vinicio explained. "Have you ever wondered why the outlands are between the fourth and the sixth region instead of remaining in numerical order?"

Of course, she had wondered—everyone did at one point or another. "I always assumed it was because it was the least desirable land and the furthest away from the castle."

"Both are valid points, but the paramount reason is soul placement," he explained.

Pouring another glass of wine, Vinicio motioned to a servant to pick up her plate.

"The Starry Wood is the center of our world. It is the forest where the monsters reside, but it is also the largest source of water. The first circle of Hell is the smallest, but it shares the largest border with the woods, giving us the best land.

"From there, the second, third, and fourth regions go clockwise around the woods. But after the fourth region lay the seventh, sixth, and fifth regions. Not quite chronological, is it?"

Bella shook her head and smiled before drinking more wine.

"The fourth region is dedicated to the souls who pride themselves in the aristocracy. These people are in a constant battle of social climbing. Even if an outlander did make it past the barriers, they would find the culture a barrier within itself. The fundamentalists won't accept them, and the social climbers would sooner die than admit an outlander, leaving him with little option."

Vinicio took Bella's hand and kissed her fingertips gently. "I know we've had some bumps in the past, but I'd like to hear your thoughts on trying to conceive again," he said.

"I don't know—last time, it was so awful."

"I know. Nature can be so cruel, but we are getting on in years, and if we want a child, we must keep trying. I don't want anyone debating the legitimacy of our marriage."

"Are people doing that now?" Bella asked. Vinicio had struck the correct fear, it seemed.

"People talk, but it's nothing for you to worry about. Just focus on being as healthy as you can—and on me, of course," Vinicio teased.

He laughed, and Bella laughed along with him.

She told Vinicio more about her life before she married the steward. Growing up, she saw someone hang or burn alive every week, it seemed. Their bodies would be left on display until the next martyr came along.

She talked about how her parent's eyes came alive when they watched a person burn. They enjoyed the sense of control and piety it gave them, but it made Bella feel ill. She craved the zeal in their eyes when they saw justice served, but she didn't know where to find it.

That was when she met him. Nora's father was much older, and his clothes were ragged, but he was kind to her. He was the first person to speak to her like an adult. He told her that she needed to find her own voice and that her parents didn't have the right to punish her so severely.

Their relationship progressed as he walked her home from school each day. He said it was because he lived nearby, and he said he didn't want her walking by herself. Not long after that, she started lying to her parents to visit his little shack at the edge of town.

Bella never thought about why he lived so poorly; she just assumed he had trouble finding work. It was indeed a scarce thing in her town. Hearing this, Vinicio wondered if she simply didn't *want* to notice, but he said nothing as she told him what happened next.

"It wasn't long until it became more romantic," Bella told Vinicio. "It all happened so fast."

One minute she was crying on his bed because she was afraid to go home, and the next minute, he was on top of her. She knew what they were doing was wrong, but she loved him so much and didn't want to do anything that would push him away. If he turned her away, it would be worse than any flame. Vinicio admired her passion for love. No doubt she was a loyal and self-sacrificing wife as well.

The romance went on for several months. When Bella came down with morning sickness, she thought it was the flu. After a week of severe symptoms, her parents called a doctor. People in town hinted to her parents that she was involved with a man, but they didn't believe the town gossip. Her parents were severe, but they trusted her to be morally adept.

"I'll never forget the look on my father's face when he found out his daughter had become the town harlot."

Her father's disappointment weighed on her heart to this day. Vinicio could tell Bella loved her parents, but they couldn't forgive her, and they couldn't understand her. She kept her fond memories as close as she could despite how rare they were.

The night she found out she was pregnant, Bella's father went out with a group of his friends and found Nora's father. Poor Bella was under the impression that they were arranging a wedding. Usually, when this sort of thing happened to other girls, they would make the father of the child marry the mother. Bella waited by the window for the party to return, except it was only her father who returned. She raced down the stairs, ignoring her nausea.

Pulling open the door to her father, she asked, "When is the wedding?"

Her father didn't answer her. He wouldn't even look at her. Her mother came from behind Bella, and that is when her father finally spoke. "Darling, I told you to stay here. Send the girl to the center of town."

"That was when I knew something was wrong," Bella told Vinicio with tears in her eyes.

She had run as fast as she could to the center of town. "I still remember the smell of the pyre burning. It made me sick to my stomach."

Bella persisted despite the sickness. When she reached the town, he was already dead. There was nothing to be done. She fell to her knees and sobbed at his bonfire. She remained by his burning carcass until her father carried her home. Bella grieved wildly the following months. It was a wonder Nora survived. Bella hardly ate or slept. If anyone so much as spoke to her, she would go into fits.

"Do you think your grieving is what saved you from exile?" Vinicio asked.

Bella nodded and drank more wine. "I know it was."

The town elders deliberated on the topic, she explained. Her parents had been willing to do whatever their town decided. But when they saw the extent of her suffering, many raised questions. Did Bella know what she was doing? Did she know her lover had been an outlander? These questions needed answers before they could make a verdict, so the town leader paid Bella a visit in her ninth month of pregnancy.

"Bella," Mr. Roy had said as he sat beside her bed. "I understand you are going through a lot right now, but it is vital that you answer me honestly, okay?"

Bella looked at him but said nothing. He seemed perplexed by the animosity in her eyes.

"Why are you so angry, child?" the old man asked.

"You killed him."

"Yes, we did. Do you understand why we had to do that?"

Bella could feel the anger rising in her throat, but she needed to know why. Why didn't they arrange a marriage?

"It turns out that you are not the only young lady that man seduced," the old man explained. "Several other girls came forward, one even younger than yourself."

"You lie!" Bella hissed.

"No, my dear." The earnestness in his eyes made her recoil. "It *is* the truth, but that is not why we burned him."

"Why?" she whispered.

"He came from the outlands. We've seen his type from time to time. They make their way from the region next to us—win a lucky gamble and move to this region. It doesn't usually take this long for us to become aware of them, but that man's vices were subtle."

"I looked down at my swollen belly in disgust," Bella told Vinicio. "I was carrying an outlander's child."

The rest of her life would be tainted with a small, crying reminder of what she had done. There would be no marriage to a man who claimed to love her. He had probably sired several bastards. She realized that Mr. Roy wasn't lying.

Bella recalled a time when she was in town with her parents and saw him passing by. She pretended not to know him, as he had instructed her. But she *did* know Jessasia, and Jessasia was looking at him. Bella had always told herself that Jessasia was just infatuated with the handsome stranger, but it was an expression of longing.

"Who are the other girls?" she had asked.

Mr. Roy had shaken his head. "No, Bella, I won't tell you that."

"Is Jessasia one of them?" she demanded.

Mr. Roy said nothing.

"Is she pregnant too?"

"Bella …"

"Is she?" Bella raged.

Mr. Roy looked down. "Yes, as are two others."

"I screamed into my pillow," Bella told Vinicio. "Mr. Roy stayed with me for some time that night. Shortly after that, I went into labor with Nora."

Seventeen horrific hours later, the doctor said her hips were too narrow to pass a baby and wanted to cut the baby out. Towards the end, she begged for death. Her mother was wailing in grief as Bella's blood drenched the bed. Salvation had come at the hands of a cranky old woman.

The midwife was a witch. She practiced magic that was said to only belong to five distinct families, all within the fifth region. The woman had fire-red hair and blue eyes. Bella had no idea how old she was, but Mrs. Mason was among the oldest in the region, probably the world, from what Vinicio gathered.

"Get away from her, you butcher!" rasped the old woman, who had a crooked stance and frizzy red hair crawling down her back. Despite her age, her hair maintained its color.

The woman produced from her bag what looked to be a rubber cap attached to a rope and a pair of flat tongs.

"Here, hold these." The woman thrust the tongs into Bella and used them to widen her, instructing the doctor to hold them while she attached the rubber cap to the baby's head. The woman pulled the baby from Bella and saved them both.

Bella's life was still in danger for the next several days, but Mrs. Mason stayed with her and Nora. She applied natural salves and sang chants. Bella was too weak to remember much of those first few days, but she was nursed back to health by the witch.

"He isn't a doctor—he's a butcher," Mrs. Mason declared. "He cuts up any patient at the first opportunity. You stay clear of him."

Even Bella's father knew the man was quick to surgery. When he feared the doctor's intentions, he had gone to the pagan midwife and begged her help. Bella had never felt more ashamed of herself. Her father saved her life, and all she could do was bring him embarrassment and dishonor.

Once Bella's strength returned, the midwife left. Before she did, she asked if she could take Nora with her. Bella was inclined to say yes, but her parents said no. "The babe is Bella's burden now."

"Children shouldn't be a burden; they shouldn't be a punishment," the old woman pleaded. "She's still a child herself. That man was a lecherous outlander swine—he is to blame, not Bella, and certainly not the baby."

"If we change our minds, we will let you know."

"My parents never changed their minds. They made me keep the baby. And when I refused to pick her up, my mother would. When the baby cried from hunger, my father would feed it. I couldn't have care less," Bella confessed.

The witch had told Bella's parents that she was suffering a mother's depression, that it was common for mothers, especially those in bad situations. She gave them herbs and said she would cast spells in Bella's favor. Her parents had little love for the baby, but their pride required them to keep her. They named her Nora.

Over time, Bella did grow more affectionate towards her daughter, but her best intentions were always derailed by her desire for romance. Bella wanted to be swept off her feet and loved unconditionally by a man. Such a situation was ideal for Vinicio, who had needs of his own.

"I always think about how badly I've treated her," Bella concluded. "Nora loved me no matter what I did. Why wasn't that good enough for me?"

"You have needs just like anyone else," Vinicio told her.

"Now I've lost her forever."

Nora may have been lost forever, but perhaps that was for the best.

A knock on the door interrupted the couple. It was Rebus. His long beard and droopy eyelids wiggled as he walked towards them.

"My lord, I have a message for you." His hand trembled as it extended with a small tube of parchment. The seal belonged to Alfie, the tracker general.

"Excuse me for a moment, my love," Vinicio said as he went to his study to review the message.

The target is alive. Has the order changed?

A.

Vinicio read the note several times. Nora was still alive somehow.

He wrote a reply.

Orders remain the same. Target must be deceased before returning to the castle.

V.

Vinicio had heard little from Hacia, the hawk hunter general, but that was her way. Hacia was known for her loyalty, however. When a rebellion rose against Vinicio's father, it was Hacia who had straightened out the fray. The hawk hunters, along with a small group of followers, blamed his father for a series of missing people and the deaths of several babies. Fortunately, the trackers never aligned with the hunters. When the previous general betrayed Vinicio's father, it was Hacia who had struck the fallen general down. Alfie was young and eager to prove that he would outmatch the legendary tracker, and happily took his place.

The notion made Vinicio smile. Let the games begin.

Chapter Seven

Nora

"I've always been my mother's dirty little secret," Nora told Aegis as they traveled. "My father was an outlander. I don't know how they met or anything about him aside from that."

Even if an outlander was successful in higher regions, they would always be an outlander. Forever ostracized, their children were guaranteed the same untouchable label.

"When I was younger," Nora continued, "Mother would meet a nice man, and they would fall in love and make all sorts of plans. At first, she would tell them right away about my lineage. When upfront honesty didn't work, she would wait until they were proposing before telling her boyfriends about me. When she started seeing Vinicio, she left me with my grandparents until my grandfather went to the castle and confronted her. It was then, that Vinicio invited me to stay at the castle with him and my mother."

After a time, Aegis finally spoke. "Vampires don't have children, but we do love. I don't pretend to know what it's like to feel so unwanted, but I have lost my only love."

"What happened?" I asked, glad to change the subject.

"I don't know. I've been searching for years. She was hunting woodsmen, just like me, but one day she just vanished. I searched everywhere, but she was gone."

"Did the woodsmen get her?"

"No." He sighed. "I followed her tracks and scent to the very place I first found you. After that, she had just vanished."

"What was her name?"

Aegis smiled. "Minerva."

"Did she have a scar on her hand like you?" I knew it was random, but I wanted to know and didn't know how else to work it into a conversation politely.

"No. I'm the only one with this."

I shifted on the wooden bench. "How did it happen, if you don't mind me asking?"

"It happened before I slept in the ground. To tell the truth, I don't remember." Aegis could clearly tell I wanted a more exciting story, but he wasn't a very good liar.

"What are we going to do now, Aegis?" My voice wavered with fear.

It felt much better to be in a wagon than walking. What scared me was that Aegis hadn't mentioned where we would go next. He didn't seem to have any other friends or connections to help us, and I kept waiting for him to tell me to wait somewhere only to never return.

"Hey, everything will be okay," he told me. His eyes grew dark when he lied.

We traveled the remainder of the day in silence. When nightfall came, the driver stopped and made camp for the night. Once the horses were watered and fed, he invited us to sleep by his fire. His name was Jason. He'd inherited the caravan and trade routes from his father. This was his third trip on his own.

"I probably won't do this forever," Jason explained by the fire. "Once I get enough money saved, I'm going to the fifth region to start a small ranch."

"There's some decent pastures in the upper regions," Aegis agreed.

"You've been there?" Jason asked.

"I've been everywhere. I think the third region is my favorite, though."

Jason looked astonished. "What do you do, stranger?"

Aegis paused for a second. "I used to work for the castle."

"Wowee, who would have thought?"

Aegis laughed.

I wasn't in a mood for conversation. I was still reeling from everything that had happened over the last week. It had been eight days since I had been forced from the castle, and Aegis stirred doubt in my mind about Vinicio's motives. I assumed it was because my father was an outlander, but no one seemed to care about that aside from the people in the town I grew up in. Not once did Peter, Myrtle, Sarah, or anyone else mention it. Why did I think Vinicio cared about who my father was?

In truth, I just assumed Vinicio was to blame because I didn't like him. I always felt uncomfortable around him. Maybe it was a mistake. Or maybe it wasn't Vinicio. There was a shadow of a doubt in my mind, and it confused my image of the man. What if my former maid Sarah did it in retaliation for being dismissed? Or maybe someone else didn't like me? What if I was wrong?

I could tell Aegis was holding something back, but what?

I always had so many questions, but I never had the answers I needed. Aegis took off his dusty brown trench coat and laid it over my shoulders. I laid down on my side and wrapped the coat around me like a blanket. The men continued talking as I drifted off to sleep. The fire was just warm enough to ward off the chill of the night.

When I awoke the next morning, Jason was gone, and Aegis was trying desperately to keep the fire going.

"Where's Jason?" I asked.

"I sent him on his way," Aegis said.

"Why did you do that?"

Aegis's brow was furrowed, and his face drawn. "We're being followed."

We broke camp with greater care that morning. Before Jason departed, he had given us several bread rolls and water for the trip. We walked further from the road than usual.

"Last night, the same hawk made several passes over our camp," Aegis explained.

"Hawk hunters." I knew what that meant. I was being hunted by my stepfather. Trackers would be a threat to me, but could they do anything against Aegis?

"The castle trackers are not people to underestimate," Aegis said. "They would have a hard time killing me, but it can be done. We don't know how much they know or how many of them are tracking us. I'd be worried if five or six of them were ready and waiting." Then he warned me, "Trackers and hunters developed skills and tools to use against vampires should the need arise."

"Like what?" I asked.

Aegis laughed. "I can't even say for sure."

"Is there anything that will kill you outright? Like poison or something?"

"I'll tell you when you're old and gray."

I thought it was an odd sort of promise, but I realized what it meant. "You're sticking with me to the end, then."

"I guess so."

"Why?" I could tell the hardness in my voice alarmed him.

"Why what?"

"Why are you so intent on staying with me?"

Aegis walked along the trail, kicking up dust. "I'm not entirely sure myself.

I just feel like you're where I need to be."

I was grateful for that, but at the same time, it scared me. What did he expect in return? It didn't feel like he had any other motive than to care for me, but I just didn't know how to trust anyone. At the moment, I didn't have a choice but to rely on him.

"Where to, then?" I asked as I wiped my tears away.

"I thought we would cut through the Starry Wood and hop over to region three. The trackers won't go through the Starry Wood, so we could lose them."

"Why won't they go into the Starry Wood?"

"It's too dangerous."

"Wouldn't it be too dangerous for us too, then?"

"Not for me." Aegis smiled.

We reached the edge of the Starry Wood, and memories of the woodsmen flashed through my mind. I reluctantly followed Aegis into the woods. It felt so strange to be right back at the forest after only a short amount of time, but all regions touched the Starry Wood. It was the center of our world. The trees were enormous, and everything was covered in moss. Ferns grew from the ground and from stumps and burrows in the trees. Moss hung on thin branches, creating a green veil above us.

It would have been a beautiful and magical forest had I not nearly died the last time I'd gotten so close. Among the foliage, I noticed many large boulders placed randomly in the forest itself. Some of them were covered in moss, but many seemed to be recently added.

"Do the woodsmen move boulders around?"

"Yes. We never understood why. It was either some way of communicating or maybe something they did when they were bored," Aegis explained.

Aegis walked ahead and examined the forest carefully. He reminded me of a cat before a storm. I lagged, unaccustomed to the terrain. Every step I made was a loud snap and crunch behind Aegis's soft step, no doubt making his job harder. The forest was getting denser the further we got. I was up to my knees in saplings and ferns. It was like wading in a green pool.

"There are other things in this forest," Aegis warned me, "so keep your eyes peeled."

"What kind of things?"

"Bears, wolves, jaguars—all sorts of big animals that are always hungry."

We pushed onward, only taking breaks when we had to. As we stepped over rocks and soft spots on the ground and pushed through bushes, I wasn't sure how much more I could take. It was exhausting, and the humidity of the forest was stifling.

"Remind me why we are going this way again."

"The animals shouldn't be a problem. Most of them are nocturnal, like the woodsmen." Aegis paused and looked around suspiciously. "Do you smell that?"

"Smell what?" My nose crinkled as I sought the smell.

"Smells like smoke."

"Do fires happen here?" I asked. The wood seemed too damp to catch fire.

"It's too damp for a forest fire. Something is happening."

In a moment, Aegis was in action, climbing up the side of a tree to get a higher vantage point. I didn't leave the spot where I sat. A low thundering noise rumbled. I'd never heard anything like it. It grew closer, and I could make out cries of fear from various animals. The greenery began to shake as animals emerged from ahead.

They were all running in my direction, but they weren't charging at me. I stood up and looked for a place to hide. Before I could, Aegis landed on the ground, lifted me by the waist, and leaped upward into a tree. He hopped from branch to branch, tree to tree, while the animals ran below us.

I felt like a ragdoll, but it was better than being a trampled ragdoll. From the branch, I got a better view of the animals. There were great big white bears, tigers, and elephants running side by side, a horse with a horn on its head, and a large lizard I didn't recognize. Predator and prey were running together from a greater enemy.

"They're scared," I shouted.

"The forest is being smoked out," Aegis said.

"Who would do that?"

"A tracker."

The smoke's tentacles crawled slowly along the tree trunks. I could smell it, and it was starting to sting my eyes. Whatever it was, it wasn't ordinary smoke. It had some sort of chemical in it that made it hard to breathe and see. Aegis relied on all his senses for his abilities, and the smoke was affecting him more than he was willing to admit.

"The smoke is making it hard for you to see," I told him.

"I'm fine. Just let me focus."

The smoke was slowly swallowing us whole. It must have been some sort of smoke bomb created by the trackers for this very reason. We were not the first to try to hide in or cut through the Starry Wood. I worried about what they would do if they caught us. How many were there?

Aegis held me firmly as he climbed higher. The branches were thinner, making me feel even more unstable. He was hopping from branch to bendy branch, and I was countering my weight to try and save myself if he let go.

"I know you're scared," he said. "It's high up, but you need to trust me."

"I'm sorry."

I tried my best to hold still, but it wasn't until he held me so close to him that I stopped flailing around. I'd never been this close to a man before. Despite all the smoke, I could smell him. He smelled like tree sap and leather, and there was also an orange scent I couldn't place. It took my mind off the situation for a moment, but as Aegis ran out of thinner branches to use, he had no choice but to go down into the smoke.

I started coughing, and I couldn't stop. The smoke burned and clawed at my throat. I couldn't see anything but the gray fog. Aegis stopped to take off his coat and drape it over my head. His eyes were different. The whites had gone red, giving the blue a feral contrast.

"What's wrong with your eyes?" I asked as he pulled the coat over my head.

"This will help protect you from the smoke."

"Aegis?" I asked, my voice muffled under his coat.

"It's okay; it's just something that happens sometimes."

"When you are in danger?"

"When I sense danger, yeah."

With my face covered, I could still smell the smoke. If we could have gotten lower, the smoke wouldn't have been so bad, but the stampede of animals was still running beneath us. I just wanted a strong wind to blow the smoke in the other direction, just long enough for Aegis to find his way out. Those eyes scared me.

I prayed for wind as I coughed. Then, something flew past my head.

"What was that?" I asked.

"A stone shot from a sling."

"They're gaining on us?"

"It seems so. They can navigate the smoke better than I can. Nora, I may have to get down and fight them."

I didn't want him to do that. If something happened to him, I wouldn't stand a chance. But it was more than my own well-being; I had feelings for him. There was still a part of me that didn't trust him, but despite my misgivings,

I felt safe in his arms. More than anything, I wanted him to come out of this alive.

"Don't do that," I told him.

My tears stung through the smoke. Big, fat, tears fell from my eyes, and I couldn't wipe them away with the coat over my head. I didn't care. I let the rain fall. Bitterness bit at me harder than the smoke. Was I going to lose Aegis too?

"I may not have another option," Aegis said.

The commotion subsided. The animals were still running, and the smoke still threatened the forest, but the air had changed. The sounds of the forest had become muffled.

It was then that Aegis laughed.

"Why are you laughing?"

He didn't answer, but moments later, my head felt wet. It was raining. It wasn't a gust of wind, but it could bring down the smoke. I welcomed the dampness despite how it made the jacket cling to my head. It wasn't long before the rain became a downpour. The smoke was indeed clearing. My throat was sore and parched from the smoke, but my coughing became less frequent. Aegis moved faster and with a stronger sense of direction.

"Doesn't the rain make you slip?" I asked, remembering a time I had slid on a wet stone.

"It does, but the branches are so thick it's easy to regain my footing. It's an advantage our tracker friend won't have down there in the mud and the moss."

The animals began to slow and spread out. They fanned in every direction, and the rumbling of their stampede stilled. The rain was unrelenting, but a welcomed gift. Aegis no longer smelled like orange, leather, and resin; he just smelled like wet.

Aegis didn't slow down until we had emerged from the tree line and landed on the ground. Only then did he release me. Pulling the coat off my head, he put it back on and adjusted his collar. I looked out to see an increasingly deforested land. We had landed on grass, but it was patchy and yellow.

"We should keep moving," Aegis said. "Trackers won't go to the outlands."

"You said they wouldn't go into the Starry Wood."

Aegis looked at me crossly. "Let's hope they don't prove me wrong again."

"So, we're going to the outlands."

"Unfortunately, yes."

"Is it really as bad as they say?"

"Most people who say have never really seen it. Let's keep moving."

The barrier around the outlands was much more literal than I had expected. The other regions were segregated by signs, hedges, and rivers. Now, Aegis and I approached an enormous canyon that seemed to have no bottom. I wondered how we were going to cross, but we soon came to a bridge. The bridge was made of steel and wood with tracks that were far enough apart that a person couldn't walk over them. A man waited with a long cart that could glide across the rails.

"You know where you're headed, lad?" the old man asked.

Aegis nodded. "I know."

"No place for a little girl." The old man shook his head disapprovingly.

"I'm not here to sell her," Aegis explained. "Just region hopping."

The old man glared from the intense sunlight. "I suppose it's better to take your chances here than it is to go through the Wood."

We were given admission to the outlands. My knees locked up once we stepped into the cart. I could do nothing but stand frozen in terror as a chain and crank pulled the cart across an abyss. I was drenched in sweat, and not because of the heat.

A rumbling noise echoed throughout the canyon below.

"The canyon is collapsing?" I asked.

"Has been for years," the old man said. "The outlanders don't even try walking across the tracks anymore. They just find themselves an easy route to climb. It probably takes them several days, and the trackers are usually waiting for them on the other side, but they manage to get through."

Chapter Eight

The cart reached the other side with a large clank. I climbed out with shaky legs. Aegis's forehead was wrinkled with worry lines. There was nothing in sight, just orange desert.

The old man handed us a hand-carved wooden token. "Give that to any of the bridge guards, and they will let you leave. Don't show that to anyone else," he warned us.

"Thank you, my friend." Aegis said.

When we got further away from the old man, Aegis waited patiently for my next round of questions.

"So, what are we going to do?" I asked.

"We are going to cut through the city of Murdoch. Here," Aegis said, pulling all the supplies out of the bag. "Eat and drink as much as you can."

I didn't know what city he was talking about, but I was happy with this notion. It was the first time in weeks I hadn't had to ration out the food. Aegis put the silver purse around his neck and buttoned up his jacket.

"You're not hot?" I asked with a mouth full of bread.

"I am, but I won't die from it. If they see anything of value, they will rip us apart to get it."

I wasn't afraid of the outlands before, but seeing Aegis prepare made me wish I was back in the cart.

"The best way out is in," Aegis explained. "We get into Murdoch, then leave from the other side with a raiding party or slave group."

"Why not just go around?" I asked.

"The city edges the canyon, leaving only one side to go around. That would take too long, and we don't have the provisions. It would take us less than a day to get through the city."

We walked for some time. At first, it was just rubbish, broken things and fragments of pottery. Soon, the piles became larger and more sculpted, as if arranged into dome mounds.

"I don't understand—where is the city?" I whispered.

"You're in it," Aegis answered.

That was when the smell hit me. Along with the garbage were human feces and corpses. I didn't understand; where were all the people?

"During the day, most outlanders sleep," Aegis explained. "It's too hot to do anything else. They sleep in the huts they fashion out of the garbage. There's no point in building a home here because it will just get destroyed when someone wants something. Everything and nothing is worth dying for, so people build temporary sleeping arrangements. At night, they come out and take what they can from each other, fight, or do whatever they need to do to survive."

"Why are dead bodies in the huts?"

Aegis didn't want to tell me; I could tell. "If someone dies, they try to keep the body as cool as possible to reduce rot," he said.

"Why do they care if the bodies rot? Because of the smell?"

"Because it's dinner."

I didn't want to be here anymore. These people were beasts that came out after sunset to rape, murder, and eat the rotting flesh of their neighbors. No one had ever told me about this, not even Peter. Everyone made this place sound bad, but they had no idea what it was really like.

I had noticed food became scarcer from region to region. The quality and type of food decreased from region five to region six. I figured it was because we were on the run, but only in this pile of rubble and death did I fully understand. When food was traded, it was traded to neighboring regions. Very little of that food would be traded two regions over, leaving almost nothing for regions six and seven.

"Aegis, are we going to get out of here before dark?" It wasn't a question so much as it was a prayer. I was so scared, I could hear my voice trembling as I asked.

"We have yet to get into the heart of the city. This is the seventh region's suburbs. We're not even halfway in."

The sun would set in a few minutes, and all the creatures in this region of Hell would rise from their rubble huts and eat whoever wasn't moving.

"Take my hand," Aegis said. "Whatever you do, don't let go. Just keep your eyes on your feet, and don't respond to anyone."

I did just as Aegis said. I gripped his hand as hard as I could and kept my eyes down on the ground. I watched the dirt change color from an orangish-brown to a red clay before it started taking on a bluish hue. The air around me felt much cooler and damp, a relief from the heat of the day, but that relief was short-lived.

I started hearing people stir from their rubble piles. People were shouting crudely, and somewhere, a small child screamed in agony.

They are bad souls, I told myself, *and deserve to suffer this fate.* I tried to repeat this to myself over and over, but with each passing cycle, the child's scream echoed even louder. There were other screams and cries. The smell of fire and burning flesh. Burning bodies.

As we made our way through the city, more people took interest in us. I kept my eyes down as Aegis had instructed, but I could still hear them. They thought he was selling me as a slave.

"I'll trade two boys for the girl!" a man shouted.

"No one wants your used boys," another replied.

"I could use a new plaything," I heard another taunt.

The voices were coming closer. I could feel people surrounding us, and I wanted to disappear. Aegis was squeezing my hand tight as if he were silently apologizing for bringing me here.

You need to know, the voice in my head told me. *You need to know what's at stake.*

"Let's have a look at that face." A man without a nose and with gray mud streaked across his face peered into my narrowed line of sight.

Before I could react, Aegis punched in the man's head. The skull broke, and his fist smashed into the man's brain. For a few horrible moments, Aegis's hand was stuck in what remained of the skull. He shook it free, and the man fell to the ground. His eyes were filled with insanity even in death—the eye that was left at least.

"Anyone else want to piss me off?" Aegis roared at the crowd.

He had no other challengers.

The further into the city we got, the more controlled it felt. Aegis told me I could look up if I wanted to. I really didn't, but it was the least I could do for the children who were forced to live here. It was cleaner than the parts I had seen initially. There were actual buildings, ones that resembled the buildings in region six: clay buildings with holes cut out for windows and doors.

"Aegis, where are we?" I whispered.

"This part of the city is under control by a gang. It's the closest thing they have to a justice system. Everyone pays the gang in charge, and they have a safer means of living. If they don't have something worth trading, they live in the garbage like we just saw."

"We're safer here, then?" I asked.

"If anything, we are in even more danger. At some point, we will be approached by a member, maybe several. They will want to take you, and I will need to pay them off."

The people here didn't have money, food, or anything of value. The only things they could trade were children and women as slaves. If they couldn't leave the region to trade slaves, they would give up their own to live in the city of Murdoch. I imagined many gave away the product of rape, and others got pregnant intentionally to gain a bartering chip in the future.

"This is where all the slaves are being sold?"

"Yes, but it wasn't like that until recently."

I found myself wondering what Aegis considered to be recent, but before I could ask, he continued. "The gangs here really get off on pure souls. They will pay a hefty price for a soul from the upper regions, enough to give the slave trader two more trips for more souls. They love to see the horror on their faces. To…" Aegis paused. "To… do things to them. It's like ripping wings off an angel."

My face scrunched as a new question emerged. "What's an angel?"

"It's an immortal being with wings," Aegis replied.

"You've seen one?" I looked at him then, but he seemed just as puzzled as I was about angels.

"I don't remember."

We came across a sort of barricade in the street, a gate made of crunched metal and glass. The colors and shapes of the metal were unlike anything I had ever seen. They were large and long with various colors covered with dents and rust. They reminded me of carriages, but there were no horses to pull them.

On the barricades, men stood patrolling their territory. They were all large and mean-looking. All of them held crude weapons and glared at us. Whispers slipped through my mind but said little. Was it my other voice?

"We're looking to pass through your gates," Aegis called to them.

"What have you got to trade?" the leader asked and looked at me.

"I have silver," Aegis conceded. "It's not much, but what I have is yours."

The man motioned for us to approach, and Aegis pulled a silver token from his pocket. The man nodded in approval. "Got this from the gambler's pit," he demanded.

"I did."

"The whole piece, and you're free to go."

"It's all I have."

"Then you better win more next time. Give us all a round with your girl, and I'll half the token."

Aegis shook his head. "I need her intact for my buyer; the silver is yours."

The man pocketed the token and motioned to the men to open the barricade and let us pass. I couldn't afford to feel indignation over the conversations of rape. At the castle, such a thing was a disgusting crime. In the outlands, the powerful were entitled to any entertainment they wished.

You could change things, the voice whispered. What, though? There would always be bad people. They would always hurt those weaker than themselves. I couldn't stop it—no one could. The worst part was that these people were escaping to kidnap good souls to bring them to this place. What would happen when the borders fully collapsed? These monsters could overrun the guards and roam the rest of Hell freely. Nowhere would be safe.

We passed the barricade into the next portion of the city. I assumed a rival gang held the territory on this side. Aegis still held my hand firmly as we made our way through what was an empty city center. The men at the barricade watched us, and it made me nervous. They seemed to know something we didn't.

That was when I heard more new voices, not the usual voice that was my own with someone else's words. These voices first came as whispers and laughter. They were voices I didn't recognize. I looked at Aegis to see if he was hearing these things, but he looked onward. I couldn't make out what they were saying, but it felt evil.

"Aegis, maybe when we get out of sight, you can run through," I pleaded. "No one would know what they were seeing." I had the worst feeling about the ghosted ramparts. Aegis seemed to feel the same way.

"I don't know the way, and it would be a choppy ride," Aegis said. "We've got to be at least halfway through the city. I feel like we're being watched."

"I know we are." And I did know.

I didn't know how or why, but they were waiting for us. The voices grew louder, but I didn't have time to worry about it. I tried my best to ignore them. I couldn't explain it, but it scared me to a point where I could no longer speak. I tried to say Aegis's name, but nothing came out.

"Okay," Aegis finally said, "but you need to trust me. Don't wiggle around." He picked me up and held me as if I were some stray kitten. Holding me close, he went into motion.

The scenery changed so fast I couldn't make out what things were anymore. I saw blurs of dark alleys and buildings. Occasionally, he would stop at a dead end, and the world jerked to a halt before he resumed moving at full speed down the next alley. "Choppy ride" didn't begin to describe it. I was exhausted by my attempts to hold my head up.

Aegis eventually cradled my head and neck like I was an infant, another indignation I had no choice but to endure. This sort of thing wouldn't have bothered me a few years ago, but at sixteen, I was a woman. If anything, the older I got, the more helpless I seemed to become.

We shuddered to a halt in another dead end.

"Are you okay?" he asked me.

I wanted to answer, but I vomited instead. The remnants of dinner spewed all over my clothes and down the front of Aegis's coat. "I'm so sorry," I said, horrified.

"This wasn't a good idea after all." Aegis's brow creased, and his eyes were sad. "We can't afford for you to become dehydrated, not in a place like this."

"At least it would kill me faster," I replied.

Aegis frowned, unsure of how to respond. He didn't understand, but the sheer malevolence of the city was overwhelming. It was like it had a life and intent all its own. It fed on my happy memories, leaving me with only violent thoughts.

I thought back to my last night at the castle, with Vinicio drugging me and leaving me for dead. I thought about ways to get my vengeance on both him and Mother. As we made our way through the maze of Murdoch's streets, my imagination grew darker.

I imagined killing Vinicio in front of my mother, having Aegis snap his neck like a twig. The horror on my mother's face made me smile, but it wasn't enough. Perhaps I'd tie them up in the Starry Wood and let the animals eat them. That wasn't a satisfying scenario, though. Too many variables could go wrong. Maybe I'd drug Vinicio and feed him to a woodsman. Mother would watch as he was devoured, of course. She wouldn't run from the woodsmen; she'd rather die than go back to my grandparents.

The voices in my head had grown alarmingly loud. I could understand them now. They were talking about us.

Fresh meat caught in the spider's trap.

We're going to play tonight.

"Stop it," I whispered. Aegis looked at me in confusion, but said nothing.

The clinking of chains told us we were not alone. The city's residents had decided to show themselves. They were even more frightening than the last group. These men were not just wielding weapons—they *were* weapons.

Seven men stood before us with various metals protruding from their bodies. Two of the men had spikes that jutted from their fists and knees. Others had barbed wire embedded in their arms and legs. One had barbed wire wrapped around his head like a crown. They were all covered in scar tissue and tattoos.

How is that man flying? The boss would pay good money for a flying man.

The girl smells like a virgin.

Such pureness—so much pride to break.

"We've been watching you," said the man with the barbed wire crown.

"We're just trying to make our way..." Aegis started to say, but he was interrupted.

"No, you're not like us. You're something else. What are you?"

"Nothing," Aegis whispered.

"I doubt that," the man said. "Take them."

Aegis looked to me as if he were asking me what to do. He could easily jump over the building and run away, but the man was the evilest thing I'd ever encountered.

He wants to take us back to his lair. He wants to gang rape and mutilate my body in front of Aegis because he thinks he is my father. He wants to peel my skin off my body and force me to swallow broken glass before he has the same done to Aegis. The images from this man's mind were so intense it was like I was thinking them myself.

"Aegis, kill them," I commanded.

He looked at me in confusion, but he didn't have time to argue. I wiggled free of his grasp and said it again. "Aegis, I want you to kill them *now*."

The men laughed at us. Before they could utter more taunts, however, Aegis was in action. The first man was punched with neck-breaking force. The second attempted to defend himself, but it was futile. As his bladed forearms rose in defense, Aegis shoved his hand straight through the man's belly and out the other side.

The others screamed and attempted to run away, but as they ran, Aegis easily caught up to them. He bashed in one man's skull with his bare fist before grabbing two men by the head and smashed them together, killing them instantly. The two remaining men, the leader with the barbed crown and what looked like the runt of the pack, cowered.

Aegis returned to my side before acknowledging the last two men. His eyes remained their normal blue, but they were growing bloodshot from the excitement. He hissed with an inhuman sound as if challenging them to attack.

"The man with the crown last," I told him. Aegis looked at me with a smile. Was it glee?

The smaller man sobbed and begged incoherently as Aegis gently snapped his neck. Aegis didn't want to admit it, but he clearly enjoyed the kill. The man with the crown said nothing but held his arms out with a mocking smile on his face.

Aegis pulled his arms from his body as if he were pulling petals from a flower. The arms fell to the ground, and blood sprayed from the man. He screamed into the night in agony but remained standing. Again, the man smiled. Why was he smiling?

I'm taking you with me, flying man and virgin girl.

"Aegis, it's a trap!" I shouted.

In an instant, I was scooped up and in the air. There was a large boom, and the ground where we had stood was burning. The man must have had some sort of explosive device. We landed on the rooftop of a tall building and watched the chaos. People scattered, and small fires were all around. The only thing that remained of the man was part of a boot.

"What was that?" Aegis muttered.

"It was his failsafe," I explained.

Aegis didn't understand.

"He had an explosive device somewhere on his person. In the event of his death, he planned on taking his killer with him."

"How do you know that?"

"I could hear his thoughts."

Despite how crazy it sounded, Aegis didn't scoff. He didn't say anything. I thought I was going crazy at the time, but I truly could hear their voices. It seemed surreal. It happened, but maybe it didn't happen the way I remembered it. Maybe they were talking out loud, and I didn't see their lips move.

Aegis would have told me if that were the case. No, he would have heard the same thing if that were true. He didn't know anything until I told him. Aegis couldn't hear them, but I could. He also didn't seem all that disturbed by what I had told him. I wished that inner voice would explain it to me the way it explained other things, but it remained quiet.

Picking me up so that my face was on the clean side of his jacket, Aegis bounced from rooftop to rooftop until there were no more buildings. I could feel the heat in the air increasing. The sun was rising, and the people of the seventh region of Hell were constructing their garbage hovels.

"Let's rest here during the day; you're exhausted."

Aegis was right—I was tired, but I didn't want to stop, even walking along abandoned garbage hovels with my sore feet. I didn't want to sleep here.

"No. We're going to keep going," I told him. He remained unmoving as if he were calling my bluff, but I wasn't bluffing. I needed to leave this place straight away.

"After this is the wasteland," he said. "It's nothing but desert for miles before we reach the bridge."

"I don't want to stay here."

"You look like you're about to pass out."

"Then you can carry me."

Aegis stopped to look at me, not sure if I was serious or not. "What is with you? Ever since you got here, you've been acting so strange."

"Don't you get it?" I yelled at him. My voice cracked from fatigue. "I'm one of these people. My father was one of them. This is why people in the fifth region hated me. They hated me because they knew I was one of these people. More beast that human. Untrustworthy and irredeemable."

"That's not true." Aegis shook his head as he spoke. He moved towards me to hold me, and I flinched at the gesture

"And you…" I was crying now. "What's in it for you?"

"What do you mean?" Aegis brushed his hand through his hair, distressed by my question.

"Nobody does anything for free. So, what's in it for you? How long until you want this?" I asked as I rubbed my groin through my dirty yellow dress.

Aegis shook his head. He looked sad and disappointed. I hated when he made me feel that way. I stood next to a garbage teepee. It was built of various items, and I recognized one of the items to be an old dirty bedpan. I threw the bedpan at his head. It bounced off his brow, and he didn't so much as blink, but I felt better.

Aegis looked hurt, but I didn't care.

"You mean to tell me that you are protecting me out of the goodness of your bloodthirsty heart?" I asked.

"As I remember it, a certain miss was smiling while watching me rip the arms off a man."

"He deserved worse. You couldn't see the thoughts in his head."

"But you could," Aegis said. "And you have no idea why I follow you?"

I didn't know what to say. Ever since they had taken Peter away, my hurt and my anger were real. They weren't just feelings; they willed my desires and forced outcomes in my favor. I was actively participating in life for the first time despite being dragged around Hell like a child. Aegis knew why he stayed with me, even when I was only just beginning to understand.

"Go to sleep," Aegis said without looking at me.

I threw a piece of piping at his back, followed by a rock, but he wouldn't leave. I walked away. I wasn't going to sleep in the garbage, and I wasn't going to spend a minute longer than I had to in the seventh region. The longer I stayed, the more I was consumed by anger and hatred. Aegis didn't move as I walked into the distance. He stood rigid with his arms crossed in front, just watching me walk away.

Chapter Nine

I walked for a long while, but I didn't know where I was walking. I could have been heading the wrong way, and I didn't have the wooden coin needed to cross the bridge. I'd left it with Aegis, and I wasn't going to go back. Not after the way I behaved.

The desert heat was inescapable, and my mouth was dry. I was covered in filth and old vomit, and the smell of sweat had long dried. I had no choice but to sit down. I couldn't walk anymore. I would just rest for a little while. Laying my head down on the hot earth, I noted a dead piece of plant. It had either been dropped here or blown in by the wind.

It reminded me of my mother's wedding, where I had been the flower girl. The wedding had been a boring way to waste the day. I was dressed in a white lace dress with a black sash and shiny black shoes. My hair was cut to my shoulder blades before being braided and adorned with black and white baby's breath. Once I was ready, I was shuffled from one room to another. Adults fussed and chatted idly.

Eventually, I was brought into a room with three women dressed in gold dresses. They fawned and told me how adorable I was, how much healthier I looked since I'd moved into the castle. They handed me a basket of red petals covered in gold shimmer.

"Your job is to walk down the aisle sprinkling petals for your mommy to walk on," one of them told me. "We will go first, and the usher will motion when it's time for you to go. Good luck!"

I wondered who the women were as they walked down the aisle. I'd never seen them before, but they seemed to know me. They were likely my mother's friends; that would explain why they were so familiar with me despite never hearing a word from my lips.

The usher, an old suited man with a square head, motioned for me to walk down the aisle. I didn't want to do it, but the man nudged me onward, and I had no choice but to walk. Strange faces stared at me. I heard a giggle coming from behind me, and I knew it was Mother.

My face got warm. I didn't understand why, but I was angry. I didn't want to do this. I wasn't wanted here—I was just a prop for my mother to tell her friends about, an aspect of my mother's life before her fiancé rescued her. Such a good man he was to take in a misfit child.

I grabbed a fistful of petals and threw them on the ground. The guests laughed initially, but as I worked my way up the aisle, everyone could feel my anger, including Vinicio. He watched with a slight smirk, amused by my rebellious display. When I reached the front of the wedding, Myrtle, the maid, ushered me to the side.

The orchestra began playing a romantic song, and my mother glided down the aisle. The rest of the wedding went just as Mother had planned. She was too busy receiving attention to be angry with me. It appeared she would let my indiscretion go, but just before the reception, she caught me.

"Take her to her room," she told Myrtle. "She doesn't deserve sweets after that spectacle. Honestly, Nora, why do you insist on ruining everything for me?"

The maid led me away before I could answer. We said nothing as we went back to my bedroom. I didn't know why it made me so angry, but I wasn't sorry. Myrtle was a nice lady. She was close to Grandmother's age, but she always had a warm smile and checked in on me often.

"I'm going to sneak you a slice of cake. Would you like that?" Myrtle asked.

I smiled and nodded. I should have told her no. I should have said I didn't want any cake. I never saw Myrtle again after that. Mother and Vinicio got wind of her disobedience and dismissed her without a second thought. That too had made me angry, so angry that I refused to speak to Mother until she dismissed Peter and Sarah ten years later.

As arms pulled me from my childhood back and into reality, I knew it was Aegis, but I was too tired to look. He carried me until the air grew cooler. I felt nauseous again, but there was nothing left to throw up. In his hand was a small canteen.

"It's not much, but keep it in the event of an emergency."

I grabbed the canteen and drank. The water was warm, but it tasted divine. It felt as though I had woken up from a fog of heat and thirst. I emptied it, but the water only reduced my thirst. Although it no longer hurt to swallow, my teeth felt like they were covered in a layer of dirt.

Aegis insisted on carrying me the rest of the way. I didn't fight him. Even if I had wanted to, I didn't have the strength. It seemed he was determined to keep me alive no matter how terrible I was. I thought back to what he had said when I threw a bedpan at his head, something about following me.

And you have no idea why I follow you?

I'd never thought about it that way. It didn't matter where I went; he would go too. Nowhere could be worse than where we were now, so maybe he wasn't lying when he said he'd never leave me. I just had to accept it for what it was, just as I had to accept the voices for what they were.

"I can see the bridge." Aegis sighed in relief.

This bridge was like the last one, except its ferryman was a young black boy no older than nine. He peered at us from the safety of the other side with a pair of binoculars. Aegis withdrew the wooden token and held it up for the boy to see. A few moments later, the boy pushed the cart halfway and withdrew his binoculars again. Aegis obliged by raising the wooden coin into the air once more for a closer inspection. The wood of the cart banged against the edge of the rails, and the boy held out his hand.

Aegis gave the boy the token, and after careful inspection, he permitted us to board his cart.

"You folks had a rough night," the boy said, as he laughed.

Aegis could do nothing but laugh with him. We looked filthy and exhausted. I found myself laughing along with them. The cart ride didn't seem so scary this time.

At the other side of the bridge, we said farewell. It was about midday when we found a shallow river. I could feel the difference in this land. It was cleaner and had lots of birds and small creatures. There was more foliage springing up about the place.

At first, I just stuck my face in the water and drank until my stomach hurt. Once my thirst was sated, I walked into the shallow stream. The water was cool, and its currents were gentle. I sat in the creek as the water pushed against my back.

Neither of us said anything as we washed up. Aegis turned his back to me for privacy, but I washed with my clothes on. They were just as gross as I was, so I didn't think it mattered if they remained. I let my arms flow with the stream and watched the mud and vomit float away from my dress. The thoughts I had in the seventh region scared me. I didn't feel that way anymore, but what if those feelings came back?

I didn't want to kill anyone. I just wanted to find the place where I belonged. My stomach turned when I recalled the things I had said to Aegis. His interests were not sexual, but there was something else that came from that conversation. Aegis protected me and did as I said because I was someone important. No one had ever thought of me as important or special, but he did.

Aegis set up a campsite near the river. He said the water was clean and that I needed to drink a lot more and rest after the night before last. I couldn't disagree with him. We had been up for a full day and night, and I was ready to fall over. After he hung up his wet jacket on a sparse tree, Aegis went to work on a fire. As usual, he struggled to get it going. I closed my eyes and imagined a strong flame burning in the night.

"Okay, I'm getting better at this," Aegis announced proudly.

I opened my eyes, and the flame was still there. I thought back to when I last saw Vinicio, the way his hand had jerked away abruptly. If I made the flame bigger, if I could hear voices, just what was I? I couldn't stay awake long enough to form an answer. Sleep was an ocean of silence, and I welcomed the tides.

The next morning, I said nothing about what had happened in the outlands. I was too tired to talk, and Aegis wanted to keep moving in case the tracker from the woods was still on our trail.

My body ached, and I grumbled, "I'm too young to have a back this sore."

"Once you get moving again, the pain will ease," Aegis promised.

I wanted to tell him it was I who had made the fire, and it was I who had made it rain in the Starry Wood, yet I wasn't certain it was me. The snake and the gambling may have been happy accidents as well. I couldn't explain what was happening to me. Aegis seemed to know, but he wanted me to learn for myself, just like Peter did when he wanted me to understand something important.

"So, have you always been able to read minds, or was that new?" Aegis asked.

"I guess so. Sometimes a voice in my head tells me things, but it's in my voice. It's weird. I've always had thoughts that didn't feel like my own, yet at the same time, they are my thoughts. I'd never read anyone's mind before. I think I started the rain in the Starry Wood, and…"

"And what?" Aegis asked.

"My last night in the castle, I imagined stabbing Vinicio's hand. He jerked away as if someone *had* stabbed him, but I thought it was a coincidence. Now

I'm not so sure."

I'd never told anyone that before. It sounded crazier than when I said it in my head. Aegis looked into the distance in contemplation as if he understood what was happening to me, but his eyes widened at the sight of something.

"We need to go now."

"We can't; my dress is still drying."

"Now!"

For all Aegis's urgency, it was too late. A man was approaching from the distance.

"We can just run away," I told him.

"He will catch up to us again. I'll need to deal with him." Aegis sheltered me and stood in a defensive stance.

I didn't say anything and let the man approach. He was young and lean with blond hair and a cunning smile. He walked toward us with full confidence, as if he knew he would win. He probably didn't know Aegis was a vampire.

"I'm afraid to cut your time together short, but I will be taking the girl now."

I didn't want to look. I wanted to hide my face in Aegis's jacket until the man went away. I didn't want my face anymore. I wished I was someone different, a normal girl, and Aegis could be my dad, and I would never cause anyone any inconvenience ever again.

"Who are you?" Aegis asked the man.

"My name is Alfie. I was sent by the castle to collect Nora."

"What are you going to do with her?"

"Nothing more than I was instructed," Alfie promised. "Her mother is undone by her departure. The woman needs to know what became of her daughter. Peter, I know you care for the girl, but she belongs with her mother."

Aegis knew who Peter was; I had spoken of him. He looked down at me, and his face turned to one of shock and puzzlement. Quickly recovering, he answered Alfie. "I think you've made a mistake. My name is not Peter, and she is not called Nora."

Aegis spun me around to face the tracker. In an instant, I was betrayed.

What was he doing? I looked to Aegis pleadingly. Why would he just hand me over?

But after Alfie looked at me, he just walked away without another word.

Aegis helped me put on my slightly damp dress and stomped out the fire. He continued leading me along the road and said nothing for a long while. I was hurt by his strange reaction; he'd just promised he would stay with me forever, so why would he offer me up? Why did the tracker not take me?

"You could have told me about that sooner," Aegis said at last.

"About what?" I didn't understand why he was angry. If anything, it should be me who was angry with him. Was it payback for throwing a bedpan at his head? He pulled a silver tin from the bag and handed it to me. I didn't get it.

"Look at your reflection."

I did as he said. My hair was tar black, and my skin was pale and smooth. My eyes were slanted, and my cheekbones were prominent. I wasn't Nora anymore. I was someone else. I looked at Aegis to see that he didn't have the answers either.

"You've never done anything like that before, huh?" Aegis asked.

I was speechless. I shook my head, trying to grasp how such a miracle had happened.

"I think I'll stay like this for a bit," I decided.

"Is that because you don't know how to change back?"

"No," I lied.

Aegis smiled. He didn't seem alarmed at all by what was happening to me. "We need to get to region four. With the money you won, we should be able to pass. No one in the outlands has this kind of money."

"Aegis, do you think something is wrong with me?"

"I don't think anything is wrong with you."

"My face just changed!" I shouted. "That is not normal!"

"That tracker—his patch means he is the general of the hawk hunters," Aegis said as he started walking.

"You know what's happening to me. That's why you won't leave me."

"I won't leave you because I said I wouldn't."

"What do you think I am?"

Aegis stopped. He kneeled before me and held my hand. "Nora, did anyone ever tell you about the king of souls?"

I nodded. "Peter did."

"Okay. Did he tell you about the king's powers?"

"Vinicio said the king was a fairy tale," I said as I worked to connect the dots.

"Vinicio is in the minority with that opinion. Last week, you saw a woodsman and a vampire for the first time, and they were not fairy tales. The stewards have a bad habit of rewriting history, but the truth always has a way of coming out."

"But you said you can't remember the time when kings ruled."

"I don't, but I still know the history. The king had powers, powers that no ordinary soul possessed. I think the reason Vinicio wants you dead—the same reason I have an overwhelming urge to protect you, the reason all these strange things are happening—is because you're the king."

"Queen," I corrected him.

"What?" Aegis asked. I had put out the fire in Aegis's big reveal, but I couldn't help myself.

"A female king is called a queen."

"I think you're the queen," Aegis said with his chin lifted in defiance.

I nodded.

Aegis wouldn't lie to me about something so important, and it was the only logical explanation. A small part of me had always known in a way—the part that whispered to me and told me new words I was too young to understand. It wasn't just a daydream or a fantasy; it was somehow real.

That reality only brought more questions. Did Mother know? Vinicio knew for sure. It couldn't have been a coincidence that he just happened to be in the fifth region looking for a wife. Knowing my mother was potentially involved in disposing of me was too much to digest.

"What do you want to do about it?" Aegis asked.

"I just want to feel like I belong somewhere."

"We'll take this one day at a time, okay?" Aegis stood up and walked alongside me. "You need more time."

Aegis was right about that. I needed more time. I didn't want to go back to the castle; my mother was there just waiting to tell me how badly I had ruined her life. I didn't want to see my mother. She would be there with her pleading, desperate eyes, accusing me of taking away her happiness yet again. I could say it was punishment for taking Peter away from me, but it would be a lie. I couldn't win. My very existence was a punishment to her.

I remembered Peter saying something similar a week before he was sacked. We had been walking around the castle because the classroom was too hot, and I'd grown restless in the little room. Peter had taken the opportunity to talk to me about the future. We'd walked along the sandstone tiles with their black grout stained by time.

"What do you want out of life, Nora?" Peter asked.

I shrugged. I'd never thought about it before. Peter's eyes scanned my face, his brow furrowed with worry.

"You've never thought about it before?"

"I just want to be somewhere I belong," I confessed.

"You do belong." Peter stopped and made me stop to look at him. "You belong here more than anyone else. You just need more time."

"Time for what?" I asked him.

"To come into your own."

Vinicio

Vinicio's days now consisted of running a kingdom, managing souls, killing a stepdaughter, and consoling a grieving wife who hated being left alone. Bella was understandably distraught after losing her only daughter, but she made it difficult for him to complete his other duties.

While they had always had breakfast and dinner together, Bella now insisted on lunch and tea time with Vinicio as well. Bella wanted his constant reassurance and affection. She was working through grief and guilt simultaneously, so Vinicio tried his best to be available to her.

He wondered if he'd feel the same way about her if this had been required of him ten years ago when they first married. Despite his initial ploy, Vinicio had grown fond of Bella, much more so than he had thought possible—more than he should have allowed.

It had been several days since he last checked the soul safe—a duty that normally required his attention several times a day. He lacked the abilities a king would have had, and as a result, placing souls into their respective regions was far more difficult for him. The safe was no doubt overrun, and if Vinicio didn't manage it soon, the balance of the universe would be disturbed.

Bella, however, did not understand nor care about such responsibilities. She demanded his attention day and night. Vinicio had no choice but to drug Bella's after-dinner wine. Rebus procured the drug for Vinicio with no questions asked. It was a gray, odorless powder that dissolved instantly. It did leave the bottom of the wine a bit cloudy, but Bella didn't seem to notice as she emptied the glass.

Gently lifting his wife from the overstuffed red sofa, Vinicio put her to bed. She would rest easy tonight, the first time in almost a month. On Vinicio's desk awaited another message, this time with Hacia's seal. His well-manicured hands felt the rough parchment as he broke the seal.

The girl lives. Orders remain the same? H.

The informality of her note made Vinicio pause. They used protocol in messages in the event that someone was sending false letters. It was a recent development that Vinicio implemented himself. Perhaps Hacia simply forgot. Then again, maybe it was an act of defiance. He didn't have time to play games with trackers. He needed to deal with the soul safe.

Orders remain the same. V.

Vinicio decided that he'd kill the tracker that failed to produce Nora's corpse.

A heavy metal door guarded the soul safe. Only Vinicio had the key. Inside the room was nothing much—a small chair, a large oval mirror beside the safe with a map of the seven circles of Hell etched into its surface, and the soul safe.

If an intruder were to enter this room, it would appear to be an ordinary safe. The only difference was that it had seven bars that crossed on the front of the door. Inside the safe was another matter. When the safe door was opened, a gateway to a sort of soul limbo existed.

The safe had no end in sight. Instead, a tunnel extended into an unknown darkness. It was in this darkness that the souls traveled from one dimension to another, from the other life to this life. Vinicio had no way of knowing how long that dark tunnel extended or for how long the souls traveled to find themselves at the end of a closed door; he just knew they piled up at that door, waiting for life to begin again.

Vinicio opened the safe slowly so as to not disturb its residents. It was just as he feared. Many souls had collected in purgatory while he was away. With nowhere to go, the souls piled up along the tunnel. The souls glowed a variety of different colors, and the brightness of a soul gave Vinicio the idea of where it should be placed. The brightest, lightest souls usually floated at the top of the safe and went to the first region.

The darkest, densest orbs that hovered on the bottom of the safe went to the seventh layer. The others all generally floated around together for the most part, but with enough inspection, Vinicio could send them to their correct location.

Today would be difficult to sort out. The souls had become so compacted at the front of the safe that he couldn't control who came out first. If he had a king's powers, sorting could be done in minutes with complete precision, but alas, he was not a king.

Before he could start sending the souls to their regions, the glowing orbs spilled out of the safe and began floating around the room. In a panic, Vinicio shut the door, but the souls that had already escaped the safe were bouncing around mindlessly.

The map etched into the mirror began to glow. The souls gravitated towards the mirror as if they were being lured. The souls could not pass through the mirror without Vinicio's help.

Normally, he would push the orbs into their designated regions with a gentle hand. Today, the room swarmed with mismanaged souls, and Vinicio's patience was short. He simply didn't have time to deal with all these petty souls. Without regard for their destination, Vinicio began pushing souls through the map into whatever region they happened to be closest to.

Once he pushed them through the mirror, the souls would find unborn children to inhabit and be born into the world. It was unfortunate for some of the purer souls who would find themselves in lesser regions, but he had a world to rule.

If only the souls could find their way without a guide. The layers of Hell were so rigid in their societies that any misplaced souls would find their way to the correct region eventually. Vinicio just needed to clean up this mess.

Opening the safe once more, Vinicio let another surge of souls into the room before shutting and locking the safe for the night. Once again, he pushed souls into whatever region around the map they gathered near without remorse. He would need to make more of an effort to manage the soul safe more efficiently.

That night, when Vinicio lay in bed beside his beautiful, comatose wife, he wondered if one of those misplaced souls had found its way into her belly. They had talked about children, she knew he desired one, and it was only a matter of time before she became pregnant again. He would need to be far more careful with soul placement. He didn't want a tainted soul ruling Hell.

Chapter Ten

"You don't have a name, yet you've taught me so much." An old man's voice spoke softly. The man's voice was so familiar but so distant at the same time. Aegis knew the man's voice to be the voice of the first king, but he couldn't be certain. In his dream, Aegis bowed but could not see the soul he bowed before.

"I'll name you Aegis," the king said.

"Aegis, come down from there and play ball with me!" a young man shouted.

Aegis knew that voice to be the voice of the king as well, but he wasn't the same person as the king who had named him. Still, he felt an unrelenting pull towards the voice. Aegis looked down at his palm and rubbed the ache from his scar. Something he should not have forgotten was calling to him once again.

Hundreds of voices crept from the shadows of his mind, all calling to him as the king of Hell. Aegis spun around in circles to find a single voice to rise above the rest. He was blinded in a fog of names and faces that all looked the same yet different at the same time. They smiled, frowned, and cried, and some were pale and unmoving.

How many kings had he known? How many kings had died under his watch?

"Please," Aegis pleaded into the gray void. "What do I do?"

While the names, faces, and voices faded into the recesses of his mind, Aegis understood why he had slept in the dirt for so long. All those years ago, the vampires went to sleep when the last king died. They decided that the age of the vampire had ended and that souls needed to rule themselves.

It wasn't until the woodsmen overpopulated that the vampires woke again. The screams of innocent souls pierced through the cold ground and echoed within the dirt itself, waking the immortal beings once more. They had slept so long that many had forgotten their pasts.

Aegis feared his past: the memories of so many loved ones, the dull pain of loss. It would be a blink followed by nothing, but his own struggle to make sense of it. An entire existence was simply gone. It made him think about Nora. One day, she too would be gone. He would need to get up and carry on as though nothing were wrong. As if the end of the world hadn't occurred.

Even if they were wrong and she wasn't the king, Aegis loved her. It was worth the echo chamber within his dreams. He would yell into the grayness, and nothing would happen, but it didn't matter to him anymore. Aegis would stay by Nora's side until she was gone before finding another just like her. King or no king, the only way for Aegis to live on was to protect.

"Aegis," Nora's voice called.

He followed the sound as she called over and over. When Aegis opened his eyes, he realized he was being shaken violently by the young girl.

"Aegis!" she shouted.

"I'm up."

"What were you doing?" Nora shouted.

"Sleeping."

"I've never seen you sleep before."

"It happens sometimes."

Nora looked worried but tried her best to shrug it off. "It's dawn."

"Let's get moving then."

Aegis made another sad fire. He didn't have any use for it; he only built them for Nora. He checked the traps he had set during the night and found some large wild hares. With a flick of his wrist, their necks snapped. Aegis skinned and gutted them in the woods before skewering them. There was no reason to hide it from Nora; she had watched him rip a man's arms off and cleave another man's head in half, but a man had his habits.

By the time he returned, the fire was roaring. It seemed to Aegis that he was getting better at the fire building. The fire was impressive. He wondered what he'd done differently this time. Perhaps it was the better air flow or a slightly drier kindling. It had sprung to life quite suddenly.

"You need to get your strength back, so eat as much as you can," Aegis told Nora.

She devoured the rabbits. Her lips were still chapped from their time in the outlands. She looked a mess, and he felt that he was to blame. Aegis couldn't wait until they could reach civilization. Nora could have a bath and live a somewhat normal existence, at least until the trackers caught up with them again.

"Do you want to talk about the outlands?" he asked.

It was something they needed to address. Aegis had suspected she was the king of souls since her bizarre winning streak in the gambler's pit. Phineas hadn't lived long enough to confirm his suspicions, but Aegis thought Phineas was trying to tell him about her all along. Her personality seemed to shift with the regions. Aegis couldn't remember if that was a king characteristic or not.

"You seem changed," Aegis started. "I saw a side of you I didn't expect."

"I ordered you to kill people." She understood the ramifications despite her age. "And you just did it."

He nodded. "When the first king emerged, the vampires made a pact with him using the Dagger of Monsters. My kind vowed to protect the king always, and that's what we did until they stopped emerging."

"Dagger of Monsters?" she asked.

"It's a dagger that is said to control all creatures. It always finds its way to the king." He pulled his necklace from beneath his tunic to show her. The carving was of the dagger.

"Did you make this pact, or did all vampires agree to it?"

"I don't remember. It was thousands of years ago." It was beside the point. Aegis couldn't tell if she was skirting around the real issue or if it had just never occurred to her that she was the king of souls.

"You act differently in each region we cross," he said, redirecting her.

"I do?"

"If I were to ask you if you wanted to make a wager, would you want to?"

Nora shook her head.

"If you were given the choice now, would you have wanted me to kill those people?"

"No, of course not. But what other choice did we have?"

"There's always a choice. Would you make a different one now?" he asked.

"Yes." She choked the word out.

"The different layers of Hell affect you somehow. It's just something we need to be aware of."

"So, what do we do now? she asked.

"Whatever you want. Do you want to be ki—queen?"

"Yeah. I'm scared, though," she admitted.

"I don't blame you."

"That's all you have to say about it?" Nora was laughing at him. "You are probably the oldest living person in this world. You are smarter, faster, stronger, and wiser…"

"No." Aegis shook his head, cutting Nora off. "Minerva is the wisest; that's what her name means."

"You think she's still alive?" Nora asked. As always, she looked so uncertain when he spoke of Minerva; he rarely did because the memories hurt too much.

"If I were wise, I probably wouldn't think she was alive," he explained. But that's why her name is Minerva and mine is Aegis."

"Your names—you're named after your attributes?"

Aegis nodded.

"Then who named you?"

"I don't know. I just woke up with the name in my mouth, and Minerva was the first of our kind to speak to me."

"What was she like?"

"Her hair was long and silver, and her eyes were a dark brown. She was petite and reserved, but it would be a mistake to cross her. When I woke and crawled from the earth, the world around me was chaos. I emerged in the middle of a battleground. Vampires and Woodsmen were at the height of their battle, and I woke in the middle of it. It was the first time I had seen a woodsman. They were monstrously huge, and one nearly stepped on me. It was Minerva who found me and pulled me away from the fight. From that day on, I was her companion until the day she wasn't there."

The fire was dying, but they let it go. Minerva's song found Aegis's lips. She had taught him everything. The day Minerva left, she was going to meet members of a group. Minerva was always active in the castle politics, but no matter how hard she tried, Aegis was just never interested. He waited in the forest for her for days, then weeks.

"Come back to me, Aeg," a voice called.

"Hmm?" He looked up at Nora.

"It looks like it might rain soon," she said. "We can't camp outside for much longer."

"No." He jumped up and stomped out the fire. "We're going to use some of that silver."

Nora

Several hours later, we found ourselves in a small village. Unfortunately, we did not beat the rain, and we were soaked by the time we arrived. Unlike all the previous regions, region four used wood to build their buildings. The place we encountered was small, and more than a little peculiar.

People hustled and bustled around from store to store in elaborate outfits. All the ladies wore petticoats and hoop skirts with corsets and tiny little hats that didn't fit their heads. The men all wore waistcoats and long top hats.

I gawked. "Everyone is dressed so fancy here. Even the people in region one don't dress like this."

"Yeah, they really like their fine clothing. If we don't blend in with the locals, they won't give us the time of day."

As we walked through the city, we got more than a few side glances. Some paused to stare at us, and one woman held a hankie over her nose as if she feared we were contagious. I snorted out a giggle at the absurdity, and Aegis gave me a look that suggested disapproval. Only when we were far enough away did the people resume their activity.

The tailor and dress shop was naturally the largest store in the village. It was at least three times the size of all the others. There were several shopkeepers and patrons, all of whom stopped what they were doing to stare at us.

"We require new clothing," Aegis said loudly and shook our bag of silver.

A man with a tiny mustache and flamboyant gestures led us to the far back corner of the shop. Once he confirmed that we did indeed have a healthy budget—"a very healthy budget indeed"—he proceeded to pick out items to show us.

Aegis was first because he was an easier customer. He wanted black slacks with a black jacket and a white undershirt with a blue jacquard print on the waistcoat. While the tailor was fitting Aegis, I looked at the various gowns and fabrics.

My former maid, Sarah, was from region four. The people of this region reminded me of her with their poise and false politeness. No wonder the red fabric meant so much to her. It was clear that fashion was the highest priority in these parts.

"You, sir, are an impeccable fit. You wear a suit beautifully," the man declared.

"This one, however. . ." The snotty man's attention was now turned to me, and he shook his head. In my bitterness, I wanted to rip his waxed little mustache off his face. Before I could respond, however, he was already measuring me with his little tape. His little noises made his assessments of my figure unclear. Despite how much I disliked him, I still felt the need for his approval.

"I see," he concluded. "Underneath that hideous sack dress is promise after all!"

I smiled despite myself. The man rushed off and returned with several gowns. "You are on the cusp of womanhood, you see," the tailor explained. "Either a child's gown or a lady's gown would be appropriate, but I assumed you would prefer the latter." The man gave a knowing grin.

I liked the idea very much. I nodded and smiled, and the tailor nodded before rushing off. He selected three gowns for me to choose from and explained the nuances of lady's undergarments. Aegis decided that was his cue to leave; he couldn't care less about such things.

The dresses the tailor showed me were soft linens, silks, and lace.

"The current fashion is free-flowing whimsy," he said with pride.

I selected the lavender linen dress with cream sheer silk overlays that had lace along the cuffs and hem. The tailor's name was Andre, which I discovered while we selected dresses. I had never worn a corset before, but Andre told me how to care for one.

"You must always wear a slip under your corset so that it does not stain with sweat. Every night when you take it off, let it air on a clothesline inside out." While lacing up the corset, Andre observed, "Your waist is so naturally small. It would be best to ease into the corset. You don't need to tighten it much as of now, but as you fill it out, you'll notice the corset will fit tighter."

Andre fussed over the undergarments for several more moments before crossing his arms and nodding in approval. After that, it was finally time to put the actual dress on. It was slipped over my head and buttoned up the back.

"Perfect—go look at yourself," Andre demanded.

I stood on a small platform surrounded by mirrors. All the new hardware made me feel stiff and uncomfortable. I felt hot around my middle, but I knew in time I would get used to the restraints of the corset.

I looked at myself in the dress, and I was taken aback by the sight. The fabric was much finer than the sack dress I had gotten from Gerta's; it was soft and sheer. I was still unaccustomed to my new face with the slanted eyes, creamy white skin, and straight black hair.

"The lavender is most complimentary to your skin," Andre commented.

I meant to respond, but all I could do was stare at myself and touch the dress. Andre seemed pleased with my lack of response. Leaving me to stare at myself, Andre fetched Aegis and brought him to me. Aegis said nothing, but he smiled with surprise.

My arms seemed more rounded, as was my chest. My collarbone protruded just as it always had, but it looked more pronounced with the low neckline. The corset didn't make my waist smaller, but my waistline couldn't be seen in the yellow sack dress. The lavender silk sash sat at the smallest part of my waist to further emphasize the difference between my waist and chest.

"Your ward is quite lovely," Andre told Aegis.

We left the tailor's shop a few grams lighter, but when we stepped into the city, we looked as though we belonged. We decided to keep our old clothes in my knapsack in case we needed traveling garments again. At the moment, our goal was to find a place to stay.

This time, no one stopped to stare at us or stepped away as if we were plagued. I could see how an outlander couldn't make it in this region without a substantial amount of money. Thinking of the encounters with the crude souls in the outlands recalled harrowing screams of that small child. It would follow me in my dreams until the end of my days.

"Now that we are dressed the part, we should find a place to stay, at least for now," Aegis suggested.

"How long will we be here?"

Aegis turned to look at me. "We can stay as long as you want unless the trackers show up."

"Do you think they'll find us?"

Aegis didn't respond. Instead, he nodded towards a hotel a few blocks ahead. "That place looks okay."

It was a mansion that reminded me of a wooden castle. It had a large covered porch and towers with pointy rooftops. It was painted a dark brown and had light brown trim. There was a white picket fence that surrounded the residence and a sign that read "Abigail's B&B" in white chipped paint.

"Yeah," I agreed.

The house was ornate and well decorated, but the corners were dirty, and the sprawling staircase was worn. We stood at the front door waiting for someone to greet us, and after several minutes, a woman in a blue floral gown and a mess of reddish-brown curls pinned on her head came stomping out.

The woman greeted us enthusiastically. "Well, hello there!"

I looked at Aegis, wondering if he was still committed to this place, but he introduced us and asked for a room that had two beds.

"I have several of those available," she replied. "It's a fourth of a gram per week, and breakfast is included."

"We'll take it," Aegis said.

We were led up the stairs past the wallpapered halls and to our room. It was small, and the furniture was bland and used, but it smelled clean. The sheets on the bed were fresh, and the bathroom had soap and a small tub.

Despite bathing in the river just the other day, I felt as though a layer of dust still covered my body. A bath—it had been ages since I'd taken a bath.

That night we slept in real beds and had real meals. We spent several days at Abigail's bed and breakfast, mostly so that I could recover from our visit to the outlands. I slept most of the time, and when I didn't sleep, I ate.

"We could stay here as long as you like, you know," Aegis said as we sat in the lobby in front of a fire one evening.

"The trackers will find us eventually," I reminded him.

"They'd have a hard time finding us thanks to your new face. If we're quiet, it could work out. I could find work here, and you could make friends."

I didn't like what Aegis was suggesting. I knew he just wanted to protect me, but I had had several days to digest being the queen of Hell, and I wasn't going to sit on it any longer. The seventh layer had left me with nightmares too real for me to do nothing.

It was only a matter of time until the trackers caught back up with us, though my face change had thrown them off our scent for now. I had to admit I did like it here, but we couldn't hide for long. I had unfinished business with my mother and with Vinicio.

"I need to see my mother," I insisted. "I need to know the truth."

I woke up the next morning and stretched underneath the linens. I wasn't ready to leave my bed. Aegis was sitting cross-legged on his made-up bed, reading a book he had pulled from the small shelf above the desk.

"You're finally awake," Aegis said without looking away from his book. "I thought you would sleep through today as well."

"I love sleeping in a bed," I said.

Aegis laughed. "It beats sleeping in the dirt any day."

"I want to take a bath. Bring me up some breakfast?" I asked.

Aegis stopped reading to glance at me. "I'll let the housekeeper know you would like breakfast on my way out."

He closed his book and left the room briskly. I couldn't help feeling that he was annoyed with me, but I couldn't say why. Breakfast came rather late and was lukewarm. I didn't want to seem impolite, so I took the food and began drawing a bath. I didn't know when the next hot bath and warm meal would be.

Stepping into the hot water gave me a welcome burn. I melted into the bath and watched the bubbles close around me. This wasn't so bad; perhaps I could live here the rest of my days. I was happy to have Aegis gone, not that I was growing to dislike him or that he was in any way annoying. It was just that I wanted to be alone. The initial excitement of having a constant companion had worn away, and I could tell poor Aegis needed distance as well.

I grabbed the bar of soap and went to work on my water-wrinkled skin. Working the soap on my head, I dug my fingers into the coal black hair and scratched at my scalp. Submerging all but my face in the tub, I remained there for several minutes.

You're going to run into her sooner or later, you know, a familiar voice in my mind reminded me.

Why did I have to think of Mother at a time like this? This was the most pleasant experience I'd had since before I was left in the Starry Wood, before Vinicio had Peter removed from the castle. I wondered where Peter was. I hoped he was okay.

If I were Peter, where would I go? I couldn't remember him telling me what region he came from. Rarely did he speak about himself at all. He was very good at redirecting any questions I had that would have veered too close to his personal life. What Peter did outside of tutoring me, I did not know.

My body bobbed weightlessly in the water, anchored by my legs. With my eyes closed, the darkness began taking form. Things were moving in the dark. As I became more focused, I slowly began to interpret what I was seeing. It was a woman standing next to a barred window. She was small and had silver hair.

Was it Minerva, the woman Aegis spoke of? She was in a cell with me. It was a large cell with several beds, a tub, and a toilet. I wanted to look around, but instead, I was looking down at my hands, except they weren't my hands. These hands were large and aged. Peter!

Strong hands removed me from cold water and wrapped me in a towel, followed by a blanket. Another towel was on my head, and yet another draped my feet. Aegis was there, and he was stomping around the room in a panic. His muffled words became more coherent as I warmed up. He was pacing back and forth lecturing me.

"... I leave for a few hours, and you are still in the bathtub freezing. I can't protect someone who wants to die. Are you trying to kill yourself?" Aegis asked.

My lips were still quivering from the cold, but I said, "No."

Aegis sat down on the bed in front of me. "What were you thinking?"

I wanted to tell him that I had found Minerva, except that I hadn't found her; I'd only seen her. I wasn't even sure if it was her, or if I was looking through Peter's eyes. What if I'd just seen what I wanted to see? Aegis was looking at me with his sad eyes, waiting for something.

"I think I had a vision."

Aegis nodded. "What was the vision?"

"I was in a jail cell of some sort," I lied. Shame flushed my skin and made me nauseous.

Aegis looked down. "You don't have to tell me the truth. Sometimes visions are difficult to interpret."

Hot tears stung my eyes. "I'm sorry. I just don't know what it means yet."

Aegis nodded. "Are you hungry?"

"No." I wiped away the tears and got dressed behind the changing screen. Aegis looked out the window the same way Minerva had.

"Look, I need to tell you something," Aegis said once I had recovered. He was pacing, which meant something had gone wrong while he was in town. "That tracker we saw in the outlands was in town."

He explained the whole story to me. Alfie, the hawk hunter general, wasn't off our trail just yet. Aegis was worried because Alfie made a point of confronting him in public, which made Aegis think he knew what Aegis was.

"He told me that he was on a mission from the steward, and that he knew we had secrets. He said he would check in with us again when he found out just what they were."

"Then we can't stay here," I told him. "We need to get closer to the castle."

"There's a ferry a few miles ahead. It runs all the time." Aegis was halfway out the door as he spoke.

"I'll get packed."

The tracker wanted to know our secrets. They knew where we were, but at least they weren't entirely certain that I was Nora. It made me wonder just how much they knew already. How close had they been to us without us knowing? They could have been everywhere for all we knew, spying on us the entire time.

Would that mean we would have to fight the trackers and hawk hunters when it came time to ascend the throne? A single vampire wouldn't be enough. I'd need more help if Vinicio were to have both armies on his side.

Then there was the issue of finding Peter and Minerva. If I couldn't defeat

Vinicio, the least I could do was find them. It was the least I could do for Aegis. Vinicio had them both jailed somewhere. I doubted either had done anything wrong. Was he hurting them or just letting them rot? If I was wrong, and the vision was just wishful thinking, at least Aegis wouldn't feel let down.

Part of me didn't want to tell him because I wanted to keep him to myself. He promised to be with me until the end. Would he still be there if the love of his life were found? Minerva was beautiful. Unlike him, she looked inhuman. I could never compete with that.

What was I thinking? I didn't have time for this. I didn't need to compete with anything. I was going to be queen—his queen. At least that's what I told myself. I didn't feel like a queen most of the time, but I was trying to get used to the idea.

We checked out of the bed and breakfast and made our way to a ferry. Aegis had said little since we left the room. I wanted to be concerned about his mood, but walking had become a feat. The shoes fit well, but they were tight around the ankles. Clearly, they were intended for looks, not for use.

While my corset was not as confining as it was fashioned to be, it was still uncomfortable. It was like the corset was trapping the heat to my body, making me sweat and feel exertion over the simplest tasks. Andre had suggested that I button my shoes and stockings before I put a corset on. I silently gave a prayer of thanks to that man the first time I dressed.

The corset pressed my small breasts into visibility. As we walked toward the ferry, men noticed me and nodded, bowed, or tipped their hats. Aegis was not amused by this. He didn't say anything, but his already-sour mood was worsening with each passing gentleman.

I was relieved to see the dock after walking several hours. If we had to go on for much longer, I would have had to ask Aegis to find us a carriage.

"You can make the arrangements; I'll wait here," I told him.

He briefly clenched his jaw before strutting away. With Aegis booking our passage to the second region, several young gentlemen approached me and complimented me on my dress. I could feel Aegis's eyes looking back at me, and in my spite, I encouraged the conversation.

I giggled and chatted with the three men. They had just departed from the third region and were going home. I couldn't remember who was James, who was Steve, and who was Davey. It wasn't important. What was important was that Aegis stewed silently, watching me.

When Aegis finished purchasing our tickets, I waited for him to approach.

I imagined him shoving the men away and tossing one into the river. Instead, he stood and waited for me on the docks. Watching me with his arms crossed, he made no attempt to remove the suitors. Annoyed that he didn't come to rescue me, I excused myself from the men and went to him.

"Why didn't you scare them away?" I asked.

"It didn't look like you wanted me to," Aegis replied casually.

I scoffed at him. "It's obvious you're jealous. Why can't you admit it?"

Aegis shook his head. "I'm not jealous. I simply don't like the effect this region has on you."

The heat from my anger broiled within my corsets and splashed on my neck and face. I took a deep breath. He was right. I had become spoiled and conceited during our stay in the fourth circle. Why did he always have to be right?

The conductor's call interrupted our spat. I was so angry all I could see was red. The bellhop quickly led us to the room and gave Aegis the keys before sprinting away, aware of the atmosphere.

Aegis shut the door and braced himself for my temper.

"You said you'd stay with me until the end," I shouted.

"Does it look like I'm going anywhere?" Aegis's jaw was clenched, and his tone was harsh.

"I don't know; you tell me. You've been moody all day."

Aegis pawed at his face as if he were deeply troubled, and confessed, "It's just this place. We need to leave."

My face scrunched up as I prepared to deny that accusation, but he was right. I let this place go to my head. The desperation of Metropolis and its never-ending wall, Gerta trying to feed nine children with turning food, the screaming child in the outlands—I had forgotten about it all. The things that once motivated me to become queen were being eroded by pretty dresses, baths, and my feelings for Aegis.

"I'm so sorry I told you to murder those men in the outlands," I whispered.

"No." He shook his head. "I'd have done it without hesitation if you weren't there. Killing is my specialty."

"No, it's not," I countered. "You're a mentor. That's why your name is Aegis."

Aegis changed the subject. "We will be on this ferry for several days. It's slow but easier than walking."

I had forgotten we were even on a boat. I was so angry and confused that

I hadn't looked at my surroundings. It was a large flatboat. The wood floors suggested it was old but beautifully maintained. The furniture was finely made and cared for. I looked out the window and saw that the ship was moving.

"I've never been on a boat before," I admitted.

Aegis frowned. "Even someone as secluded as me knows the steward and his wife love to sail. You've never been on a ship?"

"They never took me with them. The only ones who took me outside the castle were Peter and Sarah, and that was only to the market."

"Let's have a look, then."

We walked around the entire ferry. Aegis was right; it did move slowly. The river was large and wild. It raged against the ferry, causing the boat to sway. It was exciting yet boring at the same time. It was the first time I had ever been on a boat, yet it lacked the stimulation that adventures brought. Perhaps I had encountered too much danger to find my first boat ride inspiring. Aegis seemed to pick up on my lack of enthusiasm, but said nothing.

"Not enough excitement for you?"

"I guess not." I laughed awkwardly.

I was still ashamed of my behavior. Aegis deserved the truth, but I wasn't ready to tell him yet. I wanted to, but Minerva's stuck in my throat. I was envious of a woman I didn't know, and for reasons I didn't understand.

Chapter Eleven

Vinicio

Vinicio and Bella had planned an anniversary river cruise before Nora disappeared. Now, Vinicio thought that with her daughter missing, Bella wouldn't want to go on a trip in case Nora came home. His feelings were mixed on whether it was a good idea, but he couldn't deny that he would enjoy the break.

"I took the liberty of canceling our trip," Vinicio said over brunch.

Bella was still in her silk red robe, her face puffy from sleeping too much. In the last week, Bella's insomnia had swung to the sleep of depression. She slept most of the day and night. Vinicio didn't mind; it helped him catch up on his duties.

"Why?" Bella asked.

"I thought, in light of everything, that you wouldn't feel up to it."

"No, I want to go," Bella insisted as she took a sip of juice.

"You've been so tired as of late…"

"I want to go," Bella pleaded.

"Well, if you really want to, I'll see to it."

Bella smiled, and Vinicio decided it was worth it. The souls could wait. When he received word from the hawk hunter requesting more defined orders, Vinicio felt uneasy and wanted to distract his wife anyhow. It seemed that Nora still lived. Perhaps it had been a mistake to send Hacia and Alfie. He'd assumed they would be so engrossed in competition and quarry that they wouldn't ask questions. He thought back to what Alfie's note had said.

Target may have company. Description of tutor, Peter, requested.

A.

Vinicio knew for a fact that Peter was not involved, yet it seemed Nora had found herself a protector. Who would go to such lengths to protect a young girl? It seemed that Nora had inherited some of her mother's charm. She must have seduced a man.

Peter is not the companion. Seek her out and dispose of him if you must.

V.

Nora needed to be eliminated before her powers fully manifested and people started noticing. The return of the king would spread like wildfire among the seven regions of Hell. The souls would risk everything if they saw even a glimmer of hope.

There would be dissent among the trackers and the court, and even the souls of region one would involve themselves. It was rare for the purest of souls to concern themselves with the rest of Hell, but for the king, they would emerge from their meditations and music to rally.

What was worse was Bella. Despite her usual complacency, she had grown more inquiring. She wanted to know why it was taking so long to find her daughter. Between her long periods of sleep, she would wake at odd hours and look for someone to talk to about Nora. It was almost as if she didn't fully believe that Vinicio was doing everything he could to find the girl.

Of course, he was, but what he intended to do with her was the part Vinicio hid from his wife. At one point, Rebus found her wandering around the barracks looking for a hawk hunter to speak with. An excursion was just what she needed. She would be confined to the boat with Vinicio's preferred guards. There would be romance and champagne—and no talk of Nora.

Vinicio had grown rather fond of Bella over the years. He had only married her to keep a closer eye on Nora, who at the time showed little promise of being king. It wasn't until the night he fired Peter that Nora exhibited any kingly traits. It was tragic, really. In the years he had spent with his wife, Bella's devotion and charm had won him over. Vinicio truly had nothing against Nora except that she was the rightful heir.

This was his home, and it was all he had ever known. He felt especially territorial about his domain, since he was trying to start a family. His legacy was one of responsibility. Unlike the kings of old who were simply born with a special glow around their soul, a steward had to learn to become a good leader. Vinicio felt that he deserved the title.

A downside to responsibility was making unsavory choices. During his reign, Vinicio had murdered four children, soon to be five. On his deathbed, Vinicio's father had confessed to him that he had killed three infant kings.

Vinicio's grandfather had also admitted that he'd killed one. Infanticide and regicide were an unfortunate inheritance of the steward line. The birth of kings was increasing throughout the generations, and those dead infants haunted Vinicio the way they would haunt his descendants.

If he had killed Nora as an infant, none of this would have happened, but those deceased babes weighed heavily on his soul. When Vinicio saw the golden glow of another king's soul, he cursed. They had been coming more frequently. Assigning the soul to the fifth layer was the easiest way to gain the upper hand on the situation. People in the fifth region never questioned anyone from the castle.

Bella was a pregnant teenage girl. He had a tracker recruit the unborn baby for the trackers and offered a large sum for it. The grandparents happily agreed. The baby would be born, and a tracker would buy the baby with the promise of a prestigious life at a handsome sum. Bella didn't want the child; no one in the fifth region did. But when the baby was born a girl, Vinicio thought perhaps there had been a mistake.

He recalled his recruiter after learning the child's sex and opted to observe her from a distance. There was no sign of the girl manifesting powers. The tracker Vinicio assigned to the region was loyal. Being from the fifth circle of Hell herself, she did not question those who outranked her.

As the years went on, Nora displayed unusual behavior for a young child, but no powers. She was sad and reserved. Even as a toddler, she sat at her bedroom window and watched the street for hours the way an old maid would.

Vinicio thought perhaps if he saw the girl himself that he would know for certain. His father's reign had been so heavily scrutinized that Vinicio did not want to take any unnecessary risks. If the girl didn't seem unusual, he'd leave her be. Having made up his mind, Vinicio paid the fifth region a visit. He kissed babies and shook hands as part of a tour to celebrate his coronation.

He had hoped Nora would be in the crowd, but she had not attended his visit. Among the masses, a beautiful, blonde woman in a blue housedress smiled at him. Vinicio was interested in the woman and, once he learned that she was Nora's mother, it seemed an opportunity had risen.

Before Nora, all the kings had been male. There was no term for a female king in Hell. Vinicio researched the stories of other worlds and found the correct word for a female king. Nora was a queen—or rather, a princess. In other worlds, this happened frequently.

If Nora discovered the truth, it would only be a matter of time before she returned to the castle. He would be removed from office and would probably be executed. The conspirators in the castle dungeon would be free and dubbed heroes for attempting to champion the rightful king. Vinicio's hands grew moist with sweat—he had never felt nervous before, and he didn't like it. Nora's death would resolve those anxieties. So would a small excursion with his wife.

Approaching his wife from behind, he wrapped his arms around her waist while nuzzling and kissing her neck. "Darling, if we don't go now, the rivers will run too low to visit the fourth region. I know you want to go dress shopping," he said.

Bella's resilience surprised him. "I'll need some new dresses, and soon. Are we taking the yacht?"

"It is the fastest," Vinicio said. "We could make it to region four in a day or so and then take our time coming back to the castle."

The yacht waited, along with several guards and crew. It was a rather ornate ship, bronzed and brilliant in the sunlight. They boarded the boat and went south. Bella took to sailing well. Her eyes looked brighter than they had in months. She giggled and smiled until he, too, was infected with happiness. Vinicio put his troubles aside and spent the remainder of the day with his wife, forgetting all about the impending murder of her daughter.

Nora

The rocking motion of the ferry lulled me to sleep, and it was the motion that woke me. Aegis was staring motionless out the window. He looked like a man in his late thirties or early forties, the peak of a man's life. He had some wrinkles and creases, but they added character to his smooth skin and bright blue eyes. Aegis was lean, but not small like Vinicio. He was built broader despite how lean he was.

I was attracted to him. He was handsome and brooding, pensive and expressive. I didn't realize it before because we were in constant danger, and I always considered myself too young. I still felt too young for him, and I wondered if I would feel the same when I grew up. I didn't want to grow old in front of him. There was no ending where he wouldn't end up heartbroken.

"You were restless," Aegis commented.

"The softer the bed, the harder it is to sleep."

"Well, I imagine you have a lot more energy now that you're not forced to walk ten hours a day on half-rotting food," Aegis said bitterly.

"Seems so far away," I murmured into my pillow.

"It was two weeks ago."

I sat up and looked at him curiously. "It's not over yet."

"I know." Aegis smiled sadly.

"I'm glad I saw the outlands. Now I know I want to be queen."

Aegis frowned at the idea.

"Isn't that what you want?" I asked him.

"I left the memories of my former life in the dirt for a reason. If anything were to happen to you ..." Aegis broke off.

"There's something I need to tell you." I told him the truth about the vision. The weight on my chest eased more with each passing sentence.

Aegis said nothing for a long while, and he continued looking out the porthole. "Why didn't you tell me right away?"

I took a deep breath, exhaled, and released the venom. "I've never had a vision before. I don't know if it was real or just something I wanted to see. Also, I..." I didn't know how I was going to say it. "I've changed in the last few weeks. I have a woman's thoughts, and my feelings for you have changed. I was afraid that you would run off with Minerva and leave me."

"I'll never leave you," Aegis said quickly. He didn't look at me, but I could tell he was upset.

"Are you angry with me?"

His back was turned as he looked out the window. "I'm just frustrated. It's like I've known you my whole life, but you still don't trust me."

How could he have known me his entire life? I didn't even know myself. I hadn't known I was the queen of souls until a couple of days ago. I still didn't understand what that meant to me. It didn't seem real. I was still waiting to learn that this was just a big misunderstanding and that I was being confused with someone else.

But even if it was a mistake, I couldn't sit idly by and let Vinicio get away with it. He was trying to kill me, and if it wasn't me, it would be someone else. I had to know if my mother was involved. I didn't want to believe she was, but our relationship had always been strained. I didn't doubt she'd toss me aside for a better life, but would she go this far?

"I'm trying." It was the only answer I could give him.

"This ferry goes as far as region two, but I think we should get off sooner than later. The security is tighter for those looking to enter the second region."

"Thank you," I whispered.

Breakfast was served buffet-style on the deck. There were fruits, meats, pastries, and orange juice. I hadn't had orange juice in so long. The syrupy sweetness gave me a sugar rush, and I went back for a second glass. This seemed to amuse Aeg, and he struggled not to laugh. I ignored him. I was going to drink the whole pitcher without shame.

"I'm sorry I didn't understand how you felt," I started. Everything felt lighter above deck in such a lovely setting. Aegis looked handsome sitting at the small table. He didn't bother with his hair, and his beard was slightly grown in, but gave him a rugged look.

He shook his head. "It's not your fault. You couldn't have known."

"You always have a strong bond with the king?"

"It's been so long, I can't say for sure, but it feels familiar."

"You've always felt strongly about me, or just when you discovered I was the queen?"

"Always," Aegis said quietly. "Sixteen years ago, I felt a change in the forest air. It was like the scent of a ripe spring, except it was the dead of winter. The scar on my hand started tingling. I think now that it was the day you were born. It wasn't just me; Minerva felt it too. She left to look for answers and never came back. Not too long after, I left to look for her."

"What did you find?" I asked.

"Phineas. The man we visited in region six. I wanted to find clues about Minerva; instead, Phineas talked about the king of souls. I left before he could tell me everything. I went back to the wood, and I remained there. The day we met, something pushed me to the edge of the wood. It wasn't coincidence; I was drawn to you. The woodsmen were drawn there by you as well."

"So, you knew all along?"

"I wasn't certain until you—" Aegis drew an invisible circle around my face with his index finger.

I laughed. "Yeah, I think that was when I knew too."

"Are you going to change back?"

"I've tried; it didn't work."

"Well, it's probably better to keep a disguise anyhow."

"I'm going to grab another pastry," I told him.

I approached the bar and helped myself. It didn't seem as though anyone else was interested in breakfast. A crowd was starting to accumulate on one side of the ship. Curiosity eventually got the best of me. With my orange juice in hand, I went to the side of the boat to see what all the commotion was about.

There was a tacky little boat sailing by. It was gold-plated and full of people. Other passengers were whispering about the owner of the boat. I overheard a nearby whisper, "That's the steward's yacht."

Vinicio

Vinicio remained below deck, waiting for Bella. Yesterday she was so bright and chipper, but it seemed that seasickness had caught up with her. Even her vomiting was dainty. She made a few coughs before retching, but even that was soft behind the bathroom door.

"You can go ahead of me," Bella offered.

"I don't mind. I'll wait as long as you need."

The romantic sentiment would make her sigh despite feeling so awful. However, Vinicio found himself wondering if he really would be so steadfast for her. He didn't know. Vinicio had loved a woman once, but it was nothing like this.

He had loved Kate fiercely. She was angry and wild, just as he had been. Their romantic encounters always resulted in scratches, bites, and bruises. Their lover's quarrels often resulted in the same. One night, their fight-turned-love-making reached an unprecedented height. She cut him with a knife she had hidden under her pillow. He responded by closing his hands around her throat. A throbbing pain pierced through his abdomen, forcing Vinicio to dismount.

He vaguely remembered being carried after that. Voices echoed distantly around him. When he awoke, Vinicio was in the medical ward. Kate had stabbed him, and he had nearly broken her neck. His father was furious with her, and he banished her to the outlands.

Vinicio could have defended her. He could have asked his father to let her go, but instead, he watched as the bridge keeper ferried Kate across the canyon. She sobbed and babbled for mercy. It was dusk when she reached the other side. The barbarians of the outlands were waiting for her.

Watching with his binoculars as those creatures dragged her away while she screamed in terror, Vinicio had felt nothing. If anything, a morbid fascination overcame him. What were they going to do to her? Kate's neck was still swollen and purple from their altercation. The outlanders circled her, and that was when he lost sight of her.

He figured they were taking turns with her. Once they were done, they would probably sell her to a mob boss. Kate was an attractive girl—she would sell for a high price. Vinicio mounted his horse beside his father and rode back to the castle without another word.

His love for Kate had faded away in the few days he stayed in the medical ward. It was if she had been a drug that had intoxicated him only to leave him weak and bitter when gone. Vinicio's love for Bella was different. She was fragile and welcomed his dominance. She grew in his strength, and in return, he became more assured of his feelings for her.

Bella interrupted his thoughts as she emerged from the bathroom. "Let's go," she said.

Vinicio took her by the waist to steady her, and his free hand took her hand to further guide her up the stairs. She seemed to be surefooted despite vomiting for a half hour.

"I'm fine, really," she promised.

The upper deck was elegantly prepared for breakfast with all of Bella's favorites from crepes to oranges. Vinicio poured a glass of champagne and gave it to his wife and poured some for himself.

"None for me, love," Bella said.

"You love this champagne," Vinicio reasoned.

"Yes, but expectant mothers shouldn't drink alcohol," she said with a smile.

Vinicio was floored by the revelation. Bella was carrying his child. Vinicio would soon have an heir. Dropping his glass, he rushed to his wife and picked her up by the waist, spinning her in the air. She giggled and embraced him when he put her back down on the ground. Holding her, he could see the crowd of ferry passengers watching them. They would soon have another steward.

Despite his sins, Vinicio vowed to do everything he could to raise the child properly. They would get the love and support Vinicio always felt deprived of. He knew Bella felt the same way. Her parents were repressive and unfeeling to an extent that left Bella in constant self-doubt and anxiety.

It wasn't just her parents. Bella was haunted by her failures as a mother for Nora. She had been too young to have and parent a child. Looking back, Vinicio wished he *had* recruited Nora as a Tracker. It would have spared poor Bella some unnecessary suffering and given him a better eye on the girl. Then again, if Nora had been tutored under Hacia, she would have survival and battle skills. It was hard enough to find the girl as it was.

Nora

I saw her. I saw my mother happy and smiling, being whirled around by the love of her life on her golden yacht. Her life was beautiful without me in it. It felt as though I were sinking into the floor. My tears were light. They cascaded down my unrecognizable face and onto my lavender dress. I wanted her to see me. I wanted her to know that I was watching her.

I registered nothing. Not the voices of concern nor the gasps. Not the people breaking away from me, and not the muffled shriek of a nearby woman. I wanted her to see me. I watched Vinicio go to the lower deck, and my mother stood alone.

She turned towards the ferry and locked eyes with me. Mother. At first, she looked confused, as though she didn't know what she was looking at. She took a few steps forward to get a closer look before fainting. I watched her fall; even her fainting was beautiful.

Castle security swarmed her in an instant, and the yacht moved out of sight. My energy was spent, and all I wanted to do was lay down. My knees buckled, but before I hit the deck, arms caught me before I faded into darkness.

I woke in my cabin covered in sweat. I tried to sit up but couldn't. The initial panic of being incapacitated subsided when I realized it was only due to the corset. I rolled to my side and pushed myself upright with my arms. Aegis was sitting on his bed facing me. He looked panic-stricken, and his hair was disheveled more than usual.

"How long have I been out?" I asked.

"A few hours or so," Aegis replied.

I tried to get up from the bed, but he extended his hand towards me, motioning me to remain seated.

"Have you been watching me this entire time?" I asked.

Aegis nodded and explained, "Something happened on the ship deck. Do you remember?"

I struggled through the haze of sleep before grasping what had occurred.

"I saw Mother," I said and began to bawl.

Aegis rested his head in his hands miserably as I recounted what I had seen. It was just as I feared. She didn't care at all that I was gone. For all she knew, I was dead, and she was glad to be rid of me. I knew my mother had never loved me, but it hurt even more to see the proof.

Aegis didn't know what to say, so he just sat and listened to my insecurities and the realized fears spewing from my mouth. When I finally stopped, I cried until I could no longer draw breath. This alarmed my protector. I heaved and shook uncontrollably as he undressed me.

He assumed the corset was the culprit of my breathing problems and tried to remove it. At first, he attempted to untie it, but when the laces didn't free me from the stills, he resorted to breaking the strings. Being free of the corset helped some, but it didn't stop the hyperventilation.

A knock at the cabin door only made things worse for Aegis. "Hello, this is the second mate, Mr. Torres. Is everything all right in there?"

Aegis opened the door and brought the man in. "I can't get her to stop doing that," he said in a panic.

"What were you doing to her?" the man accused.

"What?" Aegis realized what the man thought. I was half dressed and hysterical.

"No, I didn't touch her—I thought the corset was hurting her. She was upset and started making that noise, and I didn't know what to do."

Mr. Torres swung into action. He stepped into the bathroom and produced a bag. Aegis watched him suspiciously as he held it over my mouth and nose. After several inhalations, I could breathe normally. Working intermittently with the bag, I caught my breath. The pounding in my temples was so loud all I could do was close my eyes and shield myself from daylight.

Aegis sighed in relief. "Thank you so much. I didn't know what to do."

The second mate seemed confused by that statement. "You've never seen her hyperventilate? Are you newly married?"

"No, not married—I'm her escort," Aegis said.

Mr. Torres didn't seem convinced.

"I am employed by her family to take her to the third region to stay with her aunt. Normally, her mother accompanies us, but her mother was sick."

The second mate approached my bed and kneeled on the floor beside me. "Miss, is it as he says?"

"I'm so sorry," I said. "I've never done that before. It's as he says. Aegis would never do anything to hurt me."

Mr. Torres nodded in satisfaction. "It's all right. I have six girls at home, so it's an everyday occurrence in my house."

I laughed despite the looming exhaustion. "That sounds like great fun. I don't have any siblings."

"Oh, well, you're welcome to pay us a visit. Our house is the one that everyone avoids in the fourth region."

"I thought that was Abigail's bed and breakfast," I teased.

Mr. Torres laughed. "We are Abigail's ugly stepchild. Is there anything else I can do for you?"

I shook my head.

"All right. If you need me, I'll be on deck," he said.

Aegis showed the man out while thanking him profusely. He closed the door and rested his head against it. For all his worry of trackers and outlanders, it must never have occurred to him that his biggest battle would be to protect me from myself.

"Aegis, I'm sorry…" I started.

"You have every right to be upset; it just scared me. It's been a long time since I've felt so helpless."

Maybe it was the chaos in my heart, but something about that gave me a twisted sense of satisfaction.

"Do you want some water or something?" Aegis was pacing the room. He looked like a caged animal. He didn't like the confines of the space. He only tolerated the cabin because I was in it.

"I'd like some water, please."

Aegis shot to the door before pausing to regain his human movements. He shut it behind him, and I took the opportunity to examine my corset. The cords were ripped in half, of course, but as I inspected further, I could see the rivets were ripped in some areas as well. There was no saving the thing, but perhaps I could try.

I closed my eyes and imagined the torn undergarment re-stitching itself. Threads reconnected and pulled the metal rivets into their rightful places. Seams re-creased as the fabric grew taut against the metal boning. Once it was complete, I opened my eyes to see—a torn-up corset.

It seemed my abilities only worked some of the time. I threw the damaged garment into the garbage and put the top of my dress back on. I was at the last few pearl buttons when I heard the door click behind me.

"Aegis, can you fasten these?"

Fingers found the buttons and carefully pulled them through the fabric. Not his hands. I turned and came face to face with a black woman with dreaded hair. The badge on her vest identified her as the general tracker.

Chapter Twelve

Nora

"That was a neat trick you did up there," the woman said. "Your face changed from this face to Nora's face and back again. How did you do it?"

I tried to speak, but nothing came out. I was petrified, but I needed to stall her until Aegis came back. She crept around the room like a cat. Her movement was fluid, and she didn't so much as blink as she skirted around the space. She wore soft leather, and her black beaded dreads made no noise despite the ornaments.

"I'm the true queen of Hell," I told the woman.

"Queen?" The woman balked.

"Girl king."

"Is that why the steward wants you dead?"

I nodded.

"Can you do it again?"

I closed my eyes and imagined my face changing, but the woman didn't appear amazed. It didn't work. It never seemed to work when I wanted it to.

"I don't have control over it just yet," I whispered, embarrassed by the failure.

"How inconvenient."

Aegis swung the door open and charged the woman. She dodged just in time and nicked him with the edge of a small dagger. A line of blood emerged. Aegis maintained eye contact with the tracker as he wiped the blood away; the cut had vanished.

"So, you are a vampire."

Aegis said nothing.

"I wonder why a vampire would risk his life for a girl."

"She's the king."

"So she says, but I've seen no proof."

"She's a late bloomer. She just needs more time." Aegis held his arms up in surrender, but his legs moved in sync with hers. He was dancing the same dance, waiting for her to strike. The woman wasn't concerned with him in the slightest. She refused to take her eyes off me.

"I'll not waste a single soul on a pretender," she said. "If you are lying, I will find out, and I will bring your body to the steward just as he asks."

"Do you know if my mother knows he is trying to kill me?" I asked.

The tracker was taken aback by my question. Her face went through a range of emotions before she answered. "I only have orders to kill Nora, the steward's stepdaughter. It was only after we started to track you that we start asking why. You'll be seeing me again, girl king."

Before we could respond, she threw a vial on the ground and crushed it with her boot. A noxious gas filled the cabin. It burned my eyes and made me retch for air. I moved towards the door, grabbing Aegis's arm on the way out.

The poisonous gas spilled from the doorway. I grabbed the railing of the deck and inhaled the fresh air between hacks. Snot was leaking from my nose, and my eyes were still burning. Aegis was on the ground but recovering from the smoke at a faster rate.

"I think she was the same one from the woods," Aegis said at last.

I wiped my face with my sleeve. "She knew you were susceptible to the smoke."

"She had to have known I was a vampire from the beginning. She was well-prepared."

I agreed with him, but her motivations seemed off. She had time to kill me repeatedly, yet she didn't. Maybe she was afraid of Aegis, but she could have killed me and left before Aegis returned. If anything, it was like she was curious.

"We need to get out of here," Aegis said. "More will come. You could have been killed."

"But she didn't kill me," I told him.

"She could have. She could have slit your throat or kidnapped you." Aegis was growing angry at the thought. His jaw clenched between his mutterings.

"That's not what she came here to do," I insisted.

"Did you read her mind?" His voice was a mixture of curiosity and sarcasm.

"I didn't have to."

Aegis was insistent that we leave straight away. I didn't disagree with him. If the woman tracker could find us and Alfie was near, others were probably close behind. The smoke cleared from the cabin, and we gathered our things into my knapsack.

Before we left, we went to the top deck and took food from the lunch buffet just beginning to open. Most of it wouldn't keep long, so I just took some bread and cheese. I looked longingly for some orange juice, but it wasn't served for lunch. On the table was an assortment of crackers. The round ones with perforated edges reminded me of my first night in the castle.

I had been given the same crackers as a snack before bed—cheese, crackers, meat, and a glass of water. Mother wanted to give me food I was familiar with, but I'd never tasted anything so good before.

The meat was fresh and so thinly sliced I could see light through it. The cheese was soft. It wasn't dry or greasy. The crackers were fresh and salted. I made various combinations of the foods to fully appreciate their flavor.

The water was clear and crisp, and I drank three glasses before Mother stopped me.

"You don't want to wet the bed," she warned me.

After dinner, I was tucked into bed. It was much bigger than what I was used to, but it was soft and smelled clean. Grandma hadn't like washing my linens; she'd said it was Mother's job, but Mother couldn't be bothered with it. I'd started to wash them myself when my feet soiled the sheet or when I wet the bed.

"Mother, where is your room?" I asked her as she started to leave.

"It's on the other side of the dining hall."

I couldn't remember where that was. I wasn't sure if they had even shown me that part of the living quarters. A hard lump stuck in my throat, and despite my wish to be brave, I couldn't.

"Could you stay until I fall asleep?" I asked with a shaky voice.

Mother was visibly anguished by my request. "I know this is all new and scary, but you'll be fine. I promise."

"Please," I begged.

"Why must you do this? We just arrived at this amazing place, and you're going to get all these wonderful things, but all you can do is cry."

"I'm sorry."

Mother sighed impatiently. "You're just tired. Close your eyes, and you'll be asleep before I'm gone."

I didn't fall asleep before she was gone. Despite the fatigue, I hardly slept. She was right about drinking so much water. I had to use the bathroom several times during the night. Everything in my rooms had me scared. The dark felt menacing, but when I turned on the lights, I felt a sense of dread while looking at the stillness of the room. If I fell asleep, it was a light sleep, and it was only to stay the emptiness that loomed over my bed.

The next morning, I woke up with a headache. A plump woman came into my room and attempted to clean. She looked around to find that not a single thing was out of place. The bed was made, and the clothes were neatly folded in my dresser. I sat at the windowsill looking over the garden.

"Goodness, you're a tidy one. Are you hungry? Would you like some breakfast?"

I nodded, and the woman pulled a little cart with a tray of food into the room. I wasn't sure what it was. She set a tray with a plate next to me on the sill. It was a round brown spongy thing with brown sticky stuff and white fluffy stuff in the center. It smelled warm and sweet at the same time.

I cut into the round. It was like a bread, but resilient to the weight of my finger. The woman laughed at my curiosity.

"It's called a pancake. It has maple syrup and whipped cream on top."

Whatever it was, it was delicious. We had sweet foods in the fifth region Some people had cakes on their birthdays, and fruit wasn't too difficult to find. Mostly, my grandparents disapproved of displaying or giving unnecessary frivolity. They had made sweetbread for special occasions or as gifts. But between the difficulty of finding raw sugar and the cost, it had been a rare occurrence.

Aegis' voice penetrated the memory. "Nora?" he asked.

I realized that I'd been staring at the crackers for several minutes.

"We need to go," he said as he led me to the lower deck.

"How are we going to get off the ferry?" I asked.

"We're not far from the forest's edge; I can jump over."

He was more excited about this idea that I was.

"Aegis, don't you think that will draw too much attention?"

"Yeah, but why not? That tracker knows who you are, and she will probably tell others."

Maybe it was time to start asserting my right to the throne. I wanted to be queen; how else does one become queen? I didn't have the best handle on my powers, but with enough practice, I could grow to understand them.

Think of it as a campaign, my voice whispered back at me. I wasn't sure what that meant; I'd ask Aegis later.

He scooped me up in his arms as bystanders eyed us curiously. I saw Mr. Torres, so I smiled and waved. Aegis smiled and waved as well; he was enjoying the humor of the situation. Stepping back a few steps, my protector focused on the woods that awaited several hundred feet away on the other side of the river. I leaned my head against his chest and relaxed my neck, knowing full well that I couldn't withstand the speed.

Aegis ran at full sprint before leaping off the edge of the railing. As we went sailing through the air, I looked behind us to see the people on the ferry pointing and shouting amongst themselves. Aegis had overestimated how far he could jump. We landed at the shallow edge of the river. He was knee high in water, but it was close enough.

"Which way next?" he asked as we entered the forest.

"To find my mother," I told him. Aegis looked panic-stricken at the thought.

"Nora, no. Absolutely not," he said. His arms were crossed, and his feet were firmly rooted to the ground.

"Why should we wait?"

"You're not ready to go face to face with your mother," Aegis insisted. "I'm not ready for you to confront her."

I knew he was right. I wasn't ready, but I had to face her. I needed to know if she was complicit in the attempt on my life. "We know she's on the river somewhere."

"No."

"Then I will talk to just her, alone, and then we can leave," I said, trying to convince him.

"No. There are guards. There are people who want you dead. Your powers are still unpredictable, and if I'm captured, you're as good as dead."

"I need to know." My voice trembled.

Aegis looked away in exasperation. "I think it would be best if we travel around the safer regions, spread the word of your coming, and face your mother and Vinicio when your powers finally peak."

"Campaign?" I asked.

"Yes, that's a good word for it, I suppose."

"Aegis, what happens when you walk in a circle with someone following behind?"

His eyes narrowed. He was surprised by the rationale. "We can keep ahead of them."

"If we wander in the safe regions, it will only be a matter of time before the trackers catch up to us."

"I can outrun them."

"We should go to the place Vinicio would least expect," I prompted.

"Agreed. I'm thinking we go back to the fifth or sixth region…"

"By going to their very home."

Aegis kicked the dirt and an explosion of dust scattered for miles. He rubbed his face as he walked away, cursing in his native tongue under his breath. Aegis wouldn't leave me. He had no choice but to follow me.

"We are going to stalk their boat and hope to catch her alone," I explained.

"Can we just sleep on it?" Aegis bartered. "Just a night or two? The river ends not too far from the port where we boarded the ferry. They will have to come back in this direction anyway."

"We can do that," I agreed. We walked into the woods just far enough that our camp couldn't be seen. Aegis began collecting wood for the fire. I helped him stack it up before lighting it myself.

Aegis beamed with pride when the fire burst from the wood and roared into life.

"How long have you been able to do that?"

"Just now," I lied.

The forest was much more enjoyable without a smoke bomb trying to kill us. There was an awkward silence between Aegis and me that seemed to go clear into the night. It seemed we only wanted to speak to one another when we were in danger.

I spent most of the time toying with the fire, making it so large that Aegis warned me that it would start the trees burning. I made it small before putting it out entirely.

"Can you start it again?" Aegis asked.

I couldn't.

"Keep trying."

I refocused on the glow of the fire. It flared and danced to life.

"You did it!" Aegis exclaimed. "But why is it so red?"

He was right. The color of the fire was wrong. It wasn't a mixture of oranges and reds; it was just red. The base of the fire was just as crimson as the tips of the fire, making the flame look two dimensional and false. I laughed at the absurdity of it.

With additional effort, the fire went back to a natural color. I ate some bread and cheese for dinner while Aegis struggled to find a good dinner conversation topic.

"How was your life in the castle?" he asked.

I finished what I was chewing before I answered. "It was good. I spent most of my time with Peter and Sarah, my maid."

Aegis shook his head. "That man is twisted."

"Vinicio?"

"Yeah. He raised you with the intention of killing you, yet he gave you a tutor, a maid, and fancy clothes. Why not just kill you outright?"

I didn't know. I didn't understand Vinicio's motivations at all. "He gave me a room with a view of the garden. It was like he knew I would enjoy it."

"Did Peter suspect Vinicio of anything?"

"Peter suspected Vinicio of everything," I joked. "He was always sneaking around behind Vinicio's back. Part of my maid's job was to make sure Peter knew his place. She spied on us all the time, but I think somewhere along the way she joined our side."

I told Aegis about an incident from when I was young. I had to have been ten or eleven. It was when I discovered Peter snooping around Vinicio's private quarters. I was working on my studies in the classroom. Peter was running an errand, so I was left to study freely.

I caught a warm draft as I walked by a wall. At first, I thought it was a sort of furnace, but it wasn't hot enough. A framed grate within the wall about three feet tall and two feet wide was hidden behind a curtain. My fingers searched the frame for some way to open the grate. I found the lip of the frame, and it swung open on a hinge.

I understood little about why adults did the things they did, but why hinge a furnace grate? I ducked inside and closed the door behind me. The walls were painted black, and the floor was stone, just like the rest of the castle. This wasn't a furnace vent—it was a servant's tunnel. It was very small for a servant's tunnel, though—a full-grown adult would need to crawl through these tunnels.

The tunnel branched off in several directions. It was a labyrinth within the castle itself, but I was never lost. Perhaps it was the layout, or maybe I had a keen sense of direction, but I could navigate the tunnels as if I'd traveled them hundreds of times. The sound of Peter's voice in an upper level hallway made me pause. What was he doing up here?

"What are you doing up here, Peter?" another familiar voice sounded.

"Oh, Sarah. I was just looking for you."

"I only clean the steward's hall on request."

"Ah, very good," Peter lied. "I wanted to talk to you about Nora."

"I was hoping to do the same. She's a strange girl."

"What do you mean by that?"

"She doesn't behave like a child. It's like she's an adult disguised as a child."

Peter hesitated before he spoke. "She's had a difficult life."

"I know, but, the other day, I gave her a doll. She doesn't play with it. She sets it down in various places in her bedroom and looks at it like she's waiting for it to do something."

"She doesn't know how to play. Her grandparents didn't believe in toys."

"What kind of life is that for a child?" Sarah's voice grew watery.

"Hey, shh," Peter said, trying to sooth her. "She's with us now. I'll play puzzles and games with objectives to teach her how to play. She struggles with imagination, but she will get there. It will just take time."

I hurried back to the classroom. I needed to get there before Peter. I thought about telling him of my discovery, but I liked having a secret.

"That's quite the story," Aegis said. "What do you think he was looking for?"

"I don't know, but he was lucky that Sarah didn't tell on him."

"You should get to bed. I'll keep an eye out for the yacht."

"Okay." I wrapped myself in his jacket. I forgot how attractive he was in that white tunic. "Aegis?" I asked.

"Hm?"

"Did you love the kings before me?"

Aegis froze in place. "I'd like to think I did."

"I wish you would remember," I muttered as I threw twigs into the fire.

"Why?"

"I want to know if you love me more than them," I replied.

"Good night, Nora."

I woke up the next morning sore and more tired than when I had gone to sleep. I rolled over to a fireless pit that was freshly stacked with wood. I pointed at the fire with my index finger and made a pew noise, and the fire was lit.

I went back to sleep for a while longer. When I woke up, it was midday, and I was starving. Where was Aegis? I wandered near the campsite; he may have just been hunting. I was growing nervous without him. I started to wonder if the trackers had caught up to us and gotten him while I was sleeping, but that couldn't be true—otherwise, I'd be dead.

I found him on the edge of the brook, squatted down behind a large boulder overlooking the river.

"Aeg?" I called.

He didn't answer. It wasn't until I got closer that I realized he was sleeping. What a strange way to fall asleep. I shook his rigid body, and he remained unmoved. He was like stone. I kneeled beside him and tried to pry his eyes open, but even his eyelids were unyielding.

I remembered reading stories about the other life. There were people who fell asleep and couldn't wake up unless their true love kissed them. It seemed wrong to kiss him without his consent, but I was willing to try anything. I placed a kiss on his lips gently and then waited for him to open his eyes.

I thought kissing would feel magical somehow. It didn't feel like anything. It felt no different than kissing my own hand. Maybe it would have been more special if he were awake, but I didn't see how it would make a difference. Still, the idea of him kissing me made my head spin.

He remained unchanged despite my fairy tale kiss.

"Dammit, Aeg!" I screamed into his ear. "Wake up!"

"Aeg. Aeg. Aeg," I shouted over and over in the most obnoxious tone I could manage.

Still, nothing happened. He had done this once before, but it was easier to wake him then. What made Aegis sleep so hard? The river rushed on as the birds in the forest chirped. Everything was so peaceful, but it did nothing to calm the rage in my heart.

Wake up, Aegis.

Aegis opened his eyes and looked at me in alarm. "Was I asleep again?"

"You wouldn't wake up. Why didn't you wake up?" I was crying, but I didn't care.

"I didn't mean to scare you. Last night you told me you wished I could remember the past. I tried to remember."

"Is this what happens when you try to remember your past? Is this how you fell asleep in the dirt with the others?" I asked.

Aegis paused, thinking of a way to explain it. "Do you remember life as a small child?"

"A little." I shrugged. "Here and there."

He nodded sagely. "My memory works the same way. The longer the span of time, the harder it is for me to remember things. Being immortal means I carry the memories of everyone I love with me even when they're long gone. Sleeping for a few centuries is as close to death as I'll ever get."

"When you slept in the ground, it was like cleaning a slate."

"Yes, that's a great analogy. But my slate is stained, so even though I don't remember, feelings and dreams still linger. My slate is stained with so much red, you understand?"

I'd gathered this from my time with him, but this was the first I'd heard

Aegis explain it fully. He had deliberately forgotten the last life, and maybe dozens before that, because it had become too much for him. Love was scary—I was learning that more and more with each passing day. Aegis didn't have a reprieve from grief unless he slept.

When the kings stopped emerging, he lost all will to live. With no king to follow, he was left alone with his memories. He slept in the ground with the other vampires and hoped never to wake up. But he woke to fight the woodsmen, and then he was left to wander aimlessly. The very idea of remembering a life from thousands of years ago was exhausting for him.

It was my fault he had fallen asleep. It was like the last time—Aegis slept when he was sad. He had tried to remember the past, and he exhausted himself with the pain of his own memories. Aegis was strong, stronger than anyone I'd ever known, but enduring thousands of years' worth of sadness was something even a vampire couldn't do.

"I'm sorry I keep asking about things you need to forget."

"No. I want to remember again," Aegis said as he stood. "I just can't find a way back."

We returned to the campfire, and I ate what remained of our supplies. Aegis would need to hunt later, but I didn't want to ask him just then. He was still tired and a little confused with sleep.

"Did you see the yacht?" I asked.

"I did. Early in the evening, in fact. They must have turned around."

"Back to the castle," I said. Mother must have been frightened by seeing me on the ferry. "Aeg, just what did I do on the ferry?" I asked.

"You were in the crowd when your face started changing from the face you have now to the face you were born with," Aegis explained. "I don't know if your mother saw the change from one to another or if she just saw your birth face, but she fainted when she saw you. Souls were screaming and running away. It was a bit of a scene."

"She fainted. That must be why they went back."

"If they pushed hard, they could be at the castle by now."

"Good."

Chapter Thirteen

Vinicio

"I know what I saw!" Bella yelled excitedly. "It was her. It was Nora."

"Doctor, can you give her something?" Vinicio pleaded. "Something to keep her calm? This stress can't be good for the baby."

The doctor's beard was long and coarse, and his glasses thick. He muttered something before pulling a syringe and vial from his bag. "This is a mild sedative, perfectly safe for a mother and her child."

Bella struggled, forcing Vinicio and a guard to hold her down while the doctor pierced the skin and injected the drug. She fought the tranquilizer in vain until she finally succumbed to sleep.

The doctor shook his head as he cleaned his glasses. "Pregnancy has all sorts of side effects. She recently lost her first child, yes?"

"I'm afraid so," Vinicio confirmed. "Nora was her name. She ran away, last seen at the Starry Wood."

"Oh, that is awful," the doctor in sympathy.

"It was. We haven't found the remains. Now it seems she sees Nora in total strangers."

The doctor scratched at his beard. "Did the girl look like her daughter?"

"They were about the same age," Vinicio replied casually. "It's not just the daughter. Bella has miscarried several times over the years." He poured himself and the doctor a scotch.

"This could be a temporary issue, grief exacerbated by hormones," the doctor said. "I imagine she is internalizing a great deal of guilt."

"I think so," Vinicio agreed.

"My nurses and I will keep her under observation for a few days. Here in the castle, of course—we want comfort and discretion."

"Much obliged, Doctor."

Bella thought she had seen Nora, alive and well, on the deck of a ferry in the fourth region. Vinicio was inclined to believe her, but he couldn't let anyone else know that. It would be better to blame Bella's behavior on grief and pregnancy until Nora was dead. He'd had little correspondence from the general trackers he sent out, which put him in an awkward position.

Assuming Bella was right and Nora was indeed on that ferry, she was too close to the castle for comfort. Vinicio could send out more trackers and draw more attention to the situation, or he could research alternative ways to dispatch the girl and her companion. The more trackers that were sent out, the more questions they would ask. Alfie and Hacia both had a proven record of loyalty, yet they questioned his motivation in subtle ways.

There was one option available to Vinicio at any time. It was one his father had told him about when he officially abdicated.

His old father had handed him a small jeweled dagger. "This is the Dagger of Monsters," he'd said. "With this blade, you can control and command the mythical creatures of our world just as the kings once did."

"Have you ever used it?" Vinicio asked.

"No. And you must avoid using it at all cost as well. Blood magic is powerful—once cast, it will always be your undoing."

"Then how do you know it works?"

"This history has been passed down from generation to generation, from the last king to you," the steward had lectured. "The history books do not know everything."

Vinicio now considered the dagger and the creature hidden within the castle, but he pushed the thought away. He would give the trackers a little more time before unleashing such a beast into Hell. With Bella asleep and the doctor gone, Vinicio retired to his private chambers.

Withdrawing a small piece of parchment, he wrote a note.

Target was last seen in the fourth region. V.

Sealing his note with wax, Vinicio left it on his desk for Rebus to find the next morning. Hacia had given him no further correspondence since she discovered Nora was alive. She was getting old, perhaps it was slowing her down. It was hard too to tell.

The hunters were big on communication—Vinicio got updates on Alfie from time to time—but trackers didn't operate that way. Many times, he sent Hacia on missions, and there would be no sign of her for months until she returned with a head. Vinicio shuddered at the crudeness of the general tracker, but she did her job well.

Across the hall from the bedroom he shared with his wife was a locked door cast entirely from iron. Reaching underneath his tunic, Vinicio produced a key cast from the same metal. He pushed it open and walked into the small, vacant room, locking the door behind him.

If he were a king, the safe would simply open for him. Since he was a steward, though, he had learned the combination. The last king gave his steward a combination of turns to unlock the soul safe in the event a new king was not born to take his place. Perhaps the first steward never encountered a king's soul, or maybe he had killed him just as his descendants had. Vinicio did not know.

One by one, Vinicio scooped up the orbs and determined which region they were destined for by the color of their glow, then sent them through the mirror map to their designated regions. It was boring work. The steward sorted out dozens of souls. Most of them were tainted, but that was always the case.

The worst of the worst spent more time in the gateways than they did on Hell or on other worlds. They never survived long in Hell, and they did better on some worlds as opposed to others. Good souls lived in Hell longer than they did in other worlds, it seemed.

Vinicio didn't like playing favorites, but when he saw a bright soul, he always went for it first. The ache around his eyes demanded his attention. He closed the safe and gave it a good spin. He wanted to lie beside his drugged, pregnant wife and place a hand on her stomach before falling into a heavy sleep.

Nora

We broke camp and made our way towards the castle at a slow pace, partly because my shoes were not good for walking, but also because Aegis didn't want to move on the castle until nightfall anyway. He held my hand to help me over fallen trees and enormous roots that rutted from the forest floor. The long dress I was wearing snagged against bushes, and I winced as if it hurt me. I loved this dress.

"Were you and Minerva…" I regretted asking him already.

"Lovers?" Aegis finished.

I nodded.

"Sometimes."

How could they be lovers some of the time? "You mean you broke up a lot?"

"No. Vampires are different than souls when it comes to love. We accept that love changes. Romance fades into platonic love. Sometimes we go our separate ways and reunite later in a romantic way, or just as friends."

Platonic. The word echoed in my mind, and it made me feel bitter. My developing interest in Aegis was confusing and platonic. I was a virgin. I didn't know if I wanted sex or something else.

"What about you?" Aegis asked. "Was there a special boy in your life?"

I shook my head.

"Well, there will be many when you're sitting on that throne."

Dusk began to settle, and my thoughts went from Aegis to my nerves. I was going to confront my mother. I promised myself I would be tough, critical, and unmoved by her magical ability to make me feel guilty for existing. We made it to a large clearing in the forest before we prepared for our mission.

"All right, first things first," Aegis said. "Take off the corset and put it in your bag. You need to be comfortable for this trip."

"I'm not wearing a corset. You broke it, remember?"

"Good riddance," he teased.

"I get nauseous when you carry me."

"It won't be so bad this time—I know my way around here. Besides, you can't scale castle walls."

"It's also a good way to get covered in vomit, Aeg," I warned.

"I'll change into my old clothes; they're more comfortable anyway. You can puke on them all you want."

Reluctantly, we changed our clothes. In the shadowy spaces of the forest, we undressed. Aegis kept his back to me for privacy despite having already seen me multiple times. I undressed while watching him undress. I had never really seen a man before. I knew it was rude, but curiosity got the better of me. He felt my eyes on him, but said nothing.

He looked mostly the same as a woman from the back—bigger and broader, but generally the same. In the same stroke, it felt different looking at him somehow. Something about his most similar body stirred parts of me that were unknown.

He was lean, but still muscular. When he bent over to put his pants on, I could see glimpses of his male parts between his legs. I thought I would find those parts compellingly attractive, but instead, I had to stop myself from giggling. Maybe it was just the angle, but they looked funny dangling around.

"Are you done?" Aegis asked as he pulled the tunic over his head.

"Oh." I changed from my lace dress to my sack dress, the dress I didn't mind vomiting on. "Ready!"

"I think this time, I'll carry you on my back. This should be a much smoother ride since I know the forest well."

I climbed onto his back. His arms hooked me from around the knees, and I grasped firmly around his shoulders. I took a deep breath to steady myself against another jarring ride.

"Ready?" Aegis asked.

"Yeah."

In an instant, we were off. He did much less jumping around, and it was indeed much easier to endure. I still couldn't look at the passing scenery as it made my tummy cramp up, but if I looked ahead, everything felt fine. It was even somewhat fun. When he did jump, it felt more like we were floating upward before gracefully landing back on the ground.

I held him as tightly as I could, but not because I was afraid. It was because I was wanted to be as close to him as possible. He was everything I could ever want. I wondered if he could love me the way I loved him. Aegis was loyal to me, but could he love me as a woman and not just as a king?

We stopped for a short break halfway through the Starry Wood. While Aegis didn't need a rest, I did. My stomach began to unknot as soon as my feet felt solid ground. The wood was like a habitat of its own. The trees were so densely packed that they blocked out much of the moonlight.

Over a snack, we discussed our plans. It had been a while since Aegis had seen the castle, and he wouldn't be aware of the passages that I took.

"There are large caged ducts that go throughout the building. I don't know what they were for, but no one ever used them except for me."

"Like service tunnels?" Aegis asked.

"I think they were for servants, but no one seems to remember," I explained, "They lead outside the castle too."

"You mentioned those before. At what parts?"

"One exit is at the closest point to the Starry Wood. Another leads to the eastern side of the castle."

"If we get separated for any reason, I want you to take one of those, preferably the eastern side," Aegis said.

"Why can't I come to the wood? No one will follow me in here," I pointed out.

"Not unless they want to eat you," Aegis reminded me.

I had a hard time believing there were more woodsmen around, but I shuddered thinking about my last encounter with them. If Aegis hadn't been there, I would have suffered a horrific death.

"Okay. If anything goes wrong, I'll head east."

"Ready to saddle up?" Aegis asked.

I climbed back onto his back, and once more, we rushed towards the castle. We'd get there at night, but that would work to our advantage. I still hadn't figured out what I would say to Mother. What would she say to me? I rested my head against Aeg's shoulder and tried not to think about it.

The sky grew dark, and I knew we were nearing our destination. The closer we got, the more I thought about turning back. My stomach was turning, and my heart was pounding erratically.

Aegis could feel it. "You're nervous." He looked over his shoulder at me. "You have every right to be nervous. I'm nervous too," he admitted.

"I think I might throw up."

Aegis scaled the castle wall with me on his back. He told me not to look down, but I did it anyway. I couldn't look away. It felt as though I were falling without even moving. I let out a whimper, and Aegis knew that I hadn't listened to his advice.

"You're afraid of heights, Nora," Aegis said, annoyed. "I don't say these things just for the fun of it, you know."

We stopped on a lower story of the castle so I could see something beneath my feet. "I know."

"It's all right; you need to tell me which one is your mother's bedroom anyway."

"I'm not entirely sure," I admitted.

"You're joking."

"No, but it's late in the evening, and only a few lights are on. We could check those rooms."

Aegis let out a frustrated sigh and headed towards a lit room. I knew what wing of the castle it was and that it was the third story, but it looked different on the outside. Aegis crawled around as we peeked into lit windows.

"We're the worst peeping Toms ever," he told me.

I couldn't help but let out a giggle, which he shushed right away. "The last thing we need is to get caught."

"Sorry."

When we rounded a rather tall tower, we knew it was the right window. It was by far the largest and had stained glass double doors that led onto a balcony. It would have been an incredibly romantic place if it didn't hold the people who had plotted my assassination.

"If I see your stepfather, we're going to abandon this stupid mission,"

Aegis clarified.

"Yes." I did not want to run into that man. Not yet, at least.

"Can you change your face back?" Aegis asked. "I just think your mother would be more responsive if it were your face and not this one."

"Yeah, I can try."

I thought about what I had done last time. I feared the man with the hawk. I thought he was going to kill me. More than anything, I wanted a different face. I wanted to be someone else. On the boat, I wanted Mother to see me, and my face started to change.

See my face. I closed my eyes and chanted those words over and over.

I heard Aegis whisper, "Hey, you did it."

My eyes opened wide and saw Aegis looking back at me, smiling in awe. I felt my face; it didn't feel any different than before. It was a face. But it was the way Aegis looked at me that made me happy. For a moment, I forgot where we were and what we were doing.

"We should head up." Aegis said.

I looked in the window to find my mother at her mirror, combing her hair. She looked sad and tired. She was using the golden combs Vinicio had gotten her as a gift several years ago. He had gotten her several sets since, but she preferred that set. The room was draped in crushed red velvets and blacks, Vinicio's favorite colors.

"Go on," Aegis prompted me, fearful that Vinicio would appear at any moment.

I knocked on the glass. My mother jolted upright, knocking her stool over as she swung the comb around wildly. I didn't wait for an invitation. I pushed open the window and stepped into the bedroom. Its red plush carpets matched the drapes and bed. The entire room was nothing but red and gold.

My mother rushed toward me, falling to her knees as she hugged me around the waist.

"I knew you weren't dead," she said.

"Then why didn't you look for me?" I asked, tears flowing from my eyes.

"We are!" Mother exclaimed. "We were. Vinicio sent out all his best people to find you, but there hasn't been so much as a hint about where you were. What happened?"

"Vinicio," I started.

Mother looked at me strangely, shaking her head in denial. "No, he has been trying to find you. You ran away."

"I didn't run away; I was drugged and left in the Starry Wood," I declared.

Anger shook my mother's voice. "No, he wouldn't have done that. Why would he do that?"

"Because I am the rightful king. He only married you to get to me."

"Nora, stop that—it's a lie. How did you get up here?" Mother looked at the window and saw Aegis staring at her fiercely. "Who is that?"

"That's not important," I said.

Mother glared at the shadow in the window. "You can't put your trust in a strange man like that, Nora."

Like you're one to talk, Mother.

"What is important is that your husband is trying to kill me, and you're too busy going on boat rides to notice," I said in an accusatory tone.

Her eyes went wide in fear. "That *was* you," she said in realization, looking at my dress. "How did you do that?"

"I told you. I am the true king of Hell."

"Nora," Aegis cut in. "Someone's coming; we need to leave."

"I'll come back." I glared at my mother. "And you'll be sorry when I do."

"Nora, wait!" she screamed.

I didn't listen. I ran into Aeg's arms, and he embraced me tightly before giving my mother a scathing look and making his way down the castle wall and into the Starry Wood.

I didn't say anything for a long time, and Aegis let me be for the most part. We just walked along the edge of region one, the edge of the world. No one bothered us. No one seemed to care that my lavender dress was dirty, which was nice. People in this region didn't seem to mind a lot of anything. Outside the castle, there were few people who resided here. The scarce population allowed for the plants to grow.

I had seen little of the first region when I lived in the castle. I remembered the carriage ride and how the harsh grounds of region five became lush with grass and tall plants in one pace. It was as though someone had drawn a line, and anything before the line turned to ash. We could grow things in region five, but mostly roots and potatoes. Region one had so many plants they grew intertwined and hung from trees.

Peter told me that outside of the castle, only the purest souls lived in the first circle of Hell. People of all sorts came for whatever business they had, but they were never permitted to remain in the region. They were escorted from the border to the castle and back.

I knew about the border between the first and second regions. It was the only one I knew of. When Mother and I first crossed into the first region in that black carriage, we crossed a large drawbridge outside the castle. The chains that raised and lowered the bridge had once been black, but now were covered in rust. Trackers patrolled by the dozens.

"Nora, it's very important that you follow the rules here," Mother had warned me.

"Yes, Mother."

"The castle shares this region with its inhabitants. We are not region one citizens, so even royalty must respect the space of the people who live here. The castle and its markets are available to us, but we cannot go stomping around the region disturbing the souls here."

I was six. I had no intention of disturbing anything. Still, I knew the first region wasn't made for us. We didn't belong, but I wondered about what kind of people lived here. I'd never met a pure soul before. At least not that I knew of.

Everything had looked so exotic to me then, but after seeing most of the world, I still found myself floored by the beauty of it all. Aegis seemed to appreciate it as well. Every few miles, he would look to me as if he wanted to say as much, but then he would stop, remembering that I was suffering.

I hated watching his smile fade to that of worry and sadness, but I couldn't fake it, not that Aegis would ever ask me to. It had been three days since I confronted my mother, and I couldn't think about anything else. I hated that she had such power over me. It always felt as though I could never win with her, but now I knew it to be the truth.

If she were unhappy, I too would be unhappy. Even though I knew Vinicio wanted me dead, I felt guilty about it, as if it were somehow my fault for wanting to live. She wanted me to live, but she didn't want Vinicio to answer for his crimes. She wanted everything on her terms, not under the conditions that reality provided.

I still hadn't determined how complicit Mother was in my departure from the castle. She seemed genuinely happy that I was alive until I told her about Vinicio's plot against me. Her relief may have been self-serving. Perhaps she was only happy that I was alive because it meant she did nothing wrong. Being a neglectful mother weighed heavily on her mind until absolution jumped through the bedroom window.

"Come back to me, Nora," Aegis's voice called soothingly.

I looked up and saw a large building unlike any I had seen before. It had a clay-tiled roof supported by wooden beams. It was several stories high, but the walls looked as though they were made with paper. A wooden porch lined the perimeter of the building, and its pointed roof had a large spike at the top.

"What is it?" I asked.

Aegis didn't seem to know either. "Let's check it out."

Everything was quiet as we approached the building. "There are no doors," I said.

Aegis investigated himself. "No, there are doors—they just slide." His fingertips found the edge of a slider and pulled it open.

"The walls are made of paper!"

"Yeah, it seems so."

The feeling of curiosity and excitement was doused by fear. "We shouldn't be here."

"What is it?" Aegis whispered.

"The first circle of Hell is meant for pure souls, not for visitors. The trackers monitor this place heavily."

"We won't disturb anyone. Promise."

I knew what Aeg was doing. He was trying to give me a distraction, something to cheer me up and take my mind off my mother. I wanted to let go of the feelings of abandonment; I just couldn't navigate my way out. Instead of allowing her to control my feelings of self-worth, I decided I would put my trust in the hands of Aegis. I relented despite the feeling that told me to leave.

Chapter Fourteen

Inside the building, several men sat cross-legged in a trance. It appeared they were unaware of our intrusion, but perhaps they didn't care. In the center of the room was a big wooden staircase that led to the upper stories. A large copper gong was hanging from its wooden harness. Aegis gave a shrug, not knowing what to make of it. We navigated through the men in their large red robes and climbed the stairs.

The second story was almost empty aside from several large drums. It was a notably smaller room, but some of the paper walls were open, exposing a balcony. The balcony wrapped around the second story. Aegis and I both stopped and gasped at the view.

We could see for miles. The jungle held so many different shapes and colors. It was indeed a paradise. Even some of the trees seemed to have rainbow-colored wood. Climbing vines bloomed with giant flowers, and the greens were a deeper hue than I'd ever seen. Aegis seemed just as mesmerized by the scenery as I was.

"You've never been to the first region?" I asked.

"Only to the castle," Aegis admitted. "I never left the road."

Castle dwellers and castle business operated as a city of its own, away from the rest of the region. The people of this region were in an existence of their own, and disturbing them would be a crime. The souls of this region did not care for wealth or power. Their ways and ideals were a mystery to the rest of us.

A loud, echoing bell startled me, and I realized someone had hit the gong. Shortly after that, there was a quiet commotion. The monks were making their way up the stairs. Some brought other instruments with them, and others began tightening the drums. It wasn't long until everyone coordinated and began playing.

Aegis was moved to tears. "I didn't know souls could make music."

"The monks are the only ones who remember how," I explained.

Aegis looked at me curiously. "Is that what they're called?"

"Yeah."

"Peter taught you that?"

I shook my head. "No, Peter didn't know about them. Neither did I until just now."

"Then how did you know what they were called?"

"Sometimes, I just know things. They don't come to my mind. It happens when my chest feels heavy, and the feeling makes its way to my mouth. I don't always know myself until it comes out."

Aegis continued to watch the monks play their song. They played for hours. When my legs grew tired, I sat down in the same cross-legged position. Aegis felt no such fatigue; instead, he seemed to grow uneasy in the bliss.

He started pacing the balcony, constantly looking outward for any sign of movement. The concern wasn't lost on me—I knew we were still too close to the castle. Not only were we wanted by Vinicio, but it was wrong to remain in the holy region without merit.

After the sun started to set, Aegis tried to pull me away from the music. "We should get moving," he pleaded.

I could barely hear him over the drums. For the first time in my life, I was experiencing a level of peace my mother couldn't tarnish. I was my own person, a queen preparing to ascend her throne. I had a life and a future full of mistakes to make, and I couldn't allow my mother's mistakes to follow me into the light.

"Nora!" Aegis yelled in frustration.

"I just want to listen to the song," I explained.

"This song isn't for us, and we don't have time to linger."

Aegis was right, but I couldn't will myself to return to the inner turmoil. It felt as though my legs were gone. I could no longer move them. It felt as though my soul were pulling away from my body. Aegis was becoming more desperate and angry, but I couldn't hear him. I watched from afar as he shook me by the shoulder. My unresponsive body stared off into oblivion. Surrounded by the drummers, I swayed with the sound. They shone brighter than any sun.

Are you ready to understand?

Yes, I told the voice within me, the one that had told me about monks, campaigns, and how to win at Spades Fourteen. I had always heard the voice as my own before. This time, the voice was male, but the same spirit.

When it became clear the stewards wouldn't suffer us to live, we had to adapt. We intentionally held you back, delayed your powers, but gave you enough to survive. And it worked! You were born a girl without powers, and the steward let you live. He second-guessed himself, and you found Aegis. If you're ready, we can fully merge so you can better develop your powers and rise to be the king.

Queen.

The voice roared with laughter. *I have a new word for you. To be a queen, you must be crowned. And as you're not crowned yet, technically you are a princess. The Princess of Hell. Are you ready, Princess?*

I am, I promised.

I would no longer *hear* the voice; I would *be* the voice. My powers would still need development, but they would come more naturally from here on out. I would be able to do things I'd never dreamed of. I was finally strong enough to stand on my own and wield these abilities, and in doing so, I would change the world for good.

That was when I saw them—four figures. Three of them were gray, but one of them was brown. A quartet of trackers was stalking in with weapons. I could no longer see Aegis, yet I felt his presence so strongly. He stood in front of my body and prepared for battle. One of the trackers pulled out a baton and extended it. The others were similarly armed, but each of them had selected a different weapon. One had a whip, another had a bow, and the last one had a sword.

The trackers fanned out, taking stances among the drummers and making it a precarious situation for the monks. None of them seemed to notice, and they continued playing their song as though nothing were occurring within the room. They grew brighter against the dimness of the visitors. I remained in the center of the room beside Aegis, though he couldn't see me. My body remained on the balcony where I had left it.

The tracker with the baton stepped forward, challenging Aeg. Before he could launch at her, the one with the whip caught his leg, tripping him. Before he hit the ground, Aegis pushed off with his free leg and was sent hurdling towards the baton tracker. The whip tracker lost control of its whip as Aegis took the brown figure down before him. The archer had released several arrows into my protector, but they had no effect.

Did they feel alarmed? Perhaps they felt nothing. They held no gender, nor did they have faces. Their souls were gray, and the bleakness was what I saw. Aegis knocked the baton wielder down and snapped its neck before fighting the swordsman unarmed. The blade never made its mark, but Aegis was leaving droplets of blood on the floor.

Aegis was becoming agitated by the attacks. He was becoming littered with arrows. The sword jerked abruptly as he grabbed it by the blade and ripped it from the tracker's hand before turning it to decapitate his attacker. The tracker with the whip didn't see the vampire coming. Aegis was so furious at that point that he killed it where it stood, slicing the creature in half with the sword. Aegis saved the archer for last. He grabbed it by the hair before ripping the bow from its hand. The body flailed and fought desperately.

I was being pulled back. I felt as though I were being swept away by a massive wind until I was sitting in my body again. I could see Aegis, who had a dozen arrows stuck in him. In the place of the dimly lit soul, Aegis was now holding a young girl by her hair. She was crying and begging for mercy, but it had no effect on him. His rage was too deep.

"Aegis, stop!" I commanded.

My voice was drowned out by the drums, but Aegis's keen sense of hearing picked it out nonetheless. For several moments, he hesitated. It seemed he was no longer fighting the girl, but himself.

"Aegis!" I cried out.

He let go of the girl, and she fell to the floor, shaking. My legs were numb from sitting so long. It felt like thousands of needles were stabbing me. It ached when I moved around, but I knew it was the only way to get the blood flowing. Aegis was just staring at the girl.

"Aegis, we need to leave," I yelled across the music. "Pick me up and get me out of here."

Aegis seemed lost. Looking at the girl and the carnage he'd left behind, he looked as though he wanted to run away. For a moment, he almost did. His feet were pointing towards the stairs, but he took one last look at the girl and me.

Before he could take another step, I called, "Aegis! Come back to me!"

In a second, he whisked me into his arms, and we were leaping over the balcony and into the dense jungle. The young tracker made no attempt to follow us. We covered several miles before I could get him to stop.

"We need to find water," I told him.

Aegis sniffed out the scent. He found a clear pool being fed from a large waterfall. It tasted cleaner than any I had remembered—even the castle water didn't taste that good. I didn't realize how thirsty I was until I tasted that water. Aegis still looked lost.

"Let's get those arrows out of you," I told him.

I wasn't sure how to proceed. I didn't want to hurt him, but I had to pull them out. He looked like a porcupine. The idea made me giggle out loud, but Aegis wasn't in a laughing mood. I yanked an arrow from his side, and he winced in pain, but made no complaint.

"I'm sorry I didn't listen to you," I said as I pulled another from the back of his leg.

"She wasn't any older than you are," Aegis said.

"You were defending me."

I pulled one more from his lower back and watched in amazement as the wound healed instantly.

"That could have been you."

"No, it couldn't have been. I can't shoot a bow."

Grabbing an arrow with each hand, I put my foot on his butt to brace myself and pulled away, taking the projectiles with me.

"You see how easy it is for me to kill?" Aegis said morbidly.

"Yeah, I saw it," I told him. "You're going to need to sit down with me to pull out the rest."

Aegis sat at the edge of the pool, looking at the waterfall. "You saw me killing those little girls, and you weren't scared?"

"Of you? No."

That seemed to make Aegis feel better. The tension within him seemed to ease, and it made it easier to remove the arrows.

"Were you in a trance like the monks?" he asked.

"Yep," I said, prying yet another from his neck. "It was more like an out-of-body experience. I couldn't see anything but the color of the souls, anyway."

"Were the trackers good souls?" Aegis asked.

"Not really. They were somewhere in between."

Aegis considered that as I finished with his back and arms.

"What about me?"

"I saw nothing."

Vinicio

Vinicio checked in on his wife the next morning to find the doctor was already in the room conferring with the nurse. He could hear them murmur between themselves and saw that his wife was still asleep. He was puzzled by why she wasn't awake and why the doctor was here early. In his heart, Vinicio knew she had taken a turn for the worse.

"My liege," the doctor acknowledged, motioning for him to join the conversation.

"What happened?" Vinicio asked.

The nurse shook her head. "I don't know. Shortly after your visit, I left her to sleep. When I came to check on her not even twenty minutes later, she was crying so hard." The nurse looked at Bella with pity, as they all did.

"I think we must proceed with the utmost caution," the doctor said.

"Have you tried talking to her?" Vinicio could feel the heat rising in his face. It appeared they had come to some sort of conclusion without consulting Bella or himself.

"She refused to speak to us, but perhaps you could try?" the nurse suggested.

"She is not sedated?"

"No, she just won't get up," the nurse replied.

Vinicio rounded the four-poster bed and sat beside his wife just as he had the night before. Stroking her blonde ringlets, he smoothed her cheek with his thumb.

"What do you need, my Bella?"

She didn't open her eyes, but the flicker of movement suggested she was awake. Instead, her face puckered, and she began to cry quietly. Her eyes remained closed. Vinicio was disturbed by the display—the impact of Nora's departure had clearly affected Bella more than he anticipated.

"Bella, I know you're going through something very painful. There is nothing you can do to discourage me from remaining by your side. All I ask is that you stay strong for the baby."

Bella rolled to her side and sobbed.

Vinicio left the room and Bella to the doctor. There was nothing more he could say to her. The only way to end his wife's suffering was to deal with Nora once and for all. He strode across the castle to the great library, passing the court attendees and ignoring Rebus's pleas for attention. They would all have to wait. Rebus followed him for a few paces before realizing he was intentionally being unheard.

The great library's heavy doors were fifteen feet tall, ornate with carved designs and stained with various shades of wood. Closing the heavy doors behind him, Vinicio set out to learn all he could about the kings of old. Books and parchments about kings lay stacked for miles.

It was nothing personal when Vinicio dumped Nora's unconscious body at the foot of the forest, but it seemed she would stop at nothing to haunt Bella and risk the life of his unborn child. The stakes were too high, and Vinicio refused to lose to a teenage girl.

He spent the better part of three days in the library. There were so many accounts of so many kings that he often found conflicting stories. Inconsistency was an evil above all others in Vinicio's mind, and the research was becoming maddening. Just when he found the descriptions of one king's powers, his cross-reference would contradict it.

On the library desk lay several more books. One title made him smile with nostalgia. *The Emergence of the King* had been Vinicio's favorite as a child. It was the story of how the first king obtained his powers. Back when the Titans ruled, an ordinary soul had encountered a witch in a cave on a mountaintop in region two. The first king was a young man when he scaled the mountain and demanded the witch give him the powers to defeat the Titans.

The crone gave him the Dagger of Monsters. He made a pact with the witch to protect the world and all its inhabitants. Should a king fail that vow, the kings would stop returning. Vinicio felt most justified by this story. It was clear to him that the kings had indeed lost their way, and that was why he was to steward today.

Between his wife's mental troubles and the roadblocks in his research, Vinicio's hair had become unruly and his clothing wrinkled. When he caught a glimpse of his own reflection, he saw bags under his brown eyes, which were becoming puffy from exhaustion. Those who spent their time in court excused the steward's appearance. Everyone knew the pressure he was under, and Vinicio rarely paid attention to those at court in the first place.

Giving up on his reading, the steward stormed from the library to return to his wife. He took the shortcut through the court, and Rebus gave a small bow. He was stopped briefly by a few court dwellers concerned about Bella's condition. The court carried on without Vinicio, who was obviously disheveled from caring for the sick woman. Their favor was a tool that he might need to use one day.

When he arrived at the bedroom door, Vinicio got a better glimpse of himself in the hall mirror. He was taken back by his ragged appearance. He straightened himself out the best he could. Running his delicate hands through his hair, he smoothed it as much as possible. He corrected a few misaligned buttons on his vest and tucked his shirt back in.

When he looked in on his wife, she was sleeping. It had become the norm for her, sadly. Part of Vinicio missed her terribly. Another part was relieved she was sedated. He still needed to find Nora. He would have had a much harder time investigating the whereabouts of the princess if her mother was up and about.

Quietly, he closed the door and returned gloomily to the library. Vinicio took a deep breath and resigned himself to his research once more. He selected *The Curiosities of the King*. Initially, Vinicio had dismissed the book since it was an unofficial theory that involved all the kings. When the kings of old reigned, it was a tradition that a steward wrote the king's biography. The problem was that many kings had several stewards and, therefore, different accounts. When the kings stopped arriving, lesser stewards wrote the history on behalf of the reigning steward family.

King Thaddeus was a prime example of royal debauchery and multiple accounts. He was the most famous king, and he had several stewards. The man was said to be vivacious and charismatic—a force to be reckoned with, and notoriously difficult to please. According to one steward, Thaddeus became infatuated with his daughter-in-law and attempted to seduce her in the gardens.

One steward said that Thaddeus's son, Keith, had no interest in women. He suggested that Thaddeus impregnated his daughter-in-law so that Keith would finally produce a grandchild for his insistent mother. Another steward said that his animal magnetism lured the lonely daughter-in-law. Whatever the case might have been, all the stewards had different versions of the same story.

The Curiosities of the King was a compilation study written by a scholar of some sort, someone Vinicio had never heard of: Phineas Morgen. According to this study, there were not several kings, but simply one—one king's soul, reborn again and again. When the first king used the Dagger of Monsters, he bound his soul to Hell for all eternity. Morgen proposed that the king's powers hit their peak and slowly declined as the king aged, in preparation for his rebirth.

Vinicio found the evidence compelling. It made sense that only one soul would have such abilities and would return at precisely the correct point in time. Some kings fought for life despite their bodies failing, and congestion in the soul safe could account for the delay of the king's soul from surfacing. It also lined up with the first king myth. Scholars debated what the king vowed when he made the blood pact on that mountain, but most of the stewards were in agreeance.

There was also mention of the Dagger of Monsters. The first king made a blood pact with the vampires. From that point on, they were at his command. Another interesting yet false theory from Phineas was that the dagger didn't control the monsters. It served as an anchor for the king's soul. He believed the king's soul returned again and again because of a blood pact made with a witch. Vinicio knew the true nature of the Dagger of Monsters, but a simple scholar wouldn't have had access to such information.

Unlike the steward's writings, Morgen kept a laundry list of typical abilities of a king. Some kings were argued to have stronger abilities than their predecessors, but that could have been an exaggeration, a servant's pride in a particular king.

The library doors were pushed open, and Rebus came waddling into the library.

"My lord," Rebus started.

Vinicio ignored him, hoping that he would go away, but the old man wouldn't.

"My lord, I'm sorry to disturb you—"

"Rebus."

Rebus looked at the spread of books that surrounded Vinicio and then looked at him curiously. "My lord, a tracker has returned from region one. Something has happened."

Together, Vinicio and Rebus walked briskly to the tracker's lair. The makeshift barracks were quiet when Vinicio stepped in. The trackers parted, exposing one of their own. She was young, thirteen or fourteen, with her long red hair in a braided ponytail. Despite her puffy red eyes, she was otherwise unharmed.

"What happened?" Vinicio demanded.

"My team picked up the trail of two intruders. We followed them to the temple. He killed everyone but me."

"What did they look like?"

The girl explained the encounter. It was Nora—she was in region one. The man the young tracker described couldn't have been human. Vinicio felt as though Nora was mocking him. She had found a vampire guardian. Thanking the girl for her service, Vinicio walked away, leaving Rebus shaking his head in confusion.

Back in the library, Vinicio skimmed the pictures and descriptions of the king's capabilities. Along the long list of powers the kings had displayed over the years, there was one that depicted the king changing his face. According to the history, it seemed that King Earl had indeed changed his face for the amusement of his court.

Bella's frantic episode on the yacht hadn't been based on an illusion. Nora was on that ferry, passing them by. The trackers had been told to look for a little girl, not a father and daughter. The vampire must have had money, connections, something that helped them cross the borders. They had made their way to the first region.

Vinicio's hands trembled with fear. He knew he was losing.

Chapter Fifteen

Nora

The jungle grew thinner as we continued traveling southwest. The trees and all their vines and flowers were claiming more distance from one another. The jungle floor was no longer crunched from fallen plants; instead, we navigated tall grass.

"Where do you suppose the border is?" I asked.

"It's close," Aegis said, pointing at a large mountain range.

There was no way around it without doubling back through the first region, the castle, and the Starry Wood. We would need to either find a low point and climb the mountain or cross the only gate. Aegis wanted to scale the mountain, but I was willing to risk passing through the gate.

"People will be looking for us after what happened," Aegis warned.

"You said it was time for people to know of my existence."

"Yes, but maybe in a better light. I don't think invading the first region and killing trackers makes a great impression."

"Stop fretting. It won't change things."

"And neither does forgetting," Aegis pointed out.

I smirked, tempted to point out the hypocrisy of what he'd just said. However, I felt like it was better just to say nothing and let him think of all the comebacks he could. Despite his protests, we arrived at the base of the mountain. The entry to the second region was a tunnel under the mountain.

I gasped. "It's incredible."

But even the mountain was starting to erode. Along the entrance, huge cracks crawled upward. It looked as if the tunnel would collapse at any minute. Piles of dirt and rocks from landslides lined the base. Even a mountain could be brought down after centuries without a king.

There were two hawk hunters standing at the entryway with their hawks.

"So, what's the plan?" Aegis asked.

"We can distract them with something, make them leave their post."

"It could work," Aegis agreed. "I'd rather not kill anyone else today if I can help it."

I closed my eyes and focused on the screams I had heard in the seventh region of Hell. I imagined the screams coming from a boulder off in the distance. I opened my eyes and looked to Aegis, who could clearly hear it, but the guards didn't seem to hear it.

"Try again," Aegis whispered. "With feeling."

I thought about how scared and angry it made me feel when the boy screamed, how much pain was in those cries and how the helplessness I heard in him was the same that I often felt myself. This time, the cries were loud enough for the guards to hear. Both went to investigate, but they were slow to move, and Aegis was getting anxious.

He picked me up and sped toward the tunnel before I could say otherwise. The hawks fluttered, and the hunters spun in bewilderment, unsure of what had just happened. Aegis didn't stop running until the entrance was out of sight. Putting me down, he began to lead me by the hand through the darkness.

"I don't think anyone is following, and if they are, it would be hard to catch up with us," he said.

"If you had just waited a few minutes longer, they wouldn't have seen anything."

"Stop fretting."

I rolled my eyes in response. "So, what are we going to do when we encounter guards on the other side?"

"One step at a time."

Easy for him to say. He could see in the dark. I just had to trust that Aegis would tell me if there was anything in my way. We walked in the dark for what seemed like days before a hint of light became visible before us.

"Hawks couldn't fly over those mountains, so I don't imagine the guards ahead will suspect anything unusual," Aegis reasoned.

As we approached the doorway, there was no sound to indicate guards on duty. The closer we got, the less weary we became. Daylight stung my eyes when we exited the tunnel fully. I looked around for signs of trackers, but the exit was left unguarded. Then I saw something.

"Look at that," I said, pointing

On a large tree just a few feet in front of the crossing, there was a letter nailed to a tree.

Aegis went first to see what was written.

Your secrets are indeed surprising.

We'll be seeing you soon.

"That's it?" I asked.

Aegis looked over the letter and even held it in the sun to look for secret writing. There was nothing.

"I think this is from Alfie," Aegis said.

I agreed, but I didn't understand the reference, and discussion of the trackers made Aegis grumpy. I decided I'd change the conversation.

"I never told you what happened when I fell into a trance in the first region," I told him.

"You did—you said you could see the souls of the trackers."

"That's not all." I told him about the king's soul.

Aegis tried his best to remain reserved, but I could see the excitement flickering behind his eyes. "That has to be the strangest thing I've ever heard," he told me, "and I've lived a very long time."

"That's not fair—you can't remember most of it," I teased.

Aegis's smile fell, but he tried to hide it. I didn't mean to make him sad again. I didn't mind that he couldn't remember the other kings, but he did.

"Ever since you woke me up last time, I can't help but feel like I forgot something of dire importance," Aegis admitted.

"If that's true, we will figure it out," I promised. "I can be the person the world needs me to be, and I'll be the person you need."

"You already are," Aegis told me with a smile.

We continued walking until nightfall, but there wasn't a soul in sight. The air was warm, and there were trees and tall grass. Everything here looked sort of wild. It was a silly thing to say about the wilderness, but the fourth region was so well manicured. Its grass was the same length everywhere, and it was consistently the same shade of bright green.

Here, the grass was long and in patches. Everything was overgrown, but not in the same way it was in the first region. The bushes were prickly, and there was a variety of plants. A small lizard rested on a rock several feet in front of me. We watched each other for a time before he crawled away.

I waited by the fire while Aegis hunted in the cover of nightfall. I wished I could find a way to reassure him. He was reluctant to even hunt in front of me. It would have been good for me to know how to skin and clean a rabbit, maybe even catch a fish. He still saw me as the little girl he met three weeks ago, not as the princess I really was.

Back at the temple, he almost killed a girl no bigger than myself, and when the shame became too much for him, he thought to abandon me. I wasn't sure what upset him more—the fact that the girls were near my age or his inability to stop on his own. I was so engrossed in my thoughts of Aeg, I didn't realize that I was now surrounded by strangers.

I was startled by the new visitors, and my eyes grew wide. I stood and looked around for an escape. The people surrounding me were of various races, but they were all dressed in basic clothing, and their hair was either very long or shorn to the scalp.

"Are you alone, young lady?" one man with long hair and a beard asked.

I shook my head. "No, my father is with me too. He's looking for food."

"We have food; would you like some?" a woman with long hair asked.

I tried to decline, but before I knew it, the group had built up the fire and set various wooden bowls filled with food around the fire. The smell of the food overcame my sense of awkwardness. A woman with a thick blonde braid began brushing my hair as I ate.

"You've been traveling a long time," she stated.

I took another bite out of a carrot instead of answering. People were coming from all directions. It was like a swarm, and it made me nervous. They were likely indigenous to the region. Their clothing was sheer linens and rope-like material. Most of them had long, braided hair, and they wore lots of jewelry.

They seemed kind enough, but I didn't know their intentions. Peter never told me anything about the people of region two. No one ever mentioned the people of this region. Aegis had never mentioned them either. They were certainly a tribe of their own.

There were twelve of them altogether, including four children. They took turns telling stories and laughing. One woman was swollen with pregnancy. I didn't mean to, but I kept staring at the roundness of her belly. It was strange to watch her move around with such a bulge. Her tummy looked so tight, like it would burst any minute. A woman with a shaved head commanded the pregnant woman to lie down so she could rub her feet.

"You've walked too far today, Agnes," the woman scolded. "Your ankles are so swollen."

"I walk because I'm hoping it will quicken the labor."

The very idea of childbirth mystified me. I couldn't see myself having children–it didn't seem possible that I could be capable of such a thing. Obviously, I could have a child as a female, but the concept seemed so far away from me.

"You're going to have the baby tonight?" I asked.

The group laughed, and the blonde braided woman said, "It's possible. Agnes is a week overdue, but there's no way to tell until it happens. Even then, it can take days."

"Does it hurt?" I couldn't stop the questions from rolling out.

"It hurts, but it's not a hurt you remember," the short-haired woman said. "All you remember is the baby."

I wanted the woman to have the baby so I could see it happen. I had never seen a baby being born. The woman wanted the baby to come out too. I closed my eyes and wished for the woman to give birth. When my eyes opened, nothing happened.

Slightly disappointed, I turned to the woman brushing my hair, "Could you braid my hair like yours?" I asked.

The woman, who introduced herself as Carlie, had the loveliest smile.

"Tell us about yourself," she said as she braided my hair. "You said you had a father with you?"

"Yeah, he's hunting for my dinner. We're just passing through."

"From which direction?" the woman with the shaved head asked.

"We came from the first region."

"Strange. Usually, the trackers don't let anyone pass."

"There were no trackers posted," I told them.

They hid their alarm well enough, but I could see their eyes dart around.

"We worked for the castle," I explained, but it wasn't me they were alarmed with.

"We don't doubt your story," a man with long hair and a beard said. "It's just that the last time the hunters and trackers were missing from their posts, it was due to a rebellion."

"A rebellion?" I asked.

"You're too young to remember, but perhaps your father would know of it. People questioned the last steward—he was a bad steward. The trackers follow their generals over a steward any day, so when the general of the hawk hunters joined the rebellion, things got messy."

"How do you know this?" I asked.

"I'm a retired hawk hunter myself."

"Really?" I didn't know they did retire—I just thought they died.

"Yeah, the rebellion was stomped out quickly. I was young and stupid, and I thought I could take on the leader of the trackers. She could have killed me. She left me alive, but I quit after that."

"What did she look like?"

"Tall black woman with black dreads. Her name is Hacia. She's still their general now, I think."

Aegis

Aegis watched Nora from a distance. It appeared the locals had found her. They were caring for her, so he didn't feel the need to continue his hunt or to disturb them. There was no need to kill tonight. He thought about joining the group, but he decided to step back for a moment and watch Nora from afar.

Nora's resilience was inspiring. At first, Aegis had thought that the muted reaction to violence was a bad thing. She reacted so calmly to death, not the way a normal girl would behave. He came to understand that she, in one way or another, understood death in a way he did not. Aegis was, after all, immortal, so dying seemed unnatural to him. It was something he feared. Not his own death, but the death of others. Nora's death above all else.

There was also the matter of Nora's romantic inclinations towards him. He hoped that some space would redirect her. In his heart, he knew he wouldn't deny her if she demanded it of him. She was the queen, and his loyalty was practically instinctual. It was really a matter of convincing her that she didn't truly want him.

Nora would age. She would grow out of her insecure adolescence and become a woman with desires he couldn't fulfill. If she chose him instead of another soul, she would grow old, and he would remain the same. No amount of reassurance would ever convince her that she was still loved and desirable. Nora would die empty and with regret if she attempted to keep him as a mate.

The thought of their relationship becoming a fleeting romance was unbearable. If she grew unhappy with their connection, she would send him away. Aegis imagined himself lurking in the skirts of the castle, hiding in the shadows of the Starry Wood, perched on a tree watching the castle lights flicker on and off, just to know where she was. She would never ask him another question. Instead, her life would end, and he wouldn't be there the way he should be.

Thinking back to the nap he had along the river, Aegis recalled a dream of sorts. It was mostly images and sounds that didn't correlate, but he did remember standing beside others like himself. They wore similar armor and stood at attention while the world changed in front of them. A man was demanding the name of someone, but Aegis couldn't see who.

"Your name," the man said.

"That was the agreement, but—"

"Your name, beast!" the man insisted.

That was when Nora had woken him up. He didn't realize how easy it was to fall asleep. He had slept twice within the last few weeks. Prior to that was decades ago. It had a connection to his attempts at remembering. It was Nora who had kept him awake the last sixteen years, and he wouldn't lose her.

The only way they could remain together was if Aegis kept himself at a distance—not close enough to confuse her, but not far enough that she forgot about him. He watched a woman braid Nora's hair. Her face seemed changed since the last time she had worn it. She looked so grown up with her hair pulled from her face. The changes were subtle, but they were there nonetheless.

No doubt she would meet boys in the castle. All sorts of handsome young men would flock to court the young queen. Aegis just had to get her on the throne before her infatuation with him grew into a demand.

He thought about their next move. Nora was so resilient, but he was unsure if she had recovered from her mother's betrayal. He wondered if that encounter would push her toward ruling—or away from it. Would she want revenge on her mother, or would she want to avoid her?

Aegis surmised that Nora would like the third region the best. In his mind, it was the perfect place to raise children. Not that he knew anything about that, but he felt it was a place where children should live. Region two was a strange place. It seemed the people were mostly nomadic. He had heard tales of a massive city where everyone convened, but it was a place to visit and not a place to live. Eccentricities aside, the people here were kind and attentive. It seemed to Aegis that that was exactly what Nora needed.

Chapter Sixteen

Nora

"Are you the leader then?" I asked the man with long hair and beard.

"If you wish to call me that, then yes," he answered.

"Nathan is our leader because he tells the best stories," someone chimed in.

"Well, when you're as old as I am…" he said, making a silly face and pretending to walk with a cane. "You pick up a lot of stories over the years."

Nathan began telling the children a bedtime story, something about a rabbit and a turtle. I listened along, but I found myself distracted by how the people interacted with one another. Nathan had kissed Agnes earlier that evening, but now Agnes was resting in another man's lap. Carlie, the girl who had stayed by my side and braided my hair, was beginning to whisper intimately with another woman. The woman Carlie was flirting with had been holding a man's hand when they first approached me.

Trying to figure out who was a couple or *if* they were a couple was dizzying. I thought perhaps they were all just affectionate people at first, but as the night wore on, it became clear that love was on the minds of the tribe's people. A clever thought came to mind.

"Agnes," I asked, "Is the father excited, too?"

"He better be!" Agnes declared.

I looked around, waiting for someone to come forward and claim paternity, but no one did.

"We do things differently here," Agnes explained. "We believe in free love."

I had never heard of such a thing. Until Agnes said it, no one in all my travels had even mentioned love being a priority in life. The harshness in the lower regions didn't allow love—perhaps it was there, but I was unable to see it. Regions one and four had love, but what they loved contrasted so acutely. It didn't seem imaginable that anything in between could exist.

"Free love?" I questioned.

"We are in love with each other, all of us."

"So then, in a way, your baby is everyone's baby."

"And we can't wait to meet her," Nathan said, smiling.

My mind reeled with the idea of being in love with multiple people at once. How was it even possible? How did they not become jealous of each other? Another conundrum came to mind.

"What if your baby and someone else's baby share the same father?"

"I suppose that could happen," Agnes admitted, "but we are rarely blessed with children here. By the time children decide to become adults, they usually find a new tribe."

"Do you ever see them again?"

"Oh, of course." Agnes giggled. "All the time."

That made me feel better. I couldn't imagine having a mother like Agnes and never seeing her again. Carlie would be an amazing mother, too, I had no doubt. The air grew colder, and the coals of the fire grew white hot. I could feel sleep approaching. I wanted to wait for Aegis to come back, but I drifted off before he did.

When I woke the next morning, the tall grass whispered, and the sun was gently shining. Agnes was breathing funny. She was making a circle with her mouth and pushing out her breath as though she were angry. Carlie, Nathan, and the woman with the shaved head were with her, but everyone else was gone.

"It seems you get to see a baby being born after all!" Nathan kidded.

"Where is everyone else?"

"Oh, they are all hunting, gathering, playing."

The casualness of Nathan's tone did little to pacify my nerves. It felt like my head was filled up with all sorts of thoughts at once, and I couldn't figure out which one to listen to. I just wanted Agnes to be okay. I closed my eyes and wished for the baby and Agnes to be okay. Over and over, I drowned out all other voices until my prayer was all I could think of.

"Woo, that was a strong contraction—they are getting closer together!" Agnes exclaimed.

"That's good, right?" I asked.

"Yes sweetie, it means the baby will be here soon. Help me up, Sandy?" Agnes asked.

The woman with the shaved head pulled Agnes up to her feet and helped her keep her balance as she squatted on the ground. Her brown hair was tied on top of her head, and she was naked from the waist down. When another contraction came, Sandy coached Agnes, telling her to breathe and to push.

I gasped in terror as blood fell from Agnes in heaps. She let out a bellow and squeezed Sandy's hand. Carlie had her hands inside Agnes and was feeling around for the baby.

"I feel her head, Agnes," Carlie shouted.

I wanted to put my hands over my ears as Agnes let out another loud moan of pain. More blood dumped from between her legs, and her pubic area was unnaturally swollen. I had to look away. I was ashamed of myself for doing so, but I couldn't bear to see anymore. It looked like it hurt so bad, and there was nothing I could do. I thought about calling for Aegis, making him whisk me off my feet and run clear to the next region.

"One more push, Agnes!" Carlie cheered.

Agnes let out a roar as the baby ripped through her and fell into Carlie's waiting hands. More stuff came out of Agnes then. It was mostly blood, but the baby was attached to a cord, and whatever was on the other end was still inside Agnes. Falling to her knees, Agnes steadied herself with a few deep breaths and watched Carlie clean the baby.

I would never forget the way Agnes looked at her baby for the first time. She was so happy that she started crying. She sat down, and the baby was handed to her. Pulling down her shirt, Agnes exposed her bare skin to the baby and held him. The baby made gurgling noises, but I could tell even from a distance that he knew his mommy.

Carlie and Sandy interrupted the moment just long enough to get Agnes to push what looked like a sack. It was attached to the other end of the baby's cord. I was embarrassed because I had no idea what it was, and it felt as though I should have known. I knew how babies were made, but I didn't know about birth at all.

"Mothers and children have a bond that can never be severed," Sandy said to Agnes.

Nathan was preparing a bed of sorts a few feet away. He came to check on the baby and mother, congratulating everyone involved before heading off to share the good news with the rest of the tribe.

Mothers and children have a bond that can never be severed. Did that mean that no matter what I did, I couldn't be free from my mother? I wanted to hate her, but I couldn't. I wanted her love, but I wished she would leave me alone. There was no resolution, and there was no happy ending. Our bond was a metal cord, unyielding and uncuttable.

We could never bend that cord to meet in the middle because Mother had no middle. At the same time, it wouldn't break because she was my mother. Yet every time we tried to make amends, another kink would develop in the length between us.

The tribe made the area surrounding Agnes their domain while she recovered. It became the hive of all their activity. Carlie and Sandy took turns helping Agnes with the baby. I was invited several times to join the others, but I didn't want to leave. I was fascinated with the little one and all the things Agnes's body was doing. She fed the child from her breast—that was something I'd never seen before. It didn't seem like it was working very well, because the baby cried a lot.

"It can take a few days for the milk to come in," Carlie explained while we washed blankets for the new arrival in a nearby creek.

"So the baby isn't eating at all?" The idea of such a little thing being hungry was upsetting.

"Well, he is getting some nutrients, but soon the breasts will be full, and then Agnes will be squirting all over the place.," Carlie teased.

I giggled along with her, but I could still feel the worry behind my eyes.

"Why are you so sad?" Carlie asked curiously.

I hesitated for a moment, unsure of how to proceed. I felt certain I could trust Carlie, and I was tired of lying to people, so I told her. It was slow at first, and when I got to the part about my mother, I started to cry a little, but it felt good to just say it all.

". . . and then we came here." I finished my story and looked up at Carlie, half fearing her response.

Carlie's face contorted as big fat tears rolled down her cheeks. She opened her mouth to speak, but only sobs came out. She put her hand over her mouth to stifle the noise, and I felt ashamed of myself for unloading everything on her. The people in region two were so innocent and carefree. It felt as though I had destroyed her innocence.

"I'm sorry—I just need a minute," Carlie assured me.

I regretted telling her. I wished I could take it back. I closed my eyes and chanted the wish in my mind repeatedly. I imagined pulling the story from her mind like pulling a sheer scarf from her ear. The scarf was a pastel pink that contrasted against the golden grasslands and blue sky.

"Why I am I crying?"

I opened my eyes to see Carlie, her face still red and puffy from the upset, but it seemed she had forgotten everything I'd told her. She was wiping tears from her face in confusion as she struggled to remember what had happened.

"You're just happy about the baby," I told her.

It worked. I wasn't certain I could pull it off, but it had worked. I was able to pull the memories from her mind the way a girl could pull petals from a flower. This boost of confidence was just what I needed. I had done little to test my powers since the trance in region one, so I tingled with excitement despite what had just transpired. It made me feel a little guilty to be so happy because I had messed with someone's brain, but the people here were not capable of dealing with the things I had seen.

We finished hanging up the baby blankets. Before setting out to find Aegis, I told the women that I needed to find my father. He was no doubt lurking somewhere nearby. I missed him, but I didn't feel panic-stricken by his absence. Come to think of it, this was the first time he'd left me since the first time we met.

"What do you think of this place?" I heard a male voice calling from a tree after I left the nomads' camp.

"It's nice," I replied.

Aegis jumped down, and dust blew out from under his feet as he landed. "You've made some friends," he commented.

"Yeah, they are sweet people, but we can't stay here."

"Why not?"

I was heavily influenced by whichever region I stayed in, and the only neutral place was the castle. I realized that while the castle was within region one, it wasn't a part of the region itself and therefore had no influence on my behavior. Aegis was aware of this, but his solution was keeping me in safer regions. To truly be myself, though, I needed to go home.

I looked at him sharply. "Because we have somewhere we need to be."

"You don't have to become queen right away. These are good people—you could stay with them. Have a few years to experience life. It's enjoyable sometimes."

"Aegis, look at me," I said.

His eyes struggled to meet mine, and I understood what his ploy was. Aegis wanted to give me a way out.

My eyebrows rose. "I need to be queen. This world is falling apart."

"I just thought that maybe you would want something normal for once."

"I'm not normal, though. I don't belong here."

That afternoon, when the tribe settled down for their dinner, we said our goodbyes. Nathan was reluctant to let me leave at first, but Aegis promised him that I would be safe and that we would visit again. We found the old familiar road and walked it once more. Returning to our old routine, Aegis and I set up camp for the evening.

Aegis was still no better at building a fire and relied on my help. Nathan had given me lots of dried fruits and meats for the journey ahead. I wrapped the food in Aegis's nice clothing, which was still kept in my knapsack. I told Aegis about Agnes's baby and the tribe's unique outlook on love.

"Souls have unique cultures in every region, it seems," Aegis responded diplomatically.

I told him about Carlie, and how I wiped her memory. He found that far more interesting than breast milk. "I think I've figured out how to make it work," I told him.

"That's good. What's the key?"

"I need to visualize it happening, and I need to be fully committed to it. Like you said, it needs to be with *feeling*."

Aegis's eyes grew wide, and he spun around quickly, his keen ears listening for something. I wanted to ask him what he heard, but I knew it would be better to wait. Aegis motioned for me to stay where I was. After what seemed like forever, I saw two figures emerging from the darkness. Their approach chilled me—I didn't hear them any more than I heard the wind blow the grass.

It was the hawk hunter we had encountered near the outlands, and with him was the black tracker from the ferry. Nathan had said she was the tracker general. The man's gaze was locked on me, but the woman seemed more intent on Aegis. She was also much more aware that Aegis was on the verge of destroying them. The man had to be stopped by the woman, and she held her hands up in peace.

"We know for certain who you are now, and we come to swear allegiance to the rightful king of Hell," the woman claimed.

This did little to relax Aeg, but the woman kneeled and pulled her hawk hunter companion to his knees beside her. Aegis wouldn't take his eyes off the pair. The bird was capped and appeared to be sleeping.

"You are the same girl from the outlands, but you are Nora as well, yes?" the man asked.

The woman glared at him venomously, but he ignored her.

"I am."

Aegis looked at me then, and I nodded for him to stand down. He relaxed, but was still tense and on high alert. His eyes were not bloodshot, but his jaw was clenched, and he didn't so much as blink.

The woman, Hacia, and the hawk hunter, Alfie, took turns explaining their journey. They were telling the truth, which was apparent not just to me but to Aegis as well. When they finished their story, they waited for our response. I didn't know what to think.

"Nora, I knew once people caught on they would begin to follow you," said Aegis. "It won't be just me who swears undying loyalty to you."

"Could you show us something?" Alfie asked.

Hacia's eyes practically buldged from her head. Her disapproval towards Alfie's questions was obvious.

"It's okay—I need to practice," I told her.

They seemed confused by the statement, but Aegis explained. "It will take time before she reaches her highest potential. When the steward first attempted to kill her, her abilities were just beginning to emerge."

"What did you do that tipped him off?" Hacia asked.

It was a good question. Even I was unsure of just what had happened. Peter had been fired and presumably jailed, but I didn't think I had shown any kingly powers until I found Aeg.

"I don't know for sure. The last thing I remember was going to bed. I was just a normal girl, upset that my tutor had been fired."

"Your tutor?" Alfie asked.

"Yeah, Peter. Older guy with curly gray hair. Did you know him?"

"I saw him around from time to time, and I know he was under watch for some reason,"

Hacia said, nodding. "He was suspected of rebellion, but then again, the steward suspects many people of many things."

"So maybe it wasn't necessarily you," Aeg said, piecing things together, "but a secondary confirmation that made Vinicio move against you."

"Peter knew I was king?" The idea made my stomach turn. He was incarcerated somewhere because of me.

"And when Vinicio got wind of Peter's true allegiance, he decided to act," Aegis decided.

I nodded. I knew it to be true. "Peter was always trying to tell me things he wasn't supposed to about the soul safe. He said I belonged in the castle more than anyone."

All four of us stared into the fire, which was at a full blaze. Aegis pretended it didn't bother him, that he was preoccupied by bigger things than his ego. I closed my eyes and imagined the fire turning purple. In my hand was a purple dust that I tossed into the fire that changed its color. When I opened my eyes, the fire was all shades of violet, indigo, and lilac.

Alfie laughed in amusement. "You really are the king of Hell."

"It's still weird to me," I confessed.

"Well, it's not every day you learn that you're a long-forgotten myth turned reality, one that could possibly change all life as we know it," Alfie mused.

This time, it was Aeg who gave Alfie a disapproving look. "She's still a child, one that doesn't need more problems."

"We're not on our way to the castle?" Alfie questioned.

"No, she needs more time," Aegis said.

"More time for what?" If Alfie was attempting to test Aegis, it wasn't going to end well.

"She's not ready," Aegis said.

Alfie's eyes narrowed. "She doesn't need to be ready; she just needs our support."

"There's more to ruling than sitting on a throne," Aegis reminded him.

Alfie wasn't impressed by the vampire's attitude. He stood in front of Aegis then, openly challenging him. Hacia rolled her eyes at the young man's aggression, but said nothing. I didn't know how to respond. I didn't want to contradict Aegis in front of the tracker, but I agreed with Alfie.

"Who are you to decide such things, forest guardian?"

I opened my mouth to speak, but there was no gap in the argument.

"Sit down, boy," Aegis hissed.

Aegis had his back to me, but I could see Alfie's expression. It was one of terror. He was too frightened to move, and his face was pale. It was Aegis who walked away. Hacia turned her head and laughed.

"Then where are we going?" Hacia asked.

"Region three. I've seen all the regions, but that one." I realized my reason was lacking, but Hacia seemed to approve.

I was still unsure of how to speak. Aegis didn't talk to me like I was the queen of the world; he just treated me like Nora. It was unsettling to have two people of such high rank bowing before me. Everything I said they agreed with, and I wasn't sure if that was a good thing or not.

Peter wouldn't like it. I decided that no matter who bowed before me,

I would only take advice from Peter and Aegis. Maybe Minerva as well—if Aegis trusted her, I could too. I wouldn't allow flattery or the self-interests of others to cloud my better judgment.

"That would give us time to prepare," said Hacia. "If Vinicio attempts to fight your return, we will need the trackers and the hawk hunters on our side."

"What if they decide to stay loyal to him?" Aegis asked, a worry that had long been on his mind.

"Their allegiance is with us, not with the steward," Hacia promised.

"Is that why there were no guards earlier?" I asked.

Alfie nodded. "My lady Gwen," he said as he scratched under the hawk's cap, "could only reach the hunters on this side of the mountain. The guards on the other side will receive the message to pull back eventually. You did get my note?"

"Yes, but we weren't sure if it was from you," I said.

"Told you!" Hacia said as she smacked Alfie across the head. I expected him to react, but he just took the abuse from the woman without comment.

"So then, we part ways in the morning," Aegis said, "The two of you will ready your troops, and Nora and I will go to region three and lay low."

"My hawk will send word when we are ready," Alfie responded shyly, still standing where Aegis had left him.

"There's something else," Aegis said. "I'm afraid I killed some of your girls."

Hacia didn't flinch, but I could see the pain in her eyes. "Do you know which ones?"

Aegis described the girls in detail—I hadn't even known what they looked like.

"It was my fault," I told her. "We would have just run away, but the drums were so loud. By the time Aegis saw them coming, he couldn't get me out of a trance state—"

"You fell into a trance? Like the people in region one?" Alfie interrupted.

"You've seen it?" I asked.

"Yeah, I've seen it before. They are a strange group, making those noises and the trancing." Alfie's impression made me giggle.

"Nora takes on the attributes of any region she resides in," Aegis explained. "When we were in region six, she was a gambler. She was a killer in the outlands. A debutante in region four, a monk in region one, and a caretaker in region two."

Both Hacia and Alfie seemed in awe of my quirks, but the way Aegis looked at me when he said the word debutante filled me with embarrassment. It was dark, so no one could see how red my ears were, but they tingled and burned. It seemed a lifetime ago, but everything about region four was painfully awkward.

"I think it's time we go to bed," I said as I rested before the fire. Aegis stood guard while the trackers and I slept. As I dozed off, I realized just how easily sleep came when he was near.

Hacia and Alfie were gone by the time I woke up. For a moment, I wondered if they had even come or if it was a dream. Aegis had my bag packed and the fire smothered.

"Did I oversleep?" I asked him.

"You slept in, but you need the rest. Come along—we should get moving."

Aegis seemed in a better mood than he had been in the last few days. With our newfound support within the castle, I myself felt even more determined. We were no longer wandering without purpose. A plan was in motion that would not only seat me on the throne, but would spread the word of the king's return, to everyone.

"Can you know for sure that Hacia and Alfie won't betray us?" Aegis asked.

"You mean my powers?"

Aegis nodded. "I have no reason to doubt them, but I err on the side of caution."

"I can try to do what I did in region four."

Aegis scowled. "You mean when you were half-frozen in cold bathwater?"

"Well, you'll be aware of what I'm doing," I pointed out.

"I don't know; it didn't seem all that pleasant."

He was right. The first time I had a vision, it was terrifying. I was lost in my own mind until Aegis came to my rescue. But now that I was steadily developing control over my abilities, it would be easier. At least that was what I told myself.

"I didn't know what was happening. This time, I'll be ready."

"When we get to region three we will try it."

Chapter Seventeen

We walked steadily along the road until the sun was high in the sky. We took a break so I could eat, and not much was said. Aegis sped off to find fresh water to refill my water pouch. The tall, pale grass swayed in the slight breeze. It was lovely in the second region. The weather was perfect for traveling.

I wondered what region three would be like. I imagined the people would be less ideological than the second and first regions, but more practical than the fourth. When Aegis reappeared, he had a canteen full of water. Instead of making him hand it to me, I imagined the canteen in my hand. Moments later, I was sipping water, and Aeg was laughing in disbelief.

As dusk approached, Aegis began collecting sticks and debris to start a fire. The road abruptly came to a halt as the field we walked along fell off the side of a cliff. We almost walked right off the edge. I looked down to see that the road unceremoniously continued at the bottom of the precipice as though it were a slight step along the road.

I looked to Aegis with a grin. "We almost walked off the ledge."

Exasperated by the idea of his king walking off a cliff, Aegis seemed less humored by the idea. His arms were full of wood. Rolling his eyes, he dropped the bundle over the cliff, and I laughed as it scattered below. It wasn't a long way down, but far enough to hurt. Aegis extended his arm to me. Scooping me up, he stepped into space.

The rush of gravity forced us downward. My hair went wild for a moment, and then we were at the bottom as though nothing had happened. I was still grinning as I helped him collect the scattered branches. Aegis left for a quick hunt and returned with a tiny rabbit. It was better than no dinner at all.

The sunset was a red hue on the horizon. I had seen it before, but it amazed me every time I saw it. That was when an idea came to me.

"Aegis, you said that people will follow me once they know I'm here."

"You're their queen."

I closed my eyes and imagined pouring the purple dust into the sunset the way I had with the fire of the previous night. I noticed that it was harder to keep the focus on the sun. It resisted and pulled from my power until finally, the outline of the orange ball was a dark violet. The purple melted inward staining the center. I opened my eyes to see the entire sunset was a monochromatic purple. It was like an eclipse that remained as the sunset.

That brought a smile to Aeg's face. "It's incredible."

"I'll continue to practice my powers and signal to the world that I am here."

"If you can do that, you can start the fire," Aegis teased.

Still giddy from my success, I started the campfire without issue. Aegis was singing his song, obviously thinking about Minerva again.

"We will find her," I assured him.

He looked so sad when he smiled. "I've never thanked you for that."

"For what?"

"For not making me choose between you and her."

It wasn't the heat from the fire that reddened my face. I shrugged and prodded the fire. Flames bit at the rabbit on the spit.

"I understand. You love me, and you love her. It's just different."

Aegis walked towards me, and my stomach fluttered as he kneeled beside me. "Vampires don't love the same way souls do. Our lifespans are so long. We love in phases. Sometimes we go centuries without seeing our mate. Maybe when you are older and more established in life…"

"Vampires are like the people in region two, then." I cut him off, unsure that I wanted him to finish his sentence.

Aegis didn't follow, so I explained to him again how the tribes in the second region had multiple mates. "In a way, I suppose," he agreed. "Usually not multiple lovers at once."

There was an awkward moment of silence between us. I thought about Agnes having her baby, and the butterflies in my stomach turned into stones. The bond between a mother and child could never be severed. If that was true, I didn't want to have children.

I didn't want to make that sort of promise to a child when that same promise had sabotaged my entire life. My mother wanted to give me away, but my grandparents wouldn't let her, for some reason. As a baby, they wanted to keep me, but once I got a little older, they seemed to change their minds.

I think it was because they wanted to punish my mother for having premarital sex with an outlander, but they had punished me in the process. I didn't deserve to be treated so harshly, not by my grandparents or by anyone else in the fifth region of Hell. Mother didn't deserve to be punished for having me, but she *did* deserve my anger.

I didn't want to make any sort of promise to anyone. Aegis was the first person to ever need my affections. Could I even handle loving more than just him? We'd traveled the world, and I had learned almost nothing of how relationships worked aside from the small scope of my mother's marriage. And I didn't like love from what I saw.

"I don't think I want to have a mate anytime soon," I told Aegis.

"I think that is a very wise decision," Aegis said. His demeanor appeared more relaxed. His shoulders slacked, and the crease between his brows softened.

"Good night, my queen."

Vinicio

Vinicio lay by Bella's side and caressed her affectionately. She remained unmoving and unspeaking. Though she was no longer sedated, Bella refused to go on. There was nothing the doctor or nurses could do except feed and dress her.

Vinicio was given no explanation for her behavior, but he needed none. Nora had somehow gotten the message across to his wife that he was responsible for her departure, that he had made an attempt on her daughter's life.

Vinicio was unsure of just how much Bella knew, but she did know that Nora was alive and refusing to come home, which could only mean she felt unsafe within the castle. The swell of her belly was just starting to protrude. The child inside her continued to thrive despite the mother's mental decline. He was saddened by the fact that he had no secure future for the child.

If Nora intended to take her rightful place, why was she stalling? It was as if she were tormenting him on purpose. As the steward, he held the loyalties of all those at court, and the military could be bribed. No mythological powers could compete with gold. Even so, there was still a chance that this situation would not go in his favor. What then for his unborn child?

There was a commotion outside his bedroom door, and Vinicio felt annoyance tighten around his neck. Emerging from his bedroom, he yelled, "If it's not too much to ask, could you kindly keep it down?"

No one seemed to be listening. His temper was one of reservation, but if it was disturbed, the consequences were horrifying. Padding out to the great balcony, Vinicio forgot his anger as he saw what the fuss was about. The sun was purple. The entire skyline was a flurry of purple shades. The hue tickled the white marble balcony that overlooked the region, and the whispers of what it meant echoed in his mind.

Nora was coming. It seemed to Vinicio that he had only one recourse left. In his armoire was a small chest. He returned to his room, pulled it out, and unlocked the box with the same key as for the safe room. Shaky hands held the Dagger of Monsters. His father had told him that the dagger could control any magical beast in Hell, and it was his last resort.

Vinicio waited until late in the night before leaving his room. Most of the castle was asleep with the exception of the guards on duty. No one saw him as he pulled aside a bookcase and unlocked the door hidden behind it. A steep narrow staircase led downwards.

Along the wall ran a crank with pipes and wires attached to it. The bookcase had a handle on the back side, and Vinicio used the handle to conceal the entrance once again. Shrouded in darkness, he felt around for the crank and began turning it.

The more Vinicio turned the handle, the more lights along the stairway flickered, and the wires buzzed with life. Once the device was fully wound, he hurried down the stairs to reach the bottom before the lights lost their power. At the end of the stairs, another similar crank waited. Vinicio wound it as well before entering a hallway with several rooms. One of the rooms was heavily barred. He was reluctant to pass that room, and a feral roar quickened his pace down the corridor.

After several more flights of stairs, Vinicio found himself in the bowels of the castle. The air was dank and smelled of forgotten evil. This was the basement of the highest tower of the castle, and no one aside from him even knew of its existence.

Few enough knew of the dungeon, but no one had ever seen the tower basement. Vinicio's father had shared it with him. He was a young man when his father had woken him late at night for an adventure. There were many secrets to the castle, but none so forbidden as the tower basement.

"This is called electricity," the former steward said, motioning to the crank and light system. "A genius from the fifth region came up with this. We deemed it too advanced for Hell. The last thing we need is the balance of power being shifted from the castle to technological advancement."

Vinicio's father was old at this time. His slippers dragged when he shuffled, and he hunched in his nightgown. Vinicio encouraged his father to wear a sleeping shirt and trousers, but his father insisted that freeing his privates kept him potent.

"We had the young man install his devices everywhere in the dungeon before locking him away in one of those cells," the old man cackled.

The steward led his son down still more stairs. Vinicio was bored with his father's adventure. He was starting to think the old man had found a forgotten closet and was going to go back to bed. But when they reached the bottom of the stairs, the electric lights were no longer needed. The room had a golden glow of its own.

"Should you ever find yourself in danger," the old man had said, "this creature can be bartered with—but the costs are high."

Now, Vinicio stood face to face with the creature for the first time in several decades. Its incandescent gold skin crackled, and beneath it, a layer of molten crimson. It had the eyes of a goat and hooves to match.

When Vinicio stepped forward, the creature smiled. "It's been a long time, boy."

"I have a proposal," Vinicio said.

The creature nodded, his horns spiraling high into the air. "I knew you were coming. I could feel it in the air."

"You know about the girl?"

"The king." The beast laughed. "Yes, I know about her. I know about you as well. You want her dead."

"What do you want for the deed?" Vinicio asked.

The creature crossed his arms and appraised Vinicio carefully. "All I ask for is my freedom."

"Your freedom?"

"To leave this forsaken cell."

"Fair enough. Just so long as you stay away from the castle."

"Agreed." The beast smiled.

The way the creature said it made Vinicio consider whether it would be better to take his chances with Nora, but then he thought about the baby and Bella. What would happen to them if he were gone?

Surely Nora wouldn't mistreat them, but the most standard punishment was being banished to the outlands. Most would encourage the newly-anointed king to follow customary laws, and a young girl would want to do what was expected of her.

Vinicio steeled himself. He wouldn't allow his child and Bella to endure the outlands. Not like Kate. Bella was too gentle a soul; she couldn't endure the nightmares that would await her there. She wasn't strong enough. The babe would be enslaved or killed.

Vinicio pulled out the Dagger of Monsters and showed it to the Titan, who regarded it without a word. "I hold the Dagger of Monsters," Vinicio said. "If you try to betray me, I will use it to kill you."

The Titan smiled and bowed. "A pact of blood must be made."

Vinicio cut his hand and let the blood drop to the ground. "The steward pacts with the Titan. Kill Nora, the queen of Hell, and you shall have your freedom."

And just like that, the Titan was gone. Vinicio wasn't sure of what he had just done, but he would do anything to secure his child and wife from the threat of a stupid girl.

That night, while Vinicio rested, he felt foreign somehow. It was as if the bed rejected his body. He realized it was all in his mind, a fictionalization similar to the walls closing in on someone. His imagination was infested with the anxieties and strain he had been under. When his eyes adjusted to the dark, he looked at his wife. To his surprise, her eyes were wide open.

"You're awake," Vinicio exclaimed. He was genuinely happy. It was the best news he'd had all week.

"I'm always awake. I only close my eyes to keep people from talking to me."

"I want to help you, please," he pleaded.

She was quiet for a long moment before speaking. "Do you think she hates me?"

Vinicio shook his head. "No one could hate you."

"This is all my fault," she said as she fought the sobs.

"It's not your fault," Vinicio said soothingly. "It's mine, and I will make things right. You'll see."

Chapter Eighteen

Nora

The cold woke me. When I sat up, I noticed the fire had burned to nothing but coals. Aegis was perched strangely on a rock. He was squatted with his back hunched as he sniffed the air. He looked more like an animal than a man.

"Aegis, what's wrong?" I called to him.

There was no response.

Pulling his coat off, I stood alongside him and peered into the darkness. I couldn't see anything, but Aegis was electric—he was practically seething with an unchecked instinct.

"Aegis, look at me!" I commanded.

He was beginning to frighten me, but when he turned his head to face me, I stumbled backward. The whites of his eyes were so bloodshot that hardly any white remained. He looked at me as though he had never seen me before, but it was more than that—Aegis's eyes were filled with bloodlust.

Aegis turned away as he struggled to regain control. He turned his face to me once more, and his eyes had mostly returned to their normal state. "Are you afraid of me?"

"I just don't understand—are we in danger?" I asked.

"Yes," Aegis said uncertainly. "Something is coming for us. An irredeemable creature from long ago."

He was still attempting to pick up the scent in the air, and he was behaving somewhat erratically. Aegis was twitchy and raked his hair away from his face with his fingers. I noticed he was pacing as he desperately attempted to pick up the scent again.

"Something you remember?"

"In a way. It's more like an instinct."

"So, you can know things without remembering why?"

"That happens all the time—learning something doesn't always mean you'll remember the source of the information."

I brushed the damp wisps of hair away from my face. It was getting muggy, and the dampness clung to every part of me. "I guess so."

The road ahead was rocky, and a fog had rolled in. "Why do you ask?" Aegis inquired.

"It's nothing, really," I said. "I was thinking back to Peter."

"About Peter trying to tell you things he wasn't allowed to?"

I nodded. "Sometimes, when he talked about the kings of old, he told me things that I knew were incorrect."

Aegis stopped walking to look at me. "What do you mean?"

"Some of the stuff he claimed kings could do. Like he said one king could turn into mist. And another he said was impervious to flames. I know neither was true."

"Maybe it's because you know more now about what a king can do than he did then," Aeg suggested.

"No, I knew he was wrong then, too," I insisted. "Peter told me that history is often written by the victors. Maybe the stewards exaggerated the stories to make the king sound more unrealistic than he really was so that when he did come back, no one would believe it was true."

"Phineas, my friend from Metropolis, said that all the kings were linked. I never really listened to how or why, but he was probably right. He knew things like that too."

"It's not important—just something I was thinking about."

Aegis stopped me suddenly. His eyes grew bloodshot, and he quietly hissed. From the fog just ahead, a hideous creature stepped forth. He was seven feet tall and wore only a pair of pants, exposing his scarred chest. His skin was gold except for his cuts and scars, which were bright red. Horns erupted from his skull and branched out to the sky. His goat eyes were the same color as his skin. His hoofs kicked in the dirt. His arms were crossed, and his smile made the hairs on my neck rise.

"Stand aside, vampire," the beast said. "I have a pact to fulfill."

"What are you?" Aegis demanded.

The beast tilted his head as if he found the situation amusing. "You don't remember? Well, that makes things more interesting, then."

"You can't have her," Aegis said as he poised himself to attack.

The beast gave a small bow of his head before lunging at Aegis. He was just as fast—if not faster than—Aegis. A whirl of motion clamored around me as the two battled. Occasionally, the beast would look at me and smile menacingly. I wanted to help, but I didn't know how. They were moving too fast. I couldn't keep up. One moment they were in front of me and the next

Aegis was getting thrown to my left. He kicked the beast with a back-kick that sent his foe sprawling.

Back and forth they went for what seemed like hours. Aegis's breath was becoming labored. He wasn't supposed to get tired. The realization that Aegis was wearing down was like having a nightmare I couldn't wake from. The beast caught Aeg's arm and pulled it at the socket. The creature was attempting to dismember him. Aegis tried to fight him off, but with his arm behind his back, there was little he could do.

I closed my eyes and imagined barbed wires growing from the ground like vines, wrapping around the beast's hooves, climbing their way up around his legs. I heard his scream and knew it was working. I focused harder on the wires, made them grow farther up, fully wrapping around the beast. When I opened my eyes, the creature had let go of Aegis. He was fully encapsulated in barbed wire. The agony of each move enraged the beast even more, but he was tightly secured in place.

No matter how hard I made the barbed wire contract, it wouldn't kill the monster. He just screamed in rage and anguish. Aegis was on the ground looking up at him. His broken and dislocated arm dangled strangely at his side. He stood and sped towards me. Lifting me with his good arm, he ran as fast as he could manage.

"You saved my life back there," Aegis admitted.

"I tried to kill him, but I couldn't."

"That was a Titan. They don't die the normal way."

"How do we kill him?"

"I don't know. They all had different weaknesses. Nora, that thing will be back, and I don't know how I can beat him."

"For now, let's work on fixing your arm and finding a place to stay for the night," I told him. "He won't escape the barbed wire anytime soon."

We edged along the border between the second and third regions of Hell. Aegis led me in the direction of the crossing point. It was a bridge crossing a rapid river. The bridge was wide and solid as it expanded across the water. The currents were so strong, and the rocks so jagged, no one would dare cross it. Out of all the borders I'd seen, this one looked the most intact.

"This border is okay," I noted.

Aegis looked at the bridge and gave the railing a smell. "That's because this bridge is new. Trackers want it to look like the waters are this rapid everywhere, but they're likely not."

Once again, there was no one guarding the bridge.

"Looks like Hacia and Alfie cleared this border too," I said cheerfully. The worry on Aegis's face didn't abate with the good news.

The third region was all farmland. Peter had told me that most of the food was produced here, so I knew what to expect, for once. Aegis said nothing—he was still brooding over the battle with the Titan. I'd never seen anything so sinister before, yet I wasn't nearly as afraid as my protector. Perhaps it was because I didn't know any better.

The sound of an animal repeated in the distance, growing louder as we got closer to it, but I was unsure of what made the noise. When a fluffy, four-legged creature with floppy ears came running towards us, I recognized it to be a dog. Peter had talked about them all the time, but to see one in person was so exciting.

The dog was orange, and his hair was long. He bounded up the road towards us excitedly with his tongue flapping in the breeze. I let out a squeal as he ran to me. I hugged him, and he licked my face. Aegis smiled at the scene.

"I forgot about that—dogs live in the third region," Aegis said.

"Why don't they live anywhere else?" I wondered.

Aegis shrugged. "All dogs go to the third circle."

We heard a whistle, and the dog responded. It was a woman in a worn housedress. Her blonde hair was braided. Her white sweater was too big, but it looked comfortable. She was wearing thick gloves too.

"Howdy, travelers," the woman said as she approached.

"Yeah, we're new to the area," I said. "We were wondering if there was a hotel or a bed and breakfast where we could stay."

The woman looked me over before looking over Aegis, whose arm was still badly damaged.

"You're not outlanders, are you?" she teased.

"No, we came from region two. My dad fell down the cliff half a day's walk from here."

The woman nodded as if it was something she suddenly remembered. "Yeah, that ridge is a doozy. I don't know of any hotels in this area, but if you want, I have plenty of room."

I looked to Aegis, who was shocked by the hospitality. "I don't think we can do that..." he began.

"It's no trouble. Come on, let's get your arm fixed up."

"Really, we shouldn't." Aegis looked at me nervously. I knew he was right. The Titan could break free any moment and find us. Aegis didn't want to risk it, but I was exhausted. My head hurt from the tension of the fight and the lack of sleep.

"We've been expecting you," the woman explained.

"What do you mean?" I asked.

"I'll explain everything inside."

The house was large and old. The wood floors were badly scratched and in need of a polish. Everything had once been white, but the shades now varied depending on how much traffic had passed. The doors and moldings were discolored from many scrubbings. The furniture was worn in the same fashion. All of it was beautiful craftsmanship, but it was painted over and washed so much that the paint was faded and cracked.

Despite the wear, the place was lovely. Flowers hung from wall mounted vases and sat in tin can centerpieces. It felt like home—not just a place someone lived—but a real home. The house had such a warmth to it. Occasionally, a draft would send in a waft of a nearby garden.

"You can seat yourself right there," the woman said, motioning to a chair at a large dining table.

Aegis did as he was told. After several minutes, the woman returned with some supplies to dress his arm. "You don't need to go to all the trouble, really…" Aegis started.

"You want your arm to rot off?"

She reminded me of Gerta in a way. She was paler, and fairer, but there was a fire that even Aegis didn't want to provoke. He nodded his consent, and she got to work.

"What's your name?" I asked.

"Lacey," the woman replied as she examined Aegis's arm. "You sure busted this up bad. I don't know how I can reset the shoulder without hurting you. Your arm is broken in three places."

"Just do what you need to do—I can handle it," Aegis told her.

Lacey shook her head. "Okay, just don't hit me."

She laid his arm on the table, trying to decide which way would be best. "It's not dislocated as badly as I thought it looked when we were out front. Come here, girl. I'm going to need your help."

I stood on Aegis's good side and put my hands on his shoulder and arm, bracing him as Lacey pushed his injured arm back into the socket. He was counting spots on the ceiling. If it hurt, he didn't let on.

"I think I got it!" Lacey said. "That was much easier than I thought it was going to be—must be on account of that vampire lineage."

"How did you know?" Aegis asked, practically leaping from the seat.

"I've got kin with the trackers. My sister works with Hacia. They got orders a few days ago to draw their forces back. That's why it was so easy for you to region-hop the last two borders."

"I knew it!" I told Aeg, who rolled his eyes.

"The rest of the folks here don't know about you, just me. If you want to tell them, it's up to you."

"Lacey, we appreciate the help, but we have another problem," I told her.

Aegis and I took turns explaining the incident with the Titan. I could see she was apprehensive. There were a lot of people under her employment, and she didn't want to risk their lives.

"I appreciate your honesty," she said, "and it does scare me. If it's okay with you, I'd like to tell the boys and let them decide for themselves."

"I think that's a good idea," I told her. Aegis was still worried—but he always worried.

"Let's cook the boys some dinner and explain it to them then," Lacey decided.

At first, she asked me to season and tenderize the steaks she had set out. It was embarrassing not knowing how to complete such a simple task. Rather than admit I didn't know how, I tried to fake it. Before me were meat, salt, pepper, and various herbs—none of which I knew how to use.

Lacey was eyeing me curiously, so I plucked a branch of some sort of herb and put a bit of it on each steak. There was a rolling pin in the can of kitchen tools. I rolled that across the steaks a few times. It didn't take long for her to catch on that I had never cooked before. I was given the task of scrubbing potatoes, and I felt safer with that charge. I turned and saw Aeg, who was laughing so hard no sound was coming out.

As the sun lowered, people began coming into the house. A tall man with blue pants and a wide-brimmed hat was the first in the door. "Lacey, we got more hands?"

"Just passing through," Lacey told him as she brought several large steaks out of the ice box.

Several more men arrived, asking the same thing in more or fewer words. I had gotten the potatoes into the pot and onto the stove when Lacey stopped me in my tracks.

"I get inside knowledge about the trackers. I knew you were coming."

"Who is your tracker?" I asked.

"My sister. Her name is Tina. She idolizes Hacia."

"I always wanted to have a sibling."

"I have four—you can have one of them," my hostess teased. She looked back at Aegis before whispering, "Is a vampire like they say?"

"Don't worry—if he gets hungry, he'll just suck the blood out of a goat or something."

Lacey looked scared, and I laughed, despite feeling kind of bad about the joke. "They don't eat at all. Most of the myths are false. I don't even know how people came up with half the stuff they did," I told her.

"Oh, well—that's just what happens. History has a funny way of being changed. Like that rebellion business that happened a few years back—everyone has their own version of events."

"Can you tell me about it?" I asked.

"Not too much to tell, but a bunch of folks thought the last steward was imprisoning souls. Half the hawk hunters rebelled, along with a few ordinary souls. It ended nastily. Hacia and her trackers went through and cleaned house."

"She was so quick to help me, though," I said. Maybe it was a part of her plan to trap me.

"Hacia's changed since then," Lacey said. "Only after the steward's son took over did she learn the truth. She didn't like being played the fool. But if you ask the hawk hunters or the steward, you'll hear a totally different story."

Men wandered into the house, found their way to the bathrooms, washed up, and sat around with Aegis. He was a master of small talk, and soon enough, he had everyone hanging on his every word. The last to arrive was a tall, stout bloke with a thick beard.

"Lacey, sweetheart, it's my turn to clean the kitchen," he called from the dinner table.

"I know, but we got guests, and we all need to talk about a few things."

The long oval table barely contained all the people. We were elbow to elbow, but no one seemed to mind. They were hungry, and the food was hot. I waited until everyone had dished up and gotten through most of their meal before I started talking.

"My name is Nora. I am the king of Hell, and the man here is my vampire, Aegis."

Chapter Nineteen

A few of the men laughed, and a few looked alarmed.

"Okay, darling," joked a younger man, with hair the same color as his skin, as he reached for a roll.

Aegis snapped the roll from his fingers in the blink of an eye and glared at him.

That got everyone's attention. A few of the men stood in alarm, but Lacey spoke up.

"I got word from Tina a few days ago," our hostess said. "She told me about Nora and Aegis—they are the real deal. The trackers and the hawk hunters have joined forces for the first time in centuries, all for this girl, here."

Murmurs spread around the table. No one was eating anymore.

"I know it's weird," I told them. "It's still weird to me. The stewards have been lying to everyone—they have been killing the kings at birth to maintain control. Vinicio didn't kill me straight away because I was a girl, so he thought there was a mistake. I didn't develop my powers immediately, which also gave him pause, but once he was certain that I was the king, he's been trying to kill me ever since."

"Hail to the goddamned king, then," the younger man said.

"There's more, and this involves you folks, as well," Aegis warned.

I nodded. "The trackers and hunters have joined my side. I don't know if Vinicio is aware of this fact, but he released a Titan to destroy me. This Titan cannot be killed by normal means. I trapped it, but it will pursue me when it escapes."

"I think this is too important to back down on, so that's why I'm willing to risk my safety for her," said Lacey. "That being said, it's up to y'all to decide if you're willing to do the same."

The tall man with the beard was still standing in shock, but he was the first to speak. "Lacey, I don't know what a Titan is, but if the king and a vampire don't know how to kill it, it must be pretty bad. But I got to agree with you on this one. If the steward thinks it's okay to kill children and release dangerous creatures into the world, it's worth doing what little I can to protect the future king."

Most of the men nodded in agreement. It was the youngest one who spoke last. "I'd love to stay and be a hero, but I got a wife with two little ones and a baby on the way. If something were to happen to me, she'd be on her own, and I just can't do that."

"That makes you the real hero in this room," I told him. "If someone had loved me as a child, perhaps I wouldn't need to constantly rely on strangers today."

Aegis flinched at my words, but I couldn't take them back.

The young farmhand wished us all luck and left. Everyone else fumbled into their routines, despite the conversation. Soon the table was cleared and Lacey had started washing up. That was when Aegis approached.

"Why did you tell everyone the stewards killed infants?" he asked.

"Because it's true," I told him.

"How do you know it's true?"

I realized I couldn't give him an answer. "I just know."

Lacey put away a stack of dishes before returning to drying the glasses. Aegis went to visit with the men gathered around the fireplace. He told them stories of the Starry Wood, and the farm hands were enthralled. He leaned his broken arm on the table and even put weight on it—he had mostly healed already.

"Aegis, how's your arm feeling?" I asked him.

He looked at the injured limb and realized why I was asking. "It feels pretty good after a few sips from this flask," he said coyly, as he returned his arm to its intended resting place.

"Do vampires get hangovers?" Lacey asked.

Aegis grinned and shook his head, no.

"You wouldn't happen to have a bathtub?" I asked her.

Lacey showed me to the bathroom. "Here's a towel, and you can put this on while I wash your dress," she said, handing me a nightgown. I looked down at my lavender dress. It was in desperate need of washing, and some of the lace could use mending as well. I gave the gown to Lacey and thanked her for everything she had done for us.

"Well, it's not every day we get royalty to the farm," she teased.

"Oh, and one more thing—could you let Aegis know that he needs to come and help me with something in about thirty minutes? He'll know what you're talking about."

"In the bathroom?"

"Yeah." I thought about what I'd just said. "Oh, that must sound weird."

Lacey looked concerned by the idea, and it made me feel good to know she cared. "I'm still learning how my abilities work," I explained, "and last time I did this, I needed help getting out."

Lacey's expression shifted from concern to confusion and concern, but she let it go. It was one of those things she wouldn't understand, so there was no point in dwelling on it. "I'll let him know."

Once the tub was filled, I repeated the same thing I had done in region four, but this time, I focused on Alfie and Hacia instead of Peter. It wasn't long until the blackness of my closed eyelids began revealing shapes. I recognized Hacia first—her locked hair had a distinctive movement that made her easy to identify. She was talking to me. I looked down and saw a pair of large feet in sandals. I was Alfie.

"Do you think the word has spread quickly enough?" she asked.

"In the upper circles, yes, but the hunters in the fourth, fifth, and sixth regions will be slower to the news."

"Does the steward suspect anything?"

"Yeah, not sure. Rebus said the steward has been acting odd lately. He has been spending all his time in the library. It seems he's lost all interest in what we do. A mistake on his part." Alfie twiddled his fingers absently. "Oh, and I told Rebus that we didn't meet on our last assignment. Best to still look—"

"Combative?" Hacia offered.

"We have united for a special purpose, but I can't promise we will remain simply allies after this is all done."

Hacia smirked. "Neither can I."

I could tell that Alfie was let down by Hacia's answer. Either she understood what he was saying and was rebuffing him, or she didn't realize he wanted to be more than friends. He had phrased it oddly, but I knew that was because he was afraid of rejection. In either case, their troops were indeed prepared for my arrival.

I wanted to pull myself from the vision, so I imagined a weight pulling me down. It was working. I didn't need Aegis to wake me after all. Something stopped me before I left Alfie—I had something to say.

My words came out in Alfie's voice. "Tell Tina that Lacey says hi!"

"What?" Hacia asked. She tilted her head and stared at Alfie blankly.

Alfie was stuttering, unsure of what he had said. I reimagined the weight around my leg and sunk back into the water. I remerged from the lukewarm bath. Aegis was sitting on the toilet watching me.

"You were able to wake up yourself!" he cheered.

"How long were you waiting?"

"Not long. What did you see?"

I drained the tub and dried off while telling Aegis about Alfie and Hacia. He looked off into the distance as he listened.

"They are truly on our side, then," he commented.

"They are ready when we are," I told him.

"But are we ready?" Aegis asked softly.

Lacey offered us two rooms, but Aegis insisted on sharing just one. After encountering the bizarre creature in region two, he was less inclined to give me space. I didn't mind—that thing was the stuff of nightmares.

"That thing is still out there waiting for us," I said.

Standing guard beside the window, Aegis shook his head. "I don't know what to do."

"He seemed to think you would know," I pointed out. "And he knew you were a vampire."

"I know. I feel like I've seen something like him before, but I don't remember."

I sat up in my bed. "Maybe you have. What if you encountered him before you fell asleep in the ground?"

"It's possible, but I don't know—it was a lifetime ago, maybe several lifetimes ago."

"Couldn't you just try to remember?" I asked.

Aegis seemed like he wanted to snap at me, but he held his tongue. I knew it wasn't his fault he couldn't remember. I regretted asking him.

"Sorry," I mumbled, "I know you can't remember something that happened thousands of years ago."

"I have to let go of the past—I can't keep it with me," Aegis explained. "If I kept it in my head, I'd go mad."

I nodded. While I didn't understand it, I understood him. I knew he was racking his brain in an attempt to find a way to defeat that creature.

"Good night, Aeg," I whispered.

He continued looking out the window as if the monster would come charging from the hillside to do his master's bidding. Aegis wasn't used to losing, to being the weaker opponent. It was a struggle for him to be the one who needed help. Yet, while it was hard for him, I was growing stronger as a result. I wanted to tell him it would be okay, and that we wouldn't see the creature again, but I knew he would return.

Somewhere out there, a monster coiled in barbed wire bellowed as he struggled to break free of my power. The fact that I could contain him was astonishing, but I didn't speak of it because it would remind Aegis that he had failed me.

That night, I dreamed that I was a king of spades from a deck of cards. I was being shuffled endlessly with all the other cards until I slipped from the pile and fell to the ground. The breeze carried me away from the table, and I drifted until I found myself underneath a boot. I couldn't get away from the hand that picked me up—it was my mother's hand.

Mother looked at the filthy card and sneered before dropping me back to the ground. Armored knights rushed and clamored to my side, but no matter how many times they picked me up, I fell back down again. A juggler walked on his hands and tossed me a bright red apple with his feet. Suddenly, I was no longer a card, but a girl. I caught the apple and was going to eat it, but my grandmother was standing over me disapprovingly.

"You're a liar just like your father," she said in a voice that boomed across the cosmos.

I felt so small again, the way I had when I was little. I was about to cry, but I woke up instead. I gave a sigh and tried to relax. I needed to go back to sleep. Aegis still stood guard, looking intently out the window.

Come morning, he wasn't in the room, but there was a plain blue housedress on the chair beside me. It was a little big, but almost everything was too big for me. When I came downstairs, there was a stack of pancakes waiting for me. It seemed everyone had gone outside to work.

After I ate and washed my plate, I stepped onto the porch, which was concrete with metal railings. The front of the house looked out over a sea of dirt. I walked around the side of the house and discovered the barn. It was big and red with a large metal tower next to it.

I thought I would find people in the barn, but instead, I found animals. Cows and pigs lined the stalls. The hay was fresh, so I knew that people were nearby. A few families in the fifth region had cows, and many had pigs, but I'd never touched a cow before. I stretched my hand into a stall, and a brown cow sniffed it for food. I gave her a pat before she lost interest and turned away.

I heard some voices from the other side of the barn. I followed them to find a large concrete trough surrounded by cattle. I had walked into the middle of their corral. Over the noise of the animals, I heard Aegis call to me. He rode up to the gate on a gray and white horse.

"What are you doing?" I asked him.

"Well, I thought I'd help them with their chores. It's the least we can do."

That made me smile. "Yeah, I'd love to help."

Aegis motioned for me to join him on the horse. I climbed the gate, and he helped me up the rest of the way. It felt good to be so close to him again. He was wearing someone else's clothing, but he still smelled like himself. Aegis would always smell like the resin and the spices of the Starry Wood.

We trotted along fields occupied with various types of foliage. I couldn't identify most of them. It wasn't long until we came across Lacey and several others digging up radishes.

"We have another able body," Aegis announced. "Where do you want her?"

"The sooner we get these radishes up, the sooner we can get them and the carrots off to region four," Lacey said.

Aegis helped me down before returning to his mount. "Where are your carrots? I'll get them on carts."

Lacey looked up in surprise. "Did you already cart the potatoes?"

"Yes, Ma'am."

"The carrots are just north of here, on the other side of the silo."

Aegis rode off, and I noticed his arm was no longer in a sling or splinted.

I got down in the dirt and dug around for radishes with Lacey. We talked about unimportant things as we pulled the roots up from the ground and put them in bags. When our bags were full, we dumped the produce into crates.

It was hard work. My knees were sore from the constant movement, and my fingertips hurt from digging despite the gloves we wore to protect our hands. I didn't mind the aches and pains. It felt good to doing something for others. I could see how Lacey beamed with pride when she told me about how their region was responsible for seventy percent of the food in Hell.

Region three was full of farmers, ranchers, and wheat millers. They sent their foods to all but the sixth and seventh regions. Food was in limited supply in the fifth region, but that was because the first region was supposed to deliver it. It was likely that the first region sent their scraps and undesired foods to the fifth region, keeping the best for themselves.

That was why my grandparents were so stingy with food. While famine had never been an issue I was aware of as a small child, they didn't want to spoil me on the good foods they got on rare occasions. That was why so many in the fifth region had some livestock and a small garden. They never seemed to enjoy tending to them the way the people in region three did, though.

"Do you have a boyfriend?" I asked.

"Sometimes." She laughed at the question. "I'm not one for settling down. I like to do things my own way."

"Then you run this place all by yourself?"

"The men here are all hired hands. Most of them have been working here for years now, but yes, I'm the boss."

"Is it hard to be the boss?" I asked while we pulled up onions.

"It's not what I thought it would be," Lacey admitted. "When my daddy died, I took up the farm. I could have sold it or married someone to run it for me, but I thought I knew what I was doing."

"Did you?"

Lacey laughed, "No. No, I did not. I still don't, but now I'm just a little better at fessing up to my mistakes."

"It seems like you are doing a good job," I said while fighting a firmly-planted onion.

"Yeah, it's worked out all right. What about you?"

I didn't understand what she was asking. "Are you and Aegis an item?" Lacey clarified.

"No."

"You don't seem too sure on how you feel about that," Lacey assessed. She was right.

"I love him, but I'm not sure how just yet," I confessed. "And we both agree that I'm too young."

"He doesn't age like a soul does," Lacey pointed out. "I know that doesn't seem like a big deal now, but when you're older, it will be devastating for the both of you."

I nodded.

A bell echoed across the plains, and I jumped a little at the sound.

"That's just the lunch bell," Lacey said.

Everyone walked in the direction of the sound. We pulled off our shoes and washed our hands before sitting at the table, which held a large stack of sandwiches. The food here tasted better than anywhere else, even the castle. It was so fresh the taste exploded with each bite. Perhaps it was just because I was so hungry from working outside, but no sandwich had ever tasted quite as good.

After lunch, we went back to the fields and finished picking the onions. Aegis rode up on his horse to inquire about the cattle. "Are the cows supposed to be wandering around?"

Lacey's eyes rolled with annoyance. "Fergus."

"Who's Fergus?" I asked.

"One of the cows. He's been nothing but trouble since he was a calf. We had to come up with a name for him because he is always causing trouble."

"You want to round them up with me?" Aegis asked me.

With Lacey's nod of approval, I was on the back of the horse with Aeg, and we were off herding cattle. Aegis seemed to be in his element. He enjoyed this life, and so did I. Herding cattle wasn't as hard as we anticipated. Mostly, the cows were already heading back to the barn.

"It doesn't seem like they wanted to leave," I pointed out.

Worry was starting to work its way across Aeg's face. "No, it doesn't. They must have been scared off."

We rode towards the barn cautiously. The mare we rode seemed anxious as well. She kept trying to veer away.

Aegis's eyes went bloodshot. "I smell blood," he warned.

I gripped his hand with my sweaty hands as we got closer to the barn. Nothing moved in the building—it was empty—but the gates were open. Something had been dragged across the ground, something large. Smears of blood and hay made a trail out the side door, and the flies buzzed loudly. The animals all hovered around the barn, but were still unwilling to reenter their shelter. The hairs on the back of my neck stood, and I knew in my gut that the creature was back.

The bell rang a second time, and a meeting convened straight away. Everyone stopped what they were doing and came to the house. As they gathered at the table, Aegis told them about what we had seen in the barn.

"I wish I could stay longer," I said, "but if we are going to kill this thing, we'll need to get answers."

The crew shifted uncomfortably in their chairs, and Lacey tried her best to agree, but her opinion soon burst from her mouth.

"It's not right," she said. "I know you're right and there's nothing for it, but I hate seeing people getting pushed off my property."

The workmen seemed to agree.

"Next time it may not be a cow; it might be one of you," Aegis warned.

"Fergus had it coming," the tall man with the hat said, and everyone laughed.

"Markus, I won't lie to you," Aegis said directly to the tall man. "That creature scares me. Not a lot scares me."

His somber tone made everyone pause, including me. Vampires were the heroes of Hell. If they could be defeated, it meant only the worst for souls. Nowhere would be safe if a Titan roamed the seven regions of Hell freely. It would be up to me to defeat it somehow, or the world would be lost.

Aegis looked at me with his kind blue eyes and said, “I think it’s time.”

Chapter Twenty

That night, I had another dream. It started out the same way as the previous one. I was a card, shuffled in a deck. This time, instead of falling to the ground, I was being played in a game of Spades Fourteen. The man who held me was nearing his sixties with red hair streaked with gray. He was wearing black armor and had a waxed mustache. He also wore a black metal crown. It had twisted vines that blossomed with sapphire and diamond-centered flowers.

To my left was a twelve of hearts, and to my right was a nine of spades. As a face card, I only counted for one. My player had ten spades total. Not the best hand. The men beside him were anxious and desperate. My heart stopped for a moment as I paid closer attention to their faces. One of them was Aegis.

*****

The next morning, we said goodbye to Lacey and her men. Lacey offered to lend us horses, but we declined. It would be faster to have Aegis cut through the Starry Wood like we had in the past.

We walked well into the night before making a camp. I looked down at my dress, which looked as good as new.

"If you ride on my back, we'll be in the forest tomorrow night," Aegis offered.

"I'm just a little scared, I guess."

"Me too," Aegis acknowledged. "Our only chance is the castle."

He was right. Aeg was always right. I just wished I felt more confident about the process. What was I going to do? Just walk in and demand the throne?

"We need a plan," I told him.

Aegis nodded, but said nothing. "We should probably meet up with Hacia and Alfie. They will have a better idea of what to do."

"Yeah," I agreed. "I will need to perform some sort of trick to make the people at court know the king has returned."

"You could turn the sky purple again," Aegis suggested.

"No," I said. "I know what I'll do."

Aegis waited for a moment. "You're not going to tell me?"

"Trade secret," I said with a grin.

That night I did not dream, but I woke up early. I ate very little, partially because I didn't wish to puke on Aegis again, but partly because I felt too nervous to eat. My stomach churned at the mere suggestion of food. I forced one of Lacey's reheated pancakes down, but it was all I could handle.

With me on his back, Aegis raced toward the Starry Wood at full speed. We arrived much sooner than he had predicted. It was still daytime when we came within sight of the dense tree line, but something made him pause.

"What is it?" I asked.

We approached the tree line and found Fergus. The poor animal had been ripped apart, and bits were strewn from every branch and limb—everything but his head.

"Why would he do that?" I cried.

"To scare you, and to get the smell of blood in the air. All the nearby predators will be drawn to us, including any woodsmen."

"I thought you said they were all dead!"

"I said they *might* be dead."

I looked around, but could see nothing. "Do you smell one nearby?"

"Yeah, he is still investigating the cow, but if he picks up on our scent, he will surely follow it."

I clung to Aegis as hard as I could. Motion sickness wasn't an issue when several monsters wanted me dead. I tried to anticipate the leaps and falls, but it was of little use. Once I relaxed and stopped fighting it, the means of travel became less jarring.

The Wood was alive with creatures drawn to the scent of fresh meat. Aegis could fight them off, but if he were to be overwhelmed, there would be little to protect me. I wasn't going to get this far just to get eaten by a bear. A giant lizard screeched as it chased after us.

Aegis leaped into the tree branches despite knowing I hated heights. I looked over his shoulder and saw a large black cat stalking us.

"There's a cat," I warned him.

"There are several cats, a dragon, a large bear, and a woodsman."

"We're almost there," I told Aeg.

"Almost there."

The woods cleared to the same plane of grass I had woken up on all those weeks ago. Nostalgia overcame me as I remembered the first time I met Aegis. I had been so young. He looked to me as though he felt the same way. He held me for a moment before the woodsman emerged.

"Nora, I want you to hide behind that rock. This won't be a moment, but if anything happens, you need to run. Run and find Hacia and Alfie."

I nodded and did as he said. The animals heard the stomping of the woodsman, and they scattered in fear. Caught in its way, the bear wasn't so lucky. The woodsman swiped with his fist, and it smashed against a tree trunk.

The woodsman was translucent in the daytime. I could barely see him. He was different from the others—his stars were distant, and he growled as Aegis approached. He stood and waited for the vampire to attack. His movements were so deliberate, yet the others had been mindless. Aegis was reluctant to make the first move against any opponent, but this one simply waited.

My protector relaxed his posture and nodded as if he understood what the woodsmen wanted. With a leap, he was airborne and in a tree. In another swift movement, Aegis's leg went into the back of the woodsmen's neck. His spine was severed, and he fell silently to the ground. Aegis pulled his leg free from the dead giant and walked towards me.

"I don't understand…" I started.

"That was the last woodsman," Aegis explained. His eyes became bloodshot, and he whirled around, looking for the creature that stalked us. "We need to keep moving."

"Why did he just let you kill him?" I asked.

"He was the last of his kind."

"They didn't seem like social creatures."

"Not everyone communicates the same way," Aegis reminded me. I thought back to the boulders and knew that they would never be moved around the woods again.

When we approached the tall gate, the hawk hunters acted as though they hadn't seen us. It wasn't until a few moments later that a young tracker with pale blonde hair in a high ponytail came bouncing up to us.

"Hi, I'm Tina," she said with a smile.

"Tina, as in Lacey's sister Tina?" I asked.

"Hacia got your message."

Aegis was beyond confused. "What message?"

His eyes were still bloodshot, and Tina took a step back and instinctively went for her knife.

"I'll explain later," I told him. "Tina, it's okay—he won't hurt you, but we need to get to Hacia."

Still apprehensive about Aegis, Tina nodded. "Follow me."

Tina led us to the back side of the castle, where Hacia waited. She was dressed in several layers despite the weather being warm. "My king," she greeted me with a bow of her head.

"Where's Alfie?" I asked.

"The hawk hunters are on guard duty today, and he is seeing to the steward personally."

"I need to get to the throne room," I said. My confidence felt like a pane of glass.

"Aegis, Tina, and I will stay with you the entire time," she said. "I don't suspect too much interference. The steward will be forced to acknowledge your claim and relinquish his power."

Hacia led me to the front door, but I shook my head. "No, I know a better way."

The servant tunnels were empty and led us straight to the throne room.

"How did you know about these corridors?" Hacia asked in awe.

"I've always known about them."

"I've lived three of your lifetimes in the castle and never knew of them."

"Nobody does. It seems that everyone forgot about them."

"Perhaps they were an escape route for the kings back in the day," Aegis offered.

He was probably right, but before I could say another word, we had arrived at the throne room. The ornate grate was concealed by the black drapes behind the throne itself. I took a deep breath, ignoring the tremor in my hands as I unhinged the grate and pulled back the curtain.

With Aegis and Hacia on either side of me, Tina took to the nearest exit. She pulled out her knife and posed in an aggressive stance as if to dare anyone to approach her. The people in the room didn't seem all that concerned with us. Most of them were performers of sorts—jugglers, contortionists, trapeze artists, musicians, and actors.

There were sofas seated with various people, most of them looked as though they came from region four. It was Rebus, the steward's consort, who took notice of us.

"Oh." He looked us up and down nervously. "Hacia, who are your friends?" He looked at me and pointed with his mouth hanging open. "Nora! It was thought that you were dead. How…"

Hacia looked at me and motioned to the throne.

I stood in front of the golden chair. Rebus started to protest, but I forced my voice to boom over the top of his stuttering.

"I am Nora. I am the Queen of Hell."

While I had everyone's attention, I closed my eyes and envisioned a black crown with gold vines on my head. I thought about the woodsman, the last of his kind, and how sad it made me feel. The mountains were falling, and the rivers were growing still. Canyons crumbled, making way for the blackest of souls.

If I didn't become the Queen and find Minerva, Aeg would be the last of his kind just like the woodsman who welcomed death. A child screamed in the darkness. The weight on my head grew, and I knew I had been successful. The room was filled with gasps before one voice shouted, "The crown of the first king!"

The crowd murmured. I opened my eyes, and they fell silent.

Rebus, now on his knees, confirmed the crown. "That crown is locked away—there's no one who can access it except the king."

"Or a steward!" A deep voice echoed through the hallway.

Vinicio had come. I felt fear tickling my skin, but I looked at Aeg and realized Vinicio was nothing to be afraid of.

"Vinicio, steward, I demand you relinquish your stewardship," I said.

There was a glimmer of hesitation in his eye, but he kneeled at the base of the steps. "Where is my mother?" I demanded.

"Surely the court needs more proof than a stolen crown to name a little girl queen," he said.

"Are you suggesting Nora stole this relic somehow?" Rebus scoffed.

"Just as possible as a queen." Vinicio stiffened. "I wish to see her abilities for myself."

Out of the corner of my eye, I could see Aegis grow tense, and his eyes went bloodshot.

Vinicio produced a dagger with an ivory blade and a ruby gem at the hilt. "I have the Dagger of Monsters. I summon the last of the Titans."

Hacia moved to block any attack, but the steward placed the dagger on the ground.

"The king who forged that crown defeated the Titans," Vinicio said. "If she is who she claims to be, let her defeat one now."

Aegis let out a hiss.

"But there are no Titans left," Rebus said. His argument ended when the creature with the horns appeared from nowhere. Souls shrieked in fear as they scattered to the far ends of the room, unwilling to leave, yet not wishing to remain in the monster's presence.

"Vinicio, do you have any idea what you've done?" I asked. "What do you think he will do to the souls of Hell now that he is free?"

I saw the fear in Vinicio's eyes, and I knew I had struck him profoundly. He said nothing.

"I come for you, girl," the Titan stated.

"You'll have to kill me first," Aegis muttered.

The Titan laughed. "Whatever you say."

The monster strode forward, a battle axe forming in his hands. Aegis had no weapon, but Hacia and Tina did. Both women went after the Titan, giving Aegis more freedom to strike. The women blocked as he stabbed through the trunk of his opponent. He missed, but the tactic had the Titan on the defensive.

They whirled and clashed as their blades rang against each other. The Titan laughed as Aegis got a hit on his neck. "You cannot kill me with any blade, not even the Dagger of Monsters." The creature laughed as he shot a glance at Vinicio.

The expression on Vinicio's face suggested he had erred in some way.

"What does that mean to you?" I demanded.

"I have the Dagger of Monsters," Vinicio said in disbelief. "It gives me control of all creatures."

"You were given the wrong history. Now we have no idea how to kill this creature. You're an idiot if you think he will spare you."

Vinicio had nothing to say. He was not an idiot. He knew full well that the Titan was going to take great joy in ruining Hell and his great family name. The creature laughed—the rapture of the battle was something he'd wanted for centuries.

Several other trackers joined the fray, but one was killed immediately by the hilt of the axe. The Titan stepped on the body, further mutilating the boy as Hacia struggled to remain focused on the battle. The Titan could tell she loved her underlings.

I closed my eyes and envisioned the barbed wire crawling from the ground once more. It wrapped around one leg, but before it could tie the other, the Titan grabbed the wires and ripped them out of the ground.

"Not this time, your majesty!" he roared.

The Titan's hands were bloody from the wires, but it did nothing to slow him. I tried to think of ways I could help, but I was too focused on the battle to imagine anything. Tina was hit by the axe. It severed her arm just below the shoulder. Here was something I could do. I closed my eyes and imagined the limb growing back.

Tina lay on the floor, screaming in pain. Her arm was indeed growing back, but it was hurting her. That's not what I wanted. Thankfully, she passed out, but I just didn't have the attention span to focus on so much at once. I'd need to try something else.

I watched uselessly as Aegis absorbed blow after blow. He was taking hits for Hacia and the other tracker. They needed more help, and there was nothing I could do. I had led Aegis here to die. I looked away from the fight. I couldn't bear to watch him get cleaved over and over. Daylight shone through the stained-glass windows, giving the room a warm and sacred glow.

I looked at the image of the first king. He was sitting at a table playing cards with the Titan as three vampires looked on. Thinking back to my dream, I realized that Aegis was one of those vampires. Aegis was the vampire to pact with first king. The scar on his hand was proof of that pact.

Despite his lone wolf attitude, had Aegis once spoken on behalf of all the vampires? Aegis was one of the three vampires depicted on the stained glass. He was part of the first king's guard. He was there the day the king learned the Titan's fatal flaw: his name.

I closed my eyes and imagined the scene from my dream, Aegis standing beside the old king. *Remember that day, Aegis.* I imagined the memory of his days with the first king being sucked into his ear as smoke.

The battle raged on. The other tracker was down, and now it was just Hacia and Aegis left. Hacia was on the defensive as the monster focused all his attention on her, swatting Aegis away. The Titan was saving Aegis for last—he wanted him to suffer. Hacia had fallen to the floor. Aegis moved to block the Titan's swing. Without a weapon, Aegis had no choice but to take the hit from the battle axe.

It struck him in the shoulder. The hit was not fatal, but he was deeply wounded. Hacia crawled away from the battle with the Titan trailing behind. I couldn't focus and watch the battle at the same time.

Suddenly, several small blades came flying in from nowhere.

Alfie had arrived with hawk hunters and trackers. They circled the Titan and overwhelmed him. I rushed to Aegis's side and held him. Alfie was fast and proved to be a distraction for the Titan, but even he was losing ground against the beast.

"You need to help me," Aegis whispered.

I closed my eyes, this time imagining Aegis's wound vanishing into thin air. It was hard with all the noise, but when I opened my eyes, Aegis was restored. A large tear in his shirt was all that remained. The Titan laughed on, impervious to all the cuts and jabs inflicted on him. Occasionally, he would swing his ax and send the trackers flying.

I tried once more to get Aegis to remember. *Remember that life. Even if it's only for a little while, please remember.* Images of my dream came flooding back to me: visions of Aegis dressed in the king's colors. The winning hand. The beast speaking his name. I imagined smoke rolling into his mind, and his bloodshot eyes returned to blue.

Aegis stood up, looked at the Titan, and said, "Crucis."

The dagger that lay in front of Vinicio had appeared in my hand.

Aegis took the dagger from me and threw it at the Titan. "Die."

The beast roared as Aegis sent the Dagger of Monsters spinning. It pierced the Titan's heart. He let out a terrible scream as his body slumped onto the floor. I looked up and saw satisfaction on Aegis's face. He took my hand and led me to the throne.

Chapter Twenty-One

"Where is my mother?" I demanded once again.

I looked to Alfie. He snapped his fingers, and three men went running. Aegis still held my hand, and I was grateful for it. It felt as though all the energy had been drained from my body. I still had one more thing to deal with, though. The hunters returned with my mother, who couldn't look at me.

"Vinicio, your family has been killing the king souls as babes. Is this true?"

My mother burst into sobs. Vinicio simply nodded.

"You've killed some as well," I said.

"Yes."

"Vinicio, you are guilty of murder. You'll be sent to the outlands." I tried my best to keep my voice from wavering. Aegis gave my hand a squeeze to remind me he was there for me.

"Mother, you were either complicit in or denied the truth," I continued. "In either case, since you were so determined to take Vinicio's side, you shall take his side in the outlands as well."

"No!" Vinicio cried out. "Please, Nora, she didn't know. She didn't know anything."

Mother said nothing. She kept her head down and cried silently.

I glared. "She knew enough."

"Bella didn't know I tried to kill you," Vinicio explained. "She thought you ran away. I had her drugged to keep her from trying to find you."

He was no longer pleading with me but to my mother. "I tricked her. I lied to her. She wanted nothing more than to find you and to be a good mother."

I wanted to believe him, but, how could I? It was probably just a way to keep her out of the seventh region of Hell. Vinicio moved to embrace her, but Mother remained rigid in her stance. Was she angry with him? He wasn't lying. She really didn't know. She didn't try that hard to find the truth, but she wasn't a murderer.

"Nora, she's pregnant," Vinicio said.

While there were no visible signs of pregnancy, I knew it to be true. If

I looked hard enough, I could see the tiny heart beating inside her belly. I couldn't let the baby be born to the seventh region. No child, no matter how evil, deserved to live there. It was something I would change as queen.

"Mother, promise me you will do better for my sibling. I've always wanted to have a little brother or sister." I changed my sentence. "Bella is to be returned to region five with her parents."

"Will you come visit?" she asked.

I would see her again one day, I decided, but it would be on my own terms. She had a chance to be the mother she should have been for me. Perhaps she would worship this child in the way a parent should worship a child.

"Maybe one day."

She smiled and nodded before going quietly with her escort. Vinicio was led in the opposite direction. He struggled to get a last glimpse of my mother, but it seemed the spell was broken. She had lost all love for him. Instead, it was me she smiled at. It was the first time I'd ever made her smile.

Exhausted, I fell onto my throne as the rest of the room cowered in fear of what would happen next.

"What do I do now?" I asked Aegis.

"You rest."

"Actually," Rebus butted in, "there are a lot of things that need to be done. The soul safe is backlogged, and there are several decisions to be made…"

I looked at Aegis, who shrugged.

"You'll stay by my side?" I asked him.

"Always."

*****

The safe was locked before me. I didn't know how to open it, but Rebus insisted that I would know when I saw it. As it happened, though, rather than me knowing what to do, it seemed the safe itself recognized its true master. The bars spun, and the door opened when I got near.

Aegis stood at the far end of the room with his arms crossed, suspicious of the strange magic. Glowing lights of multiple shades swirled around me. I had to motion to Aeg to stay put—he acted as though he would pounce on them. I felt the urge to raise my arms outward to move the souls. They swayed with my hands as though they were following me.

I closed my eyes and recalled an image from region one. One man stood before the monks and directed their music. I began moving my hands the way he did, directing the souls to their rightful destination. I opened my eyes, and the souls were gone.

I made a point of sending all the blackest souls to the sixth region. If they proved to be beyond redemption, the souls would send them to the outlands to fend for themselves as adults. No one else would be born into such a place.

"That was incredible!" Aegis said.

By the way he looked at me just then, I realized he was in love with me. It made me sad in a way. I couldn't imagine loving someone just to watch them shrivel up and die before my eyes. The last woodsman was defeated before Aegis struck the fatal blow. What would become of Aegis? I needed to make it right.

"Peter and Minerva!" I shouted at him.

I turned to Rebus, who had stood silently watching. Reluctantly he admitted the whereabouts of the castle dungeon. He was the one in charge of feeding the prisoners. Aegis and I ran down the steps and flung open the door. There stood Minerva and Peter, smiling with tears in their eyes.

"You figured it out," Peter said as he hugged me.

"Minerva," Aegis whispered.

Peter and I left the vampires; it seemed they had some catching up to do. Likewise, Peter and I had so much to tell one another. He would be my royal advisor—along with Aegis and Minerva, of course. I would need all the help I could get.

"So, what can you do?" Peter asked, rubbing his hands together excitedly.

I led him to the balcony and turned the sunset purple. I had imagined Peter would be impressed by this ability, but he looked sort of annoyed instead.

"Of all the things you could be doing, you turn sunsets purple?"

I laughed at his sarcasm.

He frowned. "No, really—tell me you've been doing more than just that with your time."

I just giggled. I knew he was happy; he was just being a cranky old man.

"We have a lot of work to do," Peter warned me.

"I know."

I missed Aegis already.

Come back to me, Aeg. Come back soon.

About The Author

Shayna Grissom was born and raised in the Pacific Northwest. She currently resides in Seattle with her husband, two children, and her beloved pets. Shayna draws inspiration for her writings from binge-watching too many shows with far too much wine. She is a lover of the macabre, the strange, natural sciences, and films that feature vivid colors and imagery. Her favorite film director is Guillermo Del Toro, and her favorite books growing up were Anne Rice novels.

You can find Shayna on twitter @ShaynaGrissom and on GoodReads.com.